HOUSE OF
ICE &
SHADOWS

SHERRILYN KENYON

OLIVER HEBER BOOKS

0 9 8 7 6 5 4 3 2 1

Pegos

Sester

Unicorn Bay

Auderley

Licordia

Dread Waters

Ningyo

Alarium

Recmad's Death

Windy Crossing

chnal

Pyrigian Lands

Indara

Wyverns

Thassalia

Esin

Gryphons

SherrilynKenyon.com

PROLOGUE

"The Queen wants a word with you."

Gisela Bloodthorn paused in cleaning her ornate black sword to look up at the handsome blond centaur who dared disturb her during her rare quiet time.

If Adsel had entered her room for any other reason than the queen's business or had been any other creature, she'd have speared his head to the wall. But as Queen Meara's right-hand flunkey, he was spared her wrath. Dealing with the queen was enough punishment for anyone. She didn't need to add to his poor misery.

Knowing it was illegal for her to be armed in the presence of her queen, she set her sword aside.

As soon as she stood, Adsel led her from her room and down the gilded hallway to where the queen waited in her gaudy, ornate throne room that was so overdone, it was hard not to shield her eyes.

While Meara had no taste in furnishings, she was an elegant beast when it came to her personal appearance. Her brown equine half was always well groomed. She wore her long black hair in an intricate series of braids that entwined with her

1

jeweled crown. Dressed in a navy jacket similar to the dress uniforms of their military officers, she looked every bit the regal monarch.

Before Adsel could announce her, Gisela stepped around him and cleared her throat. "You summoned me, Majesty?"

That break in protocol was enough to chafe Meara, which was fine by Gisela. As Meara so often said, Gisela had been born for no other purpose than to irritate her.

It was one of many things she excelled at.

Growling, Meara moved to stand in front of Gisela. "I have need of your unique...skills."

Gisela had to lock her jaw to keep from saying something sarcastic such as..."What? You didn't summon your assassin for a sweet treat?"

After all, Meara never summoned her for any reason other than she wanted someone killed.

Another thing she was really good at. All thanks to Meara and her court.

"And that is, my queen?" She might as well play the game since Meara seemed to be in the mood for it.

"I need you to find the *apaswere* my contract with King Deciel is written on and bring it to me for protection."

Shocked, she arched a brow at that unexpected assignment. Protect someone? Was Meara sick? She never wanted anyone's life preserved. Death. Mayhem. Chaos. Those were her sustenance.

The queen was known for her cruelty and ruthlessness. Carried out by others, of course. But merciless always.

"And if this *apaswere* refuses?" Which was a good bet given that they were a warrior race that magically wrote contracts on their own flesh and guaranteed the terms with their well-honed skills. Once done, the only way for a signer to get out from under their contract was to kill the *apaswere* who held the terms on their skin.

That was a lot harder than it sounded.

Meara's eyes darkened. "I don't care if it protests or not. Bring it here. Do whatever you must, just don't let the *apaswere* die."

"And which *apaswere* am I after?"

Her queen often left out vital details as she assumed everyone around her was capable of mind-reading. Even those who found it hard at times to follow Meara's ever-shifting thoughts.

Irritated, Meara sneered at her. "Obviously the one who bears my contract with King Deciel."

That was completely unhelpful and gave her no idea which demon she was being sent after.

It made sense that the queen would want that contract. Whereas Meara was strictly queen of the centaur homeland, Thassalia, Deciel was the High King of all Thirteen Kingdoms, and ruler of the unicorn race and their lands of Licordia.

But now she was even more confused. They were at war with Dash and his army, so why go after a contract demon when the more obvious target would be to kill King Dash?

"Why not have me execute the king for you, Majesty?"

That garnered a furious huff from Meara. "Why do you think, imbecile? Aside from the fact that neither of us is allowed to invade the other's kingdom, we're not allowed to assassinate each other, either. Or cause the other any harm. At. All. Those were the terms." Shaking her head, she gnashed her teeth. "I can't believe I agreed to *that*."

Oh. That *was* an unfortunate clause and not like her queen at all. She couldn't imagine Meara ever agreeing to such a thing.

Unless she was drunk or temporarily out of her mind.

"If I know Dash," Meara sneered, "and I do, he already has one of his Outlaws searching for the demon to execute it. Probably all of them. Get to the demon first and preserve its life. Bring it here so that we can guard it. Once it's in my kingdom, it would be an act of war for them to kill it. So get it here as fast as you can."

"Yes, my queen." Gisela inclined her head and took a step back.

As she started to leave, Meara grabbed her arm. "Do not fail me." Her ominous tone was impressive.

"I never fail." Not a boast, just a mere statement of fact.

Meara released her. "And Gisela?"

"Yes?"

"If you find any of his Outlaws on your journey, kill them too. And if you succeed in doing this for me, I'll give you what you want most."

Her heart skipped at those words.

It's a trick...

It had to be. Meara never gave anyone what they wanted.

So she made sure to clarify the terms. "And that is, my queen?"

"Your freedom. On my honor. You keep the beast alive and return here with it and I'll make sure you never again have to serve me. I'll free you from my service."

She couldn't move for a full minute as those words fully sank in. Meara had never used this carrot before.

And she was right, it was the one thing Gisela wanted most. To never have to kill again...

Never have to be Meara's sword or even speak to the bitch.

It was the one thing she'd sell her soul for.

Freedom...there was nothing she wouldn't do for it. But she knew better than to get excited.

More than that, she knew better than to let Meara know her thoughts or her feelings. So, she kept her expression guarded and made sure Meara didn't know how much Gisela's heart was racing at the prospect.

Clearing her throat, she inclined her head. "Yes, Majesty." Without another word, she headed back toward her room to get her sword and small travel pack that was always kept at the ready.

Though to be honest, it'd been a while since she'd been sent on a mission. Meara normally kept her close at hand.

Not that Meara trusted her.

The queen trusted no one. Which was exactly why she kept Gisela at her side and had trained her so viciously. As the queen's personal assassin, Gisela's assignments had always been to take out whatever or whoever annoyed Meara. No matter how petty the insult. Or unintentional.

It wasn't something Gisela relished or wanted, but it was the only trade she'd ever been trained for. And one she was dreadfully good at.

Gisela grabbed her traveling cloak, grateful that she would be able to save a life this time and not take it. It felt good to have a noble cause for once.

And to finally be free?

She clenched her fists as a giddy rush went through her, and she suppressed her excitement again.

Of course, there was one serious problem. How could she find a specific *apaswere*? There were thousands of them. Literally, thousands. Tens of thousands.

It was a daunting task she was set on.

Succeed or die. That was Meara's rule. Her queen knew nothing of mercy.

And neither did Gisela.

I will seek the beast, and I'll bring it back. Whatever it took.

She just prayed she reached the *apaswere* before her enemies did.

I

Gisela hated this place. *The Beggar's Claw.* How stupid was that name? But then given the fact that it was deep in the heart of Vaskalia where trolls, giants and ogres typically lived, she was lucky it wasn't called something worse.

After all, that group wasn't exactly known for their creativity.

At least that was her thought until she passed a table of six large, tusked ogres who were drawing pictures on parchment.

"Needs more shading, Lars. But it's much better than your last. You're really improving."

That unexpected comment actually stopped her. Not just the conversation about how to improve their drawings, but the fact that their artwork was quite impressive as she looked at it.

Very well, then. She'd rethink her ogre stereotype. Apparently, they were creative. And very talented.

What she couldn't rethink was the fact that the ogres didn't care for other races.

A proven fact when Lars looked up and raked her with a sneer. "What you staring at, *human?*"

Not a human. But since she appeared as such, she didn't bother to correct him.

"Just admiring your art. Love the daisies. They're very beautiful and well done."

That caught him off-guard. He blinked his bulbous eyes twice, then smiled...maybe. With ogres it was hard to tell if they were smiling, sneezing or salivating.

She would go with pleased, especially since he didn't come after her as she drifted back into the crowd.

THAT IS nine kinds of trouble.

Being that he was all kinds of trouble himself, Xaydin Kazakh had recognized his own the moment she walked into the pub. Tall, slender and trying to remain inconspicuous...

They were like-minded creatures.

Granted he had no idea what she looked like, but she moved like water. Fluid and graceful. Every step was decisive. Her hooded, concealed head swept back and forth as she watched everyone around her while she continued to look for something or someone only she knew.

Damn.

He actually wanted to know her name, and that wasn't like him at all. His hormones had never ruled his life. Not when he had the purpose in life that he did.

Rolling a coin between his fingers, he watched her carefully. She was far too small to be a native of this kingdom. Her stature was more akin to a human, elf or sidhe. Maybe Tenmarun.

Or a shifter.

He hated shifters almost as much as an *apaswere.* Some days that hatred might be equal.

As she came nearer, she stopped to converse with a troll.

Whatever she said infuriated him. The troll rose up with a fierce snarl.

Ignore her. Not your squirrel. A phrase gifted to him by his half-brother, Masakage, that meant *Don't chase the things that aren't meant for you or that are none of your business. Tend your own yard and let others tend theirs.*

Masakage's code.

Sadly, it wasn't his. He was paid for sticking his sword into the matters of others.

The troll shoved the woman back and rose with a club in his hand. By the look on the troll's face, Xaydin could tell he planned on executing her with it.

Without hesitation, he was across the floor in time to catch the club with one hand.

The troll's eyes widened with a mixture of fury and disbelief. "Mind your business."

Xaydin glanced over his shoulder at the woman who had drawn a sword and was ready to defend herself. "Mind your manners." He punched the troll who staggered back.

When the troll started forward, his friend caught him by the arm and kept the troll pinned to his side. "Don't... Do you not see who it is?" he whispered in the troll's ear.

His eyes widened even more as he realized Xaydin's identity. That sucked every bit of fury from the beast who lowered his weapon and actually bowed. "Forgive me, lord. I didn't mean it. Never would I have knowingly snapped at you."

"I'm not the one you need to apologize to." Xaydin released the club and stepped aside for the woman to be seen.

She was frozen in place with a stern frown as her gaze went from him to her assailant.

The troll turned to bow to the woman. "Forgive me, my

lady. I meant no disrespect or harm." Then he returned peace-fully to his seat.

Gisela was stunned by the sight of the man in front of her who'd caused such a reversal in the one she was sure was about to kill her.

For one thing, her savior was huge in stature. She barely reached his shoulders, and she was exceptionally tall for a woman.

His wavy black hair fell to his shoulders and framed a face that must have been chiseled by the gods themselves. Never in her life had she seen a more handsome man or features so perfectly made. His black eyes matched the ornate black leather armor he wore. Armor that said he was most likely highborn and richer than most nobles she'd met in Meara's court.

"I didn't need your help," she whispered.

That dark, intelligent gaze went to her drawn sword. "I'm sure you could have defeated him. Eventually. But for a human to draw troll blood with a weapon in Vaskalia...victory would have ended your life even more painfully than if he'd killed you."

Gisela gasped as she realized that she didn't know their laws. So used to Thassalia where everyone brawled to the death for something as petty as stubbing a toe, she hadn't even consid-ered what would happen to her if she was attacked and fought back in Vaskalia. "I was defending myself."

"Wouldn't matter. You're not a citizen here, and they don't tolerate foreigners."

Glancing about, she realized how right he was. Everyone was staring at her with bloodlust in their eyes.

Her death was imminent and all because she hadn't both-ered to learn a stupid law that made no sense.

The man before her leaned down and whispered quietly in

her ear, "Follow me before the Watch comes and takes you into custody."

Without a second thought, she did so and then cursed herself as soon as they were on the street. Gisela stopped immediately. "Are you leading me into a trap or do you have something nefarious in mind?"

Arching his brow, he turned around slowly to stare at her in total disbelief. His expression would have been comical were it not for his lethal glare and demeanor. "For what purpose? You obviously have little to no money. And if you think I'd rape you after saving you, then you have absolutely no ability to read others."

He was right. She'd never taken the time to learn that skill. In her line of work, it didn't matter. Others fell into one of two categories: those to be ignored or those to be killed.

This stranger formed a third category that she wasn't used to dealing with.

"All I know about others is that they can never be trusted." No matter what category they fell into. "They say one thing to your face and act in complete contradiction the moment you turn your back. The troll you saved me from was willing to split open my skull because I accidentally bumped his arm so lightly, he didn't even spill his drink. For that minor offense he was willing to spill blood. No warning. Just a sick smile when he stood up to confront me."

Xaydin inwardly flinched as she gave voice to his own opinion and experience when it came to others. She was right about all that.

And they were strangers. He couldn't fault her for being suspicious. Too many creatures were cowards who preyed on those who were weaker. He had enough scars on his body to prove that.

And while she might be a formidable warrior, given her

actions and sword, she was still at a distinct disadvantage against an ogre, troll or giant.

"You're right, my lady. But I've seen enough beings preyed upon by others. My only intent was to get you out in one piece. Which I've done." He gave her a curt bow. "You're welcome." With that said, he turned to leave.

"Wait!"

Xaydin was surprised by her call. He turned back toward her slowly. "Yes?"

Gisela was as surprised by her actions as he was. She had no idea why she'd stopped him.

Other than one thing...

"Is there a safe place to stay tonight? An inn that will rent to one like me?"

He shook his head. "No...humans aren't welcome in Vaskalia. I doubt you'd find any inn in town that would let you stay even for a night."

Yet they knew him and feared him here. That much she'd gathered. Was he not human, too?

A sorcerer or shifter, perhaps?

No. Not with that armor and bearing. A mercenary more like. Some nobleman who'd fallen on hard times. That would make sense. They often drifted through the kingdoms, looking for work.

"Are you a sell-sword?" she asked.

"No."

She expected him to say more, but that one blunt word was all he seemed capable of. Interesting.

If there was no inn, she'd find an alley to bed down in. "In that case, thank you for helping me."

Xaydin cursed as she walked away, knowing what she intended to do for the night. While an alley in some streets would be fine, this wasn't one of those towns. Derthal was a lethal place for those who didn't know the customs and laws. The Watch would pick her up and probably kill her...

After they did unspeakable things to her first.

What's it to you?

Life was cheap in every kingdom. Vaskalia was no different than anywhere else on that count. But...

"If you can stomach me for one night, I'll share my room with you."

The look she gave him would freeze dragon fire. "Beg pardon?"

"I'm not negotiating a bedmate, love. I've already turned down half a dozen good offers for the night. I'm offering you a safe place to sleep until morning. You can have the bed. I'll take the floor...across the room and sleep in my clothes."

"Why would you offer that?"

He clenched his teeth as memories surged. But as always, he tamped them down with raw determination. His past would never rule him. He refused to be anchored by that weight. "I've seen the horrors of what happens to those without protectors. I'm only a predator to those who can fight back with equal skill or better. Trust me or don't. Makes no never mind to me. But if you sleep in the streets here, the Watch will take you, and your outcome won't be favorable."

Gisela didn't know why she believed those words. Trust was as alien to her as love or kindness. She didn't believe in either of those concepts.

At all.

She had no reason to trust him. Yes, he'd saved her, but that meant nothing in the world. She lived in Meara's court where hypocrisy reigned supreme. A favor always required a favor in turn, and then the one you helped would turn on you for no reason whatsoever.

The only thing she trusted in this life was that someone

would be at her throat at any moment. And often for no reason whatsoever.

Don't do it.

But where else was there to bed down? The stable wouldn't be safe. Anyone could come or go there—and often did. She'd gone to all five inns in this place, and all had refused to rent a room "to the likes of her."

Tomorrow, she'd need to go to Oath Island to begin her search for the *apaswere*. That would require a clear head, which meant a good night's sleep.

But how could she sleep in a room with this man?

You've done worse.

True. And it would be nice to sleep in a bed after being on the road this last week, sleeping in the damp brush while trying to stay alert for fear of being attacked. Really, she wanted a safe, comfortable place for the night.

Fine then. She'd keep her guard up and make sure he kept his word.

"Very well. Thank you. For everything you've done."

He inclined his head to her, then held his hand out to indicate the first inn she'd visited. The Violet Horse. Another peculiar name, but who was she to criticize?

Grateful for his unexpected kindness, she headed toward it.

He fell in beside her as if he knew she didn't like anyone at her back. Or maybe he did it to put her at ease. She noted that he also kept his arms crossed over his chest, away from his weapons.

But the most obvious telltale sign was the deliberate way he strode. Or actually, *swaggered* would be the most apropos description. His was a true warrior's lope. Smooth, steady and sexier than she wanted it to be. This was a man who was comfortable with himself and his place in the world.

One who craved a good fight and had no fear of losing.

There was also an air of refinement that clung to him. One that said he'd spent as much time at court as she had. Something at odds with his commanding warrior presence. Most warriors only came to court when summoned and left as soon as they could. Because of all the backbiting and hypocrisy, they usually avoided it at all costs.

Yet she'd been around enough courtiers to note that he held that same regal training as any nobleman.

Something proven when they reached the inn and he actually opened the door for her and let her enter first. He'd definitely had formal etiquette training.

As they crossed the nearly empty tavern room and headed for the stairs, a sharp voice called out to them.

"Oi! What are you about there?"

Her companion stopped to look at the ogre she assumed owned the place. "Heading to my room."

"We don't take her kind here. She needs to leave immediately."

A lethal aura descended over him. One she couldn't even begin to name. There really wasn't anything more than a very subtle steeling of his body and expression, yet it was unmistakable.

And terrifying.

The innkeeper audibly swallowed. "I...um...I mean we don't normally take her kind. But for you, my lord... Just keep her out of sight of the other guests, my lord...p-p-please."

Without a word, he gently took her elbow and escorted her to the stairs.

"Why is everyone so afraid of you?" she asked.

One tiny twitch of his lips let her know that question amused him. "I'm a scary being. Didn't you notice?"

She would definitely agree. "It's not that. There's something about you they know that I feel like I should, too."

He arched a brow to challenge her statement.

"I mean, you are scary. But their reactions are something more. Who are you? Really?"

"Tonight, I'm your roommate. That's all you need to know." He paused at the second door on the left and opened it.

Gisela went inside, then paused. The bed was giant, or should she say ogre and troll sized and filled with pillows. But that wasn't what concerned her.

There was another occupant swathed in a black hooded cloak that held heavy gold embroidery she assumed were alchemy symbols. One she'd almost run straight into.

Two armor clad arms came out from the folds of his cloak to lower his hood.

Her first thought was he came from Tenmaru—the kingdom to the north that was inhabited by yokai, tengu and oni. But he had elfin ears. The Tenmaru had horns, or other attributes that distinguished them from humans, fey and elves. But the one thing none of them had, to her knowledge, was pointed ears.

Then again, his armor was definitely that of the Tenmaru army, and so were his features. His dark, deep-set eyes were absolutely captivating and set in a face as perfect as her unknown companion's.

"Are you here to see the *roji no akuma?*" he asked her in a deeply accented tone.

She scowled at his question. "I don't understand that term."

"Alley demon," Xaydin said from behind her as he closed the door.

He inclined his head to the so-called demon she'd almost ran into. "Masakage...hustling fortunes in my room? Will your insults never cease?"

He laughed. "Pays for my alcohol, X. But no. I came to see you and was surprised to find a woman entering upon my arrival."

Gisela was even more concerned.

Her companion, X, cocked his head to see the bedroll on the floor behind Masakage. "Are you looking for a place to sleep since they don't take your kind, either?"

Masakage waved his hand and a long, twisted walking stick appeared in his grasp. One that held a large crystal at the top. The crystal began to glow, bathing the room with a beautiful blue light.

Only then was Gisela able to see that he'd set up a nice spot in the corner of X's room. One complete with a teapot, cup and a small bowl of food.

With a graceful sweep of his hand, Masakage gestured toward his makeshift space. "I didn't think you'd mind, brother. Had I known you weren't alone..."

They both stared at her curiously.

"I'll find another place to sleep." She took a step back.

"No one will harm you here, my lady." Masakage offered her a smile.

"He means what he says. Inshū dictates that he will care for and protect you so long as you're under his watch. You're safer here with him than you'd be in your mother's arms."

Not *her* mother's, but she understood the sentiment. Gisela glanced suspiciously toward X. "Inshū?"

X doffed his cloak. "Tenmarun hospitality law. Stay...we will protect you with our lives."

Gisela arched a brow...there was just one problem. "You're not Tenmarun."

Again, he glanced to Masakage. "He's set up camp in my room. If I interfere with his rules, he's honor bound to cut my throat. Not that I'd ever give him reason to."

Her instincts said to avoid them both at all costs. That she should also be on high alert around Masakage, but for some reason she felt more comfortable with them than she should.

And even more comfortable with the man named X and that made no sense whatsoever.

She grimaced. "I think the two of you would prefer for me to leave."

"Doesn't bother me in the least." X draped his cloak over a chair before he spoke to Masakage. "I encountered her in the pub."

Masakage arched a brow over that. "Encountered?"

X shoved playfully at him. "Get your mind from the gutter you call home. I saved her from a troll."

Masakage passed a stern frown at Gisela. "The fact you bothered to speak to her at all amazes me. That's not like you."

"I'm mellowing with age." X pulled a bedroll from his gear and placed it on the floor next to the pallet Masakage had made.

Masakage turned his attention to her. "Are you joining us in the room or leaving?"

Don't trust them.

Don't do it.

They were strangers. Never in her life had anyone ever protected her. Yet she didn't sense any treachery from either man.

If anything, they were oddly sincere, which was the most alien of all concepts.

Masakage reached into the black velvet pouch on his belt. Taking out a small coin, he studied it. "You're on a dangerous journey. And your past is one of deep sadness and hurt. It's not your nature to trust anyone. Given what I see, I understand. But you are going to have to make an awful decision soon that will either change your future for the better or relegate you to the darkness that birthed you."

He handed her the coin. "Again, you're welcome to join us for the night. Had either of us wanted to harm you, we'd already have done so."

"And as I said, his culture doesn't allow him to harm you unless you give him reason to. If he doesn't abide by the rules of Inshū, his gods will punish him. Personally, I think the gods punish us anyway and for no reason whatsoever, but I don't have his faith."

While X spoke, Gisela looked at the strange silver coin. She'd never seen anything like it. There were six swords on one side and a strange emblem on the other that looked like the image of an oni. Swollen jowls with tusks on a face that seemed to be judging her. "Are you a fortune teller?" she asked Masakage.

"I am many things." He tapped the staff against the ground, and the light went out.

Without another word, he returned to his pallet.

She started to leave, but her feet carried her farther into the room before she could prevent it.

Masakage manifested two more small clay cups and gracefully poured tea into them. He held a cup out toward X who accepted it. Then he poured another cup and held it out to her.

There was such elegance to his movements. She wished she possessed half his grace.

Sitting on the ground, she accepted it from him. "Thank you."

He inclined his head to her before he took a drink himself.

"What's your name?" Masakage asked.

"Gisela." She handed the small cup back to Masakage. "It was delicious. Again, thank you."

While X removed his armor in the corner, Masakage took the cup and glanced inside it. "Would you like more?"

She should say no, but it really had been delicious. She'd never tasted anything so soothing. It was like drinking a hug. "Yes, please."

He refilled the cup and returned it to her, then stirred his clay pot. "Are either of you hungry?"

Wearing a black linen tunic and pants, X took a seat on his makeshift bed. "You know I seldom eat."

"What about you?" Masakage asked her.

Much to her embarrassment, her stomach grumbled in response. It'd been two days since she had anything more than dried, stale bread and hard cheese to eat. And that only sparingly as she needed it to last.

With a kind smile, he manifested a bowl and spooned rice and some kind of gravy with chicken into it. It smelled incredible. "This is karee."

When he held it out to her, she didn't hesitate to take it even though she had no idea what he was serving. She really didn't care.

As he took up his own bowl and a pair of sticks that he used instead of a spoon, he glanced over to X. "She still doesn't trust us, brother."

"You blame her? I don't trust us, either...mostly because I know us."

Masakage laughed. "Have no fear, Gisela. No one will enter this room without my permission."

"Which means you'd best not sleepwalk."

Gisela was confused by X's words. "Why?"

Using powers she didn't know he had, X opened the door behind her. He tossed a small ball toward the entrance. As soon as it went through the doorway, the ball burst into pieces. "No one sets a trap better than Masakage."

That was impressive. But it made her wonder... "Then how was I able to enter?"

Masakage took a drink. "I sensed X's return to his room, so I lowered my ward to let you inside."

"And if I want to leave?"

"I've already adjusted it so that you can. No one here will hold you. I just want to make sure we all sleep in peace from anyone who might want to cause us harm."

Those were some terrifying powers. "Are you a wizard or sorcerer?"

He smiled at her. "I'm what you'd call *other*."

That last word hovered in the air between them. *Other* covered a lot of ground in their world.

She looked down at the strange coin he'd handed her and wondered exactly how powerful he was.

X paused as he caught her looking at it. "Count yourself lucky. Most have to pay handsomely to get an alley rat reading. Only a very small few get free ones."

"Really?"

Masakage shrugged. "We all have to make a living. And I'm an alley demon, not rat." There was a note in his tone that told her he knew what she did for her trade.

"So what brings you to the ogre lands?" she asked X.

"I live here."

That caught her off guard. A human in the homeland of ogres, trolls and giants? Given their innate hatred of humans or those who looked human, she'd never heard of anyone living here before who wasn't one of them.

"You live in the inn?"

X leaned back against the wall. "Not this one. I normally haunt the northern lands."

"Then you're passing through?"

"You could say that."

Giving up on X who was even more cryptic than she was, she turned her attention to Masakage. "What about you?"

"Also passing through on my way to Kernan."

The Stoneman kingdom. Interesting. "I wouldn't think they'd be any more receptive to us than the ogres are." Then again, she'd never been around Stonemen before. They were very much creatures of their own kingdom who seldom ventured beyond their borders.

"They're actually very tolerant. Being made of stone, they feel no threat from any other species. Only a sorcerer or wizard can kill them. It's why such creatures and all magic are strictly banned from their homeland and why they don't often leave their kingdom."

X snorted at that. "You will die without your magic. It's as second nature to you as your skin."

"I'll make do."

X scoffed. "Famous last words. Should I put them on your tombstone?"

They were so at ease with each other. She admired them for that. She'd never had a real friend and couldn't imagine being so comfortable with anyone else.

"How long have you two known each other?"

"Childhood," they said in perfect synchrony.

That explained it. They were probably more like family than friends. Not that she knew what either felt like. But she had witnessed others who were lucky enough to have close relationships.

A part of her that she didn't want to admit existed was jealous of such people.

"How long have you been an assassin for Queen Meara?"

Her breath caught at X's unexpected question. "Pardon?"

"Your black sword with the Thassalian crest. It gives you away. As do your attentive glances, accent and demeanor."

Of course it did. Gisela considered running. *I should never have agreed to bed down with them.* She knew better. No one could ever be trusted, and being this close to them gave them the opportunity to study her and her habits.

"She's bound for Oath Island." Masakage sat back to stare at her. "I think we both know why."

"To kill an *apaswere* so her queen can invade Licordia. But you needn't bother."

His words made her instantly curious. "Why would you say that? Have you already killed the demon?"

He laughed. "No."

"Then the demon could still be alive."

The men exchanged a look she didn't understand.

"Not for long." X handed his cup to Masakage. "Xaydin Kazakh has been put to the task."

That name went through her like a lightning bolt. "Xaydin Kazakh?" she repeated.

Masakage arched his brow as he put the cup away. "You know him?"

"Only by reputation." He was a prince whose father had been dethroned and then killed by an *apaswere*. As such, Xaydin had made it his life's quest to kill as many of them as he could. His exploits were legendary.

As was the rumor that he was insane.

Her assignment just became a lot harder.

Which meant she needed more information. "I'm surprised the High King would entrust a fallen prince with such a task."

Another odd look passed between the men. They definitely knew something about this that she didn't.

The question was what?

"You know the High King?" she prompted.

X shrugged with a smirk. "We've crossed paths a few times."

That formed a lump in her stomach as a bad feeling went through her. "Are you one of his Outlaws?"

His expression turned dark. "Why would you ask such?"

Because if they were, she'd have to kill them.

"Call me curious."

"You seem more sleepy than curious." Masakage glanced toward the bed.

An unexpected wave of exhaustion hit her. It'd been a long day of travel...a full week of it as she made her way toward Oath Island where the *apaswere* lived.

She'd only stopped here because she needed to find a ferry or boat to take her across to their island. Something she couldn't do this late at night, as she'd been told no one piloted a boat there after dusk.

Before she could stop herself, she let out a large yawn.

"Perhaps you should go on to bed?" Masakage asked her.

She nodded as she climbed, fully clothed, into the bed that was large enough to hold a giant.

He waved his hand in a circle, and as he did so, a soft blanket covered her. It was amazingly comfortable.

And made her even more tired.

"Thank you."

He inclined his head to her.

The sane part of Gisela told her to get up and find a private spot to sleep. But leaving comfort like this was hard.

No, it was impossible.

If she didn't know better, she'd swear the bed was holding her in place.

Unable to resist, she yawned again, then fell down to sleep.

Xaydin smirked at his half-brother. "What did you do?"

"Small sleeping spell. She'll never know."

"You better hope not. By the way she carries herself, I suspect she's one hell of a warrior. Did you pick up on anything?"

Masakage gave him a droll stare. "You know I did."

"Are you going to share?"

He set aside his cup. "I don't play well with others."

That was certainly true. Xaydin still remembered the first

time they'd met. Masakage had been covered in pig shit. Struggling with the chores Meara's flunkey had heaped on the poor child. Back then, Masakage's powers had been undeveloped and unpredictable.

Not knowing they were related, Xaydin had felt awful for the boy, as he'd been terribly bullied by others.

Being the bastard son of a troll, Xaydin had been born with his strength and powers intact. Powers no one expected courtesy of his fairy mother. He'd used them to fry the assholes who'd picked on any of his friends.

But that hadn't gone well for him.

The more he resisted, the worse his punishments. Sadly, resistance was his best trait.

At least it gave him an inhuman pain tolerance. And a bitterness in his soul that had never healed.

That was fine by him. With the exception of his handful of friends, Masakage and their sister, he didn't like being around others, anyway. He found most people too taxing to deal with.

Masakage was one of the few exceptions. While his half-brother had been held hostage in Meara's court with the rest of them, he'd never officially been admitted as one of their "Outlaws." No one knew why he'd refused to claim their kinship. His brother was mysterious that way and it wasn't in Xaydin to judge anyone else.

Masakage tucked away his dishes. "What do you think we should do with her?"

Xaydin shrugged. "Not quite sure. I suppose it depends on her reaction once she finds out who I am."

"And the fact that she's been sent to protect the beast you're here to slay."

He arched a brow at that. "Pardon?"

"That was her final thought before she went to sleep. You're her archenemy, X."

That was nothing new. He seemed to be most people's arch-enemy. "And?"

Masakage put away his things, then stretched out on his pallet. "Indeed."

He shook his head at his brother's weird one-word comment.

But this news was definitely something to ponder as he considered how Gisela would react to their conflicted goals.

Xaydin used his own powers to pull the blanket up around her so that she wouldn't get cold. She was a creature of great beauty, and he was trying to reconcile how she'd come to serve the centaur bitch queen.

Probably a hostage like they'd been. Only he'd never seen her while they'd been held.

Which meant nothing. There had been dozens of hostages, and they hadn't all been kept in the same place.

Meara had taken a great deal of pleasure in turning her prisoners against everyone and everything. Had he not had the Outlaws as his brethren, there was no telling how he'd have ended up, especially after he'd been told about his father's death.

He was grateful every day of his life for the stroke of luck he'd had in finding his fellow Outlaws. They alone had kept him safe and relatively sane.

"Should we kill her?"

Xaydin was shocked by that question. "When did you become so bloodthirsty?" Normally, those kinds of thoughts were his domain.

"Life...as well as my older brother...has taught me that some-times it's best to strike first."

I am an asshole.

He should have taught his brother more productive things. Like crochet or pottery.

"What about Inshū?" Xaydin reminded him.

"The gods will understand."

Wow. Masakage was in a foul mood tonight. "She's after the *apaswere*. Let her waste her time chasing it."

Masakage took her cup and held it out toward Xaydin. "Can you read the leaves?"

"Not my talent." But he took the cup anyway and looked into it. All he saw were grinds in the bottom.

"There's more to her journey than just Oath Island."

Xaydin wondered how Masakage could know that based on nothing more than some grinds swirled in the bottom of a clay cup. It made no sense to him. "What else do you see?"

"Whatever you do, don't tell her you serve Dash."

That was easy enough. "I don't serve him."

Masakage rolled his eyes. "You know what I mean."

He did, but something in his soul loved to antagonize his brother. "Why?"

"She's been ordered to execute any Outlaw she finds." He took the cup back from Xaydin, rinsed it with water, then put it into his pack with his other dishes. "That means you."

"Then perhaps we should execute her."

"Not based on what I see."

Xaydin didn't like that tone of voice. "Tell me why you've changed your mind. You were so willing to just a few seconds ago."

Masakage didn't answer. "Rest. You'll need it."

That made his stomach cramp. "I hate your ability to see the future, especially when you don't share that knowledge."

"You're not the only one. I find it most annoying myself."

That was something Masakage had never admitted to before. Interesting. "Is there any way to control it?"

He shook his head. "Believe me, I've tried."

Damn. He didn't envy him, then. While others might want

to know the future, he didn't. Here and now was all that interested him. The future would come regardless, and he had no
plans for it.

"Has your vision ever been wrong?"

Masakage shook his head. "As much as I hate the ability to
see the future, I hate it even more when it doesn't show me
anything and I'm blindsided."

"That's so fucked up."

"Yes, it is." Sighing, he rolled over to face the door. "Get a
good night's sleep, X. We need to rest while we can."

"Is that a warning?"

Masakage rolled back over to offer him his bag of coins.

Normally, he'd refuse.

Tonight, however, he was curious, so he reached in and
pulled one out. It held the image of an oni on one side and
something that looked like swords on the other.

He handed it off to Masakage who scowled at it. "Six
swords."

"What's that mean?"

"Your journey is tied to hers."

"Is that from my brother or from the alley rat?"

"Alley demon," Masakage corrected.

Xaydin wrinkled his nose. "The Masakage I know was an
alley rat like the rest of us."

He scoffed. "Don't live in the past, X. Wallowing in tragedy
isn't good for anyone and especially not trolls."

Maybe, but as much as he did his best to move on, he had a
hard time letting go. Losing his father had gutted him in a way
nothing else had. What they'd endured in Meara's court was
even harder. "How do you manage?"

"One breath at a time, brother. One breath at a time." And
with that, he rolled over again to sleep.

Xaydin listened to the quiet. Living above a very active

tavern, silence wasn't something he heard often. As a child in Meara's court, it'd been the sounds of agonized screams and those begging for mercy that had lulled him to sleep.

Sounds that still rang in his ears. Which was why he lived above a tavern. Silence, to him, was disturbing and he did his best to avoid it.

All his life, he'd tried to right wrongs. It was a burden his father had tasked him with.

You're stronger than your older brother. Smarter. It's why you must go and why I need to keep Zagrun at home. He'd never survive on his own.

Zagrun...

His other half-brother whom he hated with every breath he drew. If only his father had held Masakage's sight, then he'd have known he was signing his own death warrant by keeping his full-blooded troll at home with him while he sent Xaydin off to suffer.

Zagrun had been stupid and easily led astray by their father's enemies, and especially their uncle.

At least you don't have his fate.

True. He'd only been enslaved for a short time as a child. Zagrun would never again know freedom so long as their uncle lived. It was why he didn't kill him. He wasn't about to spare his brother one single day of misery given the nightmare their father had endured.

It was also why the other trolls respected him and why the current king didn't dare come after him even though everyone knew Xaydin was the rightful king of Vaskalia.

To try and come for him would be the last mistake King Gregun would make. If he ever came for him or sent an assassin, Xaydin would take the crown from his head and choke him with it.

Uncle or not.

Forcing his thoughts away from that topic, he glanced over to the woman in his bed.

And here I am on the floor...

His father was wrong. *He* was the idiot, not Zagrun.

Now he had something else on his mind, and a body that was rife with unsated pain.

Bloody figures. Who else would he lust for other than a woman with orders to kill him? One whose *raison d'être* was diametrically opposed to his.

Protect an *apaswere*. What a laughable thought. Oath Keepers didn't need a bodyguard.

Except for when they were being pursued by him.

Oh, the irony.

Poor Gisela. There was no telling what Meara would do to her once she failed her mission. And sadly, she would fail. He'd promised Dash the head of the *apaswere* who bore their contract, and that was exactly what he intended to deliver to him.

Pretty temptations be damned.

He owed his sanity to Dash, and he owed the death of all *apaswere* for what they'd done to his father.

No one would stop him from this.

2

Gisela came awake slowly to a delicious smell. For one heartbeat, she thought she was at her imaginary childhood home, and warmth flooded her.

Until she remembered the truth.

What she was and where she'd been sent.

Then, her thoughts went to the men.

Shit!

Sitting up, she started to panic until she saw that she was still fully dressed.

More than that, she was alone in the room. What had happened to X and Masakage? She looked to their corner and saw that all their items had been picked up. There wasn't a single trace of them.

Not even a stray thread.

She should be elated to find herself alone. Instead, she was oddly disappointed.

Which made no sense. She should be grateful that they'd kept their side of the bargain. They'd allowed her to sleep in peace and without being molested.

Men of their words...

She wouldn't have believed it possible. Yet here she was. Safe.

Unmolested.

And what a sad indictment of her life that "safe" made her uncomfortable. She was so used to living on high alert, ready to be attacked, that she couldn't relax enough to enjoy a moment of tranquility.

I'm so broken.

And she had a task to see to. Gathering her things, she made ready to leave.

Just as she reached the door, it opened.

Gisela stepped back, preparing herself to fight.

Until she saw X who paused as he met her gaze. "Relax, my lady. I come in peace."

It was only then that she realized she'd drawn her sword. "Sorry." She quickly sheathed it. "Old habits."

"Understood." He held the platter in his hands out toward her. "I brought you something to eat."

"Oh. I thought the two of you had left already."

"We were about to, but I wanted to make sure you had something to tide you over as those below won't feed you." He made an uncomfortable face. "Might feed *on* you...but they won't allow you to break your fast."

How kind of him to care. "Thank you." She really meant that, too. It wasn't the automatic response that people gave out of habit.

Inclining his head, he carried the platter to a small table beside the bed and set it down.

Without another word, he headed toward the hallway. "X?"

He paused in the doorway to look back at her. "Yes?"

"What does X really stand for?"

He hesitated. At first, she didn't think he'd respond, but after a hefty pause he gave her a wry grin. "Xaydin."

Then, he closed the door.

That name hit her like a fist.

Xaydin? Had she heard that correctly?

He was the one after her *apaswere?*

"Oh my God..." She couldn't breathe as everything played through her head.

Her X was the troll prince who'd sworn himself to killing all *apaswere...*

Xaydin Kazakh the Oathbreaker.

How in the name of everything holy could that be the man of legend? Then again, it made sense why everyone was so afraid of a human.

Only he wasn't supposed to be human.

"You don't look like a troll." At all. Nothing other than his huge, muscled body and even that looked more human than troll.

Or at least what she knew of them.

But what if it *was* him? That meant he was on his way to kill the same *apaswere* she was supposed to protect.

And he knew what her mission was! How could she have been so stupid as to even mention it? She should have stopped talking. Or never talked at all.

I'm an absolute idiot!

No, she'd been alone on the road for too long and had welcomed the company, even though she knew better.

Furious at herself and them, she left the room immediately to chase after one of the most lethal creatures in the Thirteen Kingdoms.

Maybe the most lethal of all.

Which explained why her knees were weak. Something that

infuriated her even more because she hated fear. Most of all, she hated this feeling of vulnerability. *I'm better than this.*

She was a trained assassin who'd killed dozens of men.

But they weren't the ones who were renowned for brutality. Ones who hunted other warriors who had thousands of years of experience. That took an unbelievable skill.

An unparalleled degree of stupidity.

Don't let your fear lead you...

It reminded her of the first time she'd been sent by the queen to kill someone. Her hands had trembled and her entire body had ached. Her heart had throbbed in her ears. Every part of her being had been out of sorts to the point that she felt like she was in an unknown vessel.

And as she looked down on herself taking that life, it'd felt as if she were someplace else. As if she saw a stranger who was taking actions she had no control over.

I'm not that child anymore.

True.

She'd come a long way since then. Been through so much more.

This shouldn't be a problem, and her stomach shouldn't be tied into a tangle of nerves.

Yet here she was.

She went down the stairs and into the inn that was now crowded with trolls, ogres and giants, eating their morning meals. Others who glanced at her with open disdain and hatred.

They weren't the ones who mattered. She was after the half-troll, wearing black armor and his wizard companion...

36

XAYDIN KNEW the instant Gisela left the inn and headed for where they were packing their gear on their horses. A rarity for Masakage who didn't need a horse to travel or even supplies that he normally conjured when he desired them. Only the fact he was heading into Kernan where he wouldn't be able to use his magic to portal there made this a necessity.

As for Xaydin...

The Oathkeepers didn't have the same dietary requirements he did. He had to load a few days' worth of supplies or make his meal from their roasted, desiccated bodies. And as much as he might be tempted to eat one to prove a point, they were so nauseating in appearance that he'd rather chew his own boots than skin one of them for nourishment.

He exchanged an amused glance with Masakage as his brother also saw her approaching.

With a determined stride, she cut across the street and didn't stop until she was beside him. "You're the Oathbreaker."

"That's one of my titles."

She gaped with an astonished expression. "You don't deny it?"

"It's the truth. Why should I?"

"Because you know I'm going to protect the one you're after."

He scoffed at her bravado. "You think that. But my experience says you're wasting your time."

Fury flared in her eyes as she stared up at him. "You're mocking me?"

"I would never do that. Besides, I admire your spirit and drive. And given that this is going to be a thing with us, I offer you a bargain."

Gisela froze at those words as all manner of thoughts went through her head at what he could mean. Some of them weren't so bad.

Others were terrifying.

"Explain this bargain."

"Yes," Masakage said with an interested grin. "Explain your thoughts, brother."

Xaydin smirked at him. "Stay out of it, mouse." Then, he turned his attention to her. "Since I don't want to have to keep watching my back for you, I'll escort you to the *apaswere* I seek. If you can stop me from killing him, then, he'll live. Otherwise, I'll send his head to Dash and let Dash have at your queen."

His nonchalance made the hair on the back of her neck stand up. "Is this a trick?"

"Absolutely not. I'm not your queen. I don't play tricks."

Masakage approached her. "He really doesn't. Not even when we were kids. He just sits around, brooding."

Xaydin shoved at him. "Don't you have someplace to be?"

"I do. Are we taking the ferry to the island?"

A scowl furrowed Xaydin's brow. "I didn't give you an invitation."

"You did not. My curiosity is such that I can't leave now. This is going to be spectacular. My errand can wait." Masakage smiled. "But yours...this I wouldn't miss for all the kingdoms."

Xaydin growled. "I hate you."

"Hate you less."

Their interaction baffled her. Of course, she knew very little about such things as she'd never spent any time around her siblings.

Maybe it was normal?

Not that it mattered. She was on a quest, and no one would stop her.

Xaydin jerked his chin toward the inn she'd just left. "Go get your things. Tell me which horse is yours and I'll saddle it while we wait for you."

There was only one problem with that. "I don't have a horse."

He arched a brow. "Foot or magic?"

She knew he was asking how she'd gotten here. That was something she definitely couldn't answer. At least not truthfully, because it was shameful to her. And it was something she never spoke about to anyone.

So she answered with the closest to truth that she could. "Foot."

"I'll get you a horse. Go collect your things."

Not sure if he would or if this was a trick, she returned to their shared room and quickly gathered her travel pack. She had to move fast before they left her.

If he really intended to take her to the *apaswere*, then she couldn't let this chance pass.

While she knew this was going to be a fight to see who won their way, she was determined to be the victor. No one would stop her from her task.

Because if she returned home without the *apaswere*, Meara would have her killed.

This wasn't just a mission for her.

It was everything.

3

"Is this a trick?"

Xaydin blinked at Masakage's question as he finished saddling his horse. "No."

"You're really going to let her go with you?"

"That's what I said."

"Why?"

He had no idea. Not really. It wasn't in his nature to care for anyone or anything. His soul was blacker than his heart, and he honestly liked it that way and had no desire to change.

No entanglements. Just him and his vengeance quest. He'd never wanted company or even conversation.

All he wanted was to behead the beast for Dash and go back to his solitary ways.

But the one thing he knew about creatures like Gisela, she wouldn't stop as long as she had a mission.

Because we're just alike.

Only he wasn't as passionate. He did what he did and that was it.

She still had feelings and convictions, which made her dangerous and unpredictable. And the last thing he needed was such a person trailing after him, mucking up his mission as she sought to slow him down or stop him.

So, he smirked at his brother. "Better to keep my enemy at my side, in plain sight, than to risk her coming up behind me when I least expect it."

Masakage winced. "Understood."

"You still coming with us?"

"Wouldn't miss it for anything." He levitated into his saddle. His long black hair fell to his waist as his powers perfectly draped his robes around him.

Xaydin rolled his eyes. "Should I call you princess from now on?"

"Only if you do so in a loving manner."

Stifling a laugh, Xaydin went to pay for the horse. Hopefully, Gisela would be a bit more appreciative than his brother.

"Can I help you..." The stable master drew up short as he caught sight of Xaydin. His greenish-tinted skin paled noticeably. "Your Highness." He fell into a proper bow.

"Please, don't." Those formalities angered him. "I'm no prince."

The stable master glanced about nervously before he whispered, "You'll always be our prince."

He appreciated the loyalty. But such words were dangerous. His uncle would have both their heads if he ever caught wind of this conversation. Not that Xaydin really cared about himself. He'd welcome the fight.

No, he was *wanting* that fight. Nothing would please him more than to feel his uncle's blood on his hands. The only thing that saved that beast's life was the fact that he didn't want the crown.

Oh, the irony of that.

His uncle had killed his father for something Xaydin would

have handed over to him had he only asked. Power had never appealed to him. Not in any way.

In fact, his last conversation with his father had been over that very truth.

You will be king. It's your destiny.

It was one he might have embraced had his father not sent him off as a hostage. Meara's court had soured him forever on power and royalty.

Now...

His father was dead, and he was technically a fugitive. A very public one, but a fugitive, nonetheless. It was why he chose to stay in Vaskalia. Forever a thorn in his uncle's ass.

Anger boiled inside him, but he forced it down and focused on what he needed to do.

"I'm here to buy your finest horse and a saddle."

The stable master's eyes widened. "Of course, High...my lord." He scurried away.

Xaydin peered outside where Masakage waited.

Gisela still hadn't returned.

Why are you looking for her?

If he didn't know better, he'd think he cared. But that was ridiculous. The only thing that mattered to him was avenging his father. One day, he would find the Oath demon who'd killed him, and when he did...

He'd have a new moniker.

Oathbreaker was far too mild for the havoc he intended to unleash. Deathdealer, maybe...

Or monster. He really liked that one.

"Will this work, my lord?"

Xaydin turned back toward the stable master to see the fine black gelding. It was a beautiful beast. "Perfect. How much do I owe you?"

He handed over the reins. "Nothing. Your father was a

good troll and a great king. When I was young, I was conscripted into the army even though my father was ill. As soon as your father found out that I was the only son, he sent me home to be with my parents during my father's last days. Had I not been here, my mother and younger sister would have been thrown to the streets. It's a kindness I've never forgotten. Consider this my honor to take care of King Benesh's son now."

Those words touched him and hurt him. Mostly because his father had been much quicker to defend and protect others than he'd been to protect his own child.

I'm sending you because it wouldn't be right for me to send another's son to Meara. How could I ask for that sacrifice from another if I'm not willing to make it myself?

That was the good and bad of his father. Had he kept Xaydin at home, his father would still be alive.

But then Xaydin wouldn't be the ruthless bastard that he was. Or nearly as accomplished a fighter.

To that, he owed both his father and the centaur bitch who'd carved him into the animal he currently was.

"Thank you." Xaydin took the reins and headed back toward Masakage who sat on the horse with his hands tucked into his sleeves. It was a strange, arrogant stance, but then his brother was a strange, arrogant being.

"Is that mine?"

He paused to see Gisela behind him.

How had she done that? No one ever snuck up on him. And he definitely didn't like it.

It was enough to make him want to lash out at her. But he wasn't that big an ass. He'd just make sure that he watched her in the future. Make sure she didn't ever do that again.

"It is. Need a hand up?"

She approached the horse slowly. "I'll be fine, thank you."

Gisela said that, but the horse nickered and stepped away as if it feared her.

"Sh..." She held her hand out to gently stroke its nose. Still, the horse was unsettled.

Xaydin snorted. "Must smell the centaur on you."

A peculiar light darkened her eyes before she offered him an amused, timid smile. "Horses have never particularly liked me. It's why I prefer walking."

Xaydin held his hand out to hover over the horse's eyes. Using his powers, he soothed the beast. Even so, the horse wasn't happy. There was something about Gisela that bothered it.

How strange. Stranger still was the fact that his powers picked up nothing from her. She seemed human.

But looks could be deceiving. No one could look at him or Masakage and guess their heritage. Other than his size, no one would ever know that he was part troll or sidhe.

With that thought in mind, he helped her mount, then turned toward his brother. *Can you tell what blood flows in her veins?*

He shook his head. *Why do you ask?*

A hunch.

There was more to her than what he saw. He just didn't know what, and he didn't like unsolved puzzles.

Trying not to think about it, he went to his horse and swung himself up into the saddle. He took a minute to scowl at them. "Ready?"

Gisela nodded, even though she wasn't sure about this. If she didn't know better, she'd swear the two men were talking to each other with their thoughts.

Did Xaydin have telepathy? Meara didn't and neither did she. But she had no idea what powers trolls possessed. Other than physical strength and height.

45

And apparently sarcasm that wouldn't stop.

Xaydin swept his gaze over them, then kicked his horse forward.

Gisela followed with Masakage riding by her side.

"Have you ever been to Oath Island?" she asked Masakage.

"No. Not exactly the kind of place I venture to."

There was a peculiar note in his voice. "What kind of places do you frequent?"

"Ones with real monsters."

Xaydin scoffed. "You don't think real monsters are those I fight?"

"Didn't say that. The *apaswere* are their own special hell. I don't envy you those fights. Or your mission."

"His mission?" Gisela asked.

Masakage looked away.

After a brief hesitation, Xaydin answered. "My father was killed by an *apaswere*. One day, I'm going to find him and make sure he never takes another life."

"How long have you been searching?" The question was no sooner out of her mouth than she regretted it.

Thrice more given the amount of anger in his eyes. It was such that they flashed red.

"Since your father died," she answered for him. "Sorry for the thoughtless, stupid question."

Given her own feelings for her father, she had a hard time remembering that other people didn't feel the same way about theirs.

Paternal love. The most alien of concepts for her. Well, aside from maternal love. She didn't understand that one either.

Or any other kind of love, really. Her world had been too harsh for that.

How any kind of love could survive this hell of a world, she had no idea. People betrayed and they lied.

Never trust anyone.

Yet here she was, trusting two creatures who were her enemies. Well, maybe not trust. It was impossible to trust those she knew had opposing goals.

More than that, she knew the troll prince would kill her if he ever discovered the truth about her.

Get in line.

He wouldn't be the only one who'd cause her harm. That was a long and mighty list of foes who would relish her death. Starting with her mother if that secret was ever revealed.

How she hated this world. This mission.

She should probably hate her companions as well. Yet they were oddly amusing.

And as they rode, she could imagine meeting them in other circumstances. More normal ones such as a ball.

What an utterly ridiculous thought... She'd never been the ball type. Meara loved such things. Mostly because they allowed her to flaunt her money and wardrobe. The queen never passed up a chance to show off to others. It was also a well-known secret that no one could outshine her, as those who did were often fed to ravenous beasts Meara kept in her stables.

Or she ordered them strangled.

Another reason Gisela always kept to the shadows. She had no intention of being a rival for the queen.

"You've grown silent." Masakage moved his horse closer to hers. "Are you lost in your thoughts?"

She was, but she'd never admit it. "Trying to imagine the Oath Lands."

Xaydin snorted. "Looks like any place else. Except for the demons who live there. They're particularly ugly."

"How so?" She'd never seen an *apaswere* before.

Masakage lifted his hand, and when he did, a blue ball formed over his palm. Inside the swirling blues, she saw the image of a huge, twisted being. One that had wings made of flesh and other appendages she couldn't even define...all of which were covered with writing.

Literally every inch of its skin, including its eyelids and bald head. "Behold the *apaswere*."

He was right. It was all kinds of ugly. Gisela couldn't take her eyes off it. "Do they all look like that?"

Xaydin glanced over his shoulder. "They do. The more flesh, the more contracts they hold. They use their magic to elongate their limbs and grow or attach other body parts so that they can accommodate their records. When that fails, they flay the skin off others, even their own kind or they merge them-selves together to have more contract space."

Gisela grimaced at what he described. The nightmare of it. How did they live? "What started this?"

"One twisted wizard." Xaydin curled his lip as Masakage closed his hand and the image vanished. "Centuries ago, he made a pact with the sidhe king to enforce a contract with another. It was forged in blood on his skin with his promise to unleash demons to protect their contract. Once he started, other wizards, witches and sorcerers followed. Each one wanting to outdo the other until they created an entire race that had no other purpose."

Masakage nodded. "That's the curse of striving to follow another and outdo them. Sooner or later, it becomes someone's greatest folly."

"Now we have an entire race of half demonic creatures who have no souls and no purpose other than to enforce ridiculous terms." The anger in Xaydin's voice was palpable.

"What contract did your father break?"

Xaydin came to a stop in order to level the most malevolent stare toward her that she'd ever seen. "He didn't. A shape shifter pretended to be the man my father had a contract with and broke it. Thinking they no longer had a contract, my father attacked, believing he had every right to do so. He was set up, but the *apaswere* didn't care about truth...or what consequences would befall an entire kingdom. He fulfilled the contract by killing an innocent troll who'd been deceived."

"And because of that, the only thing Xaydin hates more than an *apaswere* is a shifter."

"A pox on them all. May they burn and rot. Preferably by my hands."

That made her blood run cold, and she was glad they knew nothing about her.

Except for one thing... "You don't hate King Dash. Isn't he a shifter?"

Xaydin snorted. "He's a unicorn. They only take one human form and can't become a deceptive lie that gets an innocent killed. Besides, you can look at their horns and tell if they're trustworthy or not."

True. Unicorns had several different shades of their horns. If they were treacherous, their horns were gray. If they were dangerous, red.

And black like the king's...

All bets were off. He was death incarnate and a threat to anyone who got in his way.

Masakage tsked at his brother. "In X's mind they're not the same thing. Only true shifters rattle his rage."

Good to know. She'd make sure to keep her powers in check. Just as she had to do around Meara. The queen became insane if anyone shifted forms, especially in front of her. Her jealousy over that ability was terrifying. It was why Meara hated the entire unicorn race. She took it as a personal slight that they had the ability to become fully human while she was locked in her centaur form. In the queen's mind, her entire race was a spell gone wrong. A genetic mistake.

Meara viewed her own race as unnatural. And that self-hatred had destroyed everything in her life. Nothing was enough for their queen. All she'd been gifted with and none of it made her happy.

It would never be enough.

Even if Gisela succeeded in protecting the *apaswere* or the queen found some way to attack and destroy the unicorns without incurring its wrath, Gisela knew it wouldn't satisfy the queen.

Meara knew nothing of happiness. Only brutality and misery. The queen reveled in it, and she made sure that everyone around her was equally as miserable.

Sighing, Gisela tried to put it from her thoughts. There was no need in drifting to the past or to things she couldn't change.

So she let her gaze wander into the thick trees around them. Until she saw something move. "What's that?"

"What's..." Xaydin didn't get to finish his words before a dark shadow rushed toward them. It moved so fast that she barely registered what it was before it engulfed him.

Cursing, Masakage attacked the shadow with fireballs. The darkness wrapped around Xaydin as if it were trying to devour him. Xaydin's skin and eyes turned bright red.

With a vicious growl, he slung his arm out, and as he did so, the darkness burst into embers.

Gisela stared in awe. "What was that?"

"The *apaswere* knows I'm coming for him." Xaydin's tone was flat and emotionless.

"Does this happen often?"

Xaydin gave her a wry grin as his skin and eyes returned to normal. "Enough to keep me young and primed."

How she hated the fact that smile made him so bloody handsome. Almost charming. How?

You need to hate him.

But that was easier said than done. He was irresistible, and she had no idea why. Was it some kind of glamour spell? A potion? She had no idea what to call it. All she knew was that she was drawn to a man she should hate.

One with unknown powers. Terrifying powers, if the truth was known.

"Do they always come at you?"

"No. Normally, they have no idea that I'm after them until I take their heads. But given all that's transpired with Dash and your queen, I imagine our friend is very much aware of my mission and dreading the day we meet."

"How do you intend to find him?" she asked.

"I have my ways."

Her gaze went to Masakage. "Magic, then."

Masakage shook his head. "Not the kind you're thinking. Yes, I could concoct a potion for tracking, but he doesn't need one."

"Troll powers?" she tried again.

"You know nothing of my people, do you?"

No, not really. "There weren't any in Thassalia, and I've never been sent beyond our borders before this." Meara preferred her to kill those in their court or the nobles who angered her. All of whom were inside the queen's kingdom.

"Then you don't know anything about Meara, either."

She resented Xaydin's tone. "I beg your pardon?"

"We both lived there for a number of years." Masakage's voice was much kinder and lacked the venom of Xaydin's.

But those words explained why Xaydin had become angry.

"I'm sorry."

Xaydin scowled. "For what?"

"If you were in her lands, then you were hostages and I know how she treated those she kept in bondage. No one deserved that." Not with Meara's cruelty. Even now, the horrors of those years were seared into her memories.

As bad as her time with Meara had been, it was nothing compared to the nightmares Meara had gleefully subjected her captives to.

"I wish you'd been spared her *hospitality*."

Xaydin was caught off guard by the sincerity in her tone. That was actual kindness he heard. He only remembered it because it was rare to find, and the few times he had, he'd made an effort to commit it to memory.

Most creatures were like him. Angry and bitter to the core of their souls. Aching so much that they lashed out at others just for spite.

It was the one thing he hated most about himself. He hadn't always been that way. There had been a time when he'd been a happy child.

Unlike Masakage, he'd been accepted by his father. Loved even.

No. Treasured.

His father had appreciated the fact that Xaydin was different from other trolls.

It makes you special, lad. You are a child of three distinct worlds. That means you know more than others, as you feel it in your bones. Never lose sight that you owe loyalty to your mother's blood as much as mine.

He hadn't really understood those words until he met his brother. Masakage had finally given him an appreciation for their mother and her powers. For that entire side of his family, as well as their heritage.

To this day, he was grateful for the lesson. Harsh as it'd been.

Gisela cleared her throat. "You haven't answered my question, you know? How do you track an *apaswere*?"

"How were *you* planning to find him?"

By the expression on her face, he could tell she wanted to scream at his refusal to answer. "Ask."

He burst out laughing. Until he realized she was serious. "And you thought...what? They'd tell you?"

"I'm not trying to harm him. I want to protect him from you. Why wouldn't they tell me how to find him to keep him safe?"

Mostly because they closed ranks and hated outsiders even worse than trolls and ogres.

And he couldn't help but point out another matter. "What makes you think it's a male who holds the contract?"

Confusion flickered across her beautiful face. "I thought they all were men."

"They are not. Some are even children."

Her eyes widened with horror. "You kill children?"

"No!" The mere thought offended him. What kind of monster... Well, to be fair, he *was* a monster. Just not the kind that would ever harm a child, and it bothered him more than it should that she'd think that of him. "The children aren't allowed to take contracts until they're able to defend themselves and see their terms met. Usually around fifteen or sixteen. I just wanted you to check your knowledge and assumptions. Before you seek something, you might want to understand it."

She rolled her eyes. "How easy you make it sound. As if there's a history book about them. Not to mention when Queen Meara sends you off to do something, you don't ask a lot of questions...or dawdle. You go immediately."

Those words hit him like a fist. Mostly because he knew exactly what they meant.

Gisela was right. No one asked Meara questions. To do so would awaken her nasty wrath.

"How did you get into her service?"

She glanced away. "Like you, my father abandoned me to her."

Those words also offended him. She made a lot of assumptions about things she knew nothing. "Just to be clear, my father didn't abandon me. He had no choice."

She snorted in derision. "We all have choices. Your father was king of the trolls, ogres and giants, and you're telling me that he couldn't have fought against her to keep you safe?"

"It was more complicated than that." And it was something he struggled with on his own. He loved his father dearly, but he'd never understand why his father had given in to Meara's demands without a fight. Why he'd forced Xaydin to go when he could have sent another.

As Gisela had noted, they'd had an army, and his mother's and father's magic. He would have never handed over his own child. Not for anything.

Not for any cost. He'd have fought every devil in every realm for the sake of his child.

And it was hard to forgive his father for the fact that he hadn't been so protective. But he'd never been in his father's position, and for that, he was truly grateful.

Maybe he would have done the same thing.

That was the nightmare that forever haunted him.

Would he give up his child for his kingdom?

And it made him curious about something. "If the only way to secure your kingdom and procure peace for your people meant you had to send your child to another, would you do it?"

Gisela frowned at his question. "No. Never."

"So you would send your kingdom to war rather than trust your child to protect himself?"

She nodded. "Knowing what I know...what I've seen? Yes. I would send grown soldiers to die before I'd risk my child's safety with someone I didn't know."

"What of the innocent children who would die in the conflict?"

"I would trust their parents and my soldiers to protect them. I would never send an innocent into hell to secure anything. It's not a child's place to protect their kingdom."

There it was. That note in her voice that told him she'd been a hostage too. Only she didn't want to acknowledge it for some reason.

But he knew the hatred and venom that lived within her. It was the infernal fire that stayed inside him, night and day. All of them, really. Everyone who'd been sent to Meara as a hostage. None of them had survived that trauma without being filled with darkness and rage.

How could they?

They'd spent years being beaten and tortured. And all for the centaur queen's depravity. "I'm sorry, Gisela."

"Sorry for what?"

He didn't answer. There was no need, especially since they were nearing the shop he'd come out of their way to visit.

4

Kicking his horse forward, he left Gisela with Masakage.

Gisela watched him leave with a frown. "Where's he off to?"

"Goddess and the Moon."

"Pardon?"

He jerked his chin toward the small cottage that lay before them. From this distance, it looked like a small thatched home with a well-kempt yard. "The shop ahead. X will need supplies for our crossing. I'm sure we're here to pick them up."

"In such a hurry?"

He shrugged. "I don't question my brother. I'm just along for the irritation."

But she was curious. Kicking her own mount forward, she rushed to the small cottage where strange, twisted statues lay in a rock garden off to the right side. She wasn't sure if those statues were supposed to be enemies or friends.

Or even what the statues represented.

Ignoring them, she dismounted, then went to the old iron door that she carefully pushed open.

This definitely wasn't a home. The walls were lined with hand-carved shelves. Beautiful shelves that were filled with all manner of bottles.

But not just any glass bottles...

Potions. Made of different sizes and shapes. All sealed with various colors of wax and topped with a totem of some sort.

Gisela had never seen anything like this. But the strangest of all was the fact that most of the potions were swirling with vibrant colors. As if an invisible hand was inside making the liquid twist in beautiful patterns.

Very strange.

Xaydin turned toward her. "Care to wait outside?"

"Rather not." This was too incredible a place to not explore it. "What are all these?"

"My hard work."

Gisela gasped as a deep, sultry voice sounded from behind her. Turning, she found what had to be the most beautiful woman she'd ever beheld. Tall and slender, she had jet-black hair that matched her soulless eyes. Eyes that were painted with red and black to match her lips. Two parallel lines were drawn between her eyes, and above them was a delicate sliver of a moon. Dressed in an ebony velvet gown, she had a blood-red hooded cape that had alchemy sigils embroidered along its edges —it was very similar to the black one Masakage wore.

Silently, she stepped around Gisela. "Let her stay. Unlike your brother, there's nothing in here that could cause her harm. Or that she could use against me." She smiled at Gisela. "Regular creatures are always welcome. Witches, warlocks, magicians and such...not so much."

That made the hair on the back of her neck stand up. "Who are you?"

"Her name's Candara. She's Sagarian and half elf."

"And all witch," Candara said as she headed for the huge cauldron in the hearth.

A fairy elf witch. That explained a lot. No wonder she was so...frightening and beautiful. There was no telling how much power a creature like her would hold.

Candara looked at her as if she heard her thoughts. "Quite a bit, but nothing compared to your companion outside. My half-brother has more demon in him than any of us wish."

"Half-brother?"

"Masakage who apparently is pouting with me."

"I pout with no one." Masakage appeared in the shop, next to Candara. "I was only taking a moment before entering, as I had no idea what mood you'd be in or how tolerant of my presence."

Candara scoffed. "Are you still haunting alleys?"

"It's a living. No worse than yours."

She shook her head. "Such a waste of your *noble* talents."

He plucked a purple swirling bottle from the shelf beside him. "And this isn't a waste of yours?"

"It pays my bills. Some days, very handsomely. Better than being an alley rat."

"Enough." Xaydin sighed. "I realize you two have your issues, but I need more potions before your fireballs start launching and you destroy half the shop."

Gisela's eyes widened as she realized something. "You're all three related."

Candara inclined her head. "Indeed. Our mother was a Leanan sidhe."

"And part oni," Masakage added.

Which meant Xaydin was part sidhe and oni, too.

Gisela cursed at her luck. Oni, troll and sidhe made for a lethal mixture. No wonder no one could stand against him. She was lucky she was still alive.

Unable to believe her cursed luck, she looked down, then her gaze was drawn to the fragrant red...something in Candara's cauldron. "What's that? A love potion?"

Candara laughed. "It's lunch. Would you care for some?" Snapping her fingers, a bowl appeared in her hand filled with the cauldron's contents. She held it toward Gisela.

It smelled wonderful, but she wasn't dumb enough to even try to eat something from a witch's cauldron. "No, thank you."

"Suit yourself." She sipped from the bowl as she turned toward Xaydin. "Pick your potion, brat. The trackers and warnings are behind you."

"Easier said than done." Xaydin skimmed the bottles she'd mentioned while Masakage ladled a bowl of red stew for himself.

Candara moved to sit on an old wooden stool to wait. "You may pick a potion as well, princess. But be warned. My work calls out to you for two reasons. Either you need it or it needs you. Choose wisely."

Those words confused her. "What?"

Before Candara could respond, Xaydin picked up a gray swirling mist held in a large teardrop-shaped bottle. "Angel's Envy? How did you get this?"

Candara shrugged. "Envy exists everywhere. Even the divine."

"I understand, but how did you come by this?"

She swallowed her bite of food. "I don't ask you about your skills. Why would you ask me about mine?"

"Point taken."

But Gisela definitely wanted to ask, especially as she saw the one marked Unicorn Blood. "How many potions are here?"

"No idea. I make them when I know they're needed." She took another sip of her stew, then jerked her chin toward the

60

shelf behind Gisela. "You might want to browse in that area. I have a feeling you'll find what you need there."

Masakage moved to sit beside his sister on another stool.

Gisela glanced over the bottles until she saw the vibrant red, heart-shaped bottle marked with a single word. *Love.* "I didn't think you could make someone fall in love with you."

Candara laughed. "Creatures do it every day. They fall in and out of love at whim. Therefore, love potions are easy to enact. However, that is not what you think. It's made from the tears of a lost love to strengthen a heart so that it can withstand heartache."

"Then why does it say *Love*?"

"Look at the label."

It now read *Tears of Love Lost.*

How? She could have sworn the other words weren't there when she'd first picked it up. And now that she looked closer, she realized there were all kinds of tears on the shelf. *"Tears of a Writer?"*

She nodded. "A very special and powerful concoction. Creates all manner of chaos."

"How so?" Gisela asked.

"Creativity and pain. Potent mixture. Also, very unpredictable. Not something I recommend for a novice user or anyone who's unable to magically defend themselves, as it is a *very* creative potion."

That was terrifying so she went to the next yellow bottle. *"Tears of Enemies?"*

"Also very potent, but not nearly as much as the *Blood of Enemies.* Those come with all manner of warnings."

Gisela had no response to that. Only one question. "How do you get all these ingredients?"

An insidious smile curved her lips. "I have my ways."

Xaydin took a purple swirling bottle. "I'll take this one."

Candara glanced at it. "You might also want *Dead Speak*."

"I would ask why, but I know better. Thank you." He moved to another potion shelf.

Gisela started to tell her that there were too many to choose from when one small square bottle caught her eye. Unlike the others, it didn't swirl. It was a static crimson. Picking it up, she frowned. "*Dragon Fire*?" It looked nothing like the larger bottle of *Dragon Blood* she'd seen.

Candara inclined her head. "That is a very special potion. When you throw it, it will consume its target and leave nothing behind save ashes."

This could easily come in handy. "How much?"

"Nothing for someone who travels with my brothers, but be warned...using magic will cost you, and that's a price I can't name, as the magic will take what it wants from you." She jerked her chin at the potion Gisela held. "What I do know about that one is that it will take its fire from your soul."

That sent a shiver over Gisela. "Meaning?"

"I don't know exactly. Again, I don't pick the price. The potion does. Just a warning before you use it, as they never take the same thing. The cost varies per user and per use. Just remember that the price is never what you think."

Xaydin shook his head. "She's terribly vague and terrifying. It's her most annoying quality."

"You mean endearing, big brother. Any annoying or scary traits I might have were inherited from you."

Gisela envied them their playfulness and camaraderie. She'd never been that comfortable with any of her siblings.

Masakage held his hand out and a bottle from the shelf to her left flew toward him. "I'll take this one."

Candara arched a brow. "I'm flattered. I thought you disdained my magic."

"I disdain you selling it so cheaply. But I'm well aware of exactly how powerful you and your potions are. Respect."

She ruffled his hair, then smiled at Gisela. "Any time your younger brother compliments you it is the highest form of praise."

"I'll take your word for that."

Masakage tucked his unnamed potion into the bag at his side. "Are you sure we can't pay you?"

She shook her head. "I make plenty. The love potions alone are worth their weight in gold. I'd never be so crass as to profit off the blood of my family...mother notwithstanding."

"Have you seen her lately?"

She scoffed at Masakage's question. "Not in years. We still don't speak." She turned toward Xaydin. "And I wish we spoke more often."

"Talking is a useless endeavor."

She shook her head at Xaydin. "How would you know? You so rarely do it."

He grunted at her, then headed for the door.

Gisela hid her smile. She cradled her potion to her chest. "Thank you. I appreciate the gift."

Candara inclined her head to her. "Remember what I said about using it. You may not be thanking me later. Godspeed."

Masakage waited for them to leave so that he was alone with his older sister. "What aren't you saying?"

"What you already know."

He winced at her confirmation of what he'd sensed. "How do I get the Shadows off him?"

"You can't. They've been sent for him, and I don't know how to stop them."

Masakage scowled at her. "All the potions here and you have nothing for banishment?"

"I have plenty of those spells and potions. But nothing for the Shadows. They're insidious."

Which was why he'd postponed his original trip so that he could help his brother. No one wanted to deal with them. They slipped in when one least expected.

"Who sent them?"

Candara shrugged. "You'd probably know quicker than I would. His enemies are everywhere."

"Is Gisela one of them?"

She nodded slowly. "But at least she's torn. While she fears her master, she hates her, too. She can be turned against the one holding her leash."

"How?"

"How do you win over any feral beast? Kindness."

The same for him and his brother. The rarest of all qualities. Betrayal. Cruelty. Viciousness. Those were the staples of most creatures.

But kindness...

"I wish we were dealing with unicorns."

Her frown deepened. "Why?"

"You can tell by the color of their horns if they're assholes or not."

She laughed. "True. They can't hide their natures from others."

Indeed. They wore them as trophies on their foreheads.

"And you just reminded me of something." Candara left his side to head for a small chest in the far corner.

After a few seconds of rummaging, she returned with a slender, thin wooden box.

Before he could ask her what she had, she opened it to display a long, twisted gold wand.

A bad feeling went through him. "What's that?"

"Relax. I haven't been killing unicorns. It's the wand of Amandine."

He sucked his breath in sharply at the name of the mythical queen of the unicorns. It was said that she was the mother of their entire race. "How?"

"Legend says that when she lay dying, she begged her daughter to cut her horn so that her powers would always be preserved. That way she could always protect her family and people."

That sounded like something the great queen would have ordered done.

Candara handed him the wand. "Since Xaydin is on an errand for her descendant, you should carry this to help him protect the last of her line."

The wand heated in his hand as if in agreement. "What can this do?"

She gripped his hand in hers. "You'll know when you need it. And when this journey is over, see it back to the ones who should be its caretakers."

King Dash. She didn't say his name, but Masakage knew who she meant. There was no one else who could do right by such a sacred object.

With a sad smile, she kissed his cheek. "Be safe."

"You, too."

She gave a last squeeze to his hands before she released him and stepped back.

His heart sad, he left her there and went outside to join the other two.

They were already mounted and waiting.

Xaydin frowned as his gaze went to the box, but true to his brother's form, he didn't ask about it.

Neither did Gisela.

As quickly as he could, Masakage mounted and tucked the wand away. "Lead on, my brother."

Xaydin scowled at him. "That's a rather chipper tone for you, isn't it?"

"Not always a moody bastard. I mostly leave that for you."

Snorting, Xaydin turned them away from Candara's cottage. "Should have drowned you when we were kids."

"Pretty sure you tried."

Gisela pressed her lips together to keep from laughing. She loved hearing them banter and had the feeling that Xaydin would never tolerate such cheek from anyone other than his siblings.

And she really hated to admit that she enjoyed traveling with them. Weird, considering the fact that she normally didn't like to even be around others.

Weirder still was the fact that she hadn't even known them a full day and yet she felt a peculiar sense of being part of their group.

I've lost my mind.

They were enemies. Would always be such.

Yet she was more comfortable with them than she'd ever been with her own mother. How sad was that?

Not wanting to think about it, she allowed the sun to warm her skin as they rode deep into the surrounding woods. From the maps she'd seen, they weren't far from the sea that divided the troll lands from Oath Island—land of bureaucracy. A word Meara had never heard of. They didn't do contracts in Thassalia.

Disputes were settled in the arena...while Meara watched for entertainment.

Which begged the question as to how Meara had been forced to sign a contract with the unicorns? She must have fought that with everything she had.

But then King Cratus who had ruled before King Dash was reported to have been equally as savage. Not savage enough to survive a fight with his own son, yet he'd quelled the centaur queen.

Which made her wonder about Dash. She only knew the unicorn king by reputation.

Feral and brutal. Like Xaydin. Another product of Meara's tender loving care.

To this day, Gisela wasn't sure how Meara had been chosen as the host for the hostages.

After the truce of the Thirteen Kingdoms had been signed, Cratus had sent the children of each royal house to Meara to be held as a guarantee that their parents wouldn't attack him or each other.

It'd been a peculiar deal by everyone's estimation, and yet they'd all submitted to the High King's dictate.

And screwed over an entire generation of royal children because the rulers were too afraid of Cratus to overthrow him. While Meara might hate the Outlaws who'd banded together to survive her brutal dictates, Gisela understood why they'd done so. She only wished she'd been blessed to be part of their company.

Instead, Meara had kept her imprisoned alone. Away from everyone except Gisela's trainers.

You will be my sword.

And so she was the very weapon she'd been forged into. Vicious. Cold. Always on her own. Always alone.

Until now.

What she really hated was how much she enjoyed traveling with companions. Even though they weren't currently speaking, there was something soothing about it. If she were attacked, she'd have help. If she were hurt...

Don't be stupid. There was no guarantee they'd help her. Why would they?

Because he did so last night.

Before he knew who you were.

True. But in spite of their enmity, they were still being cordial to her.

Maybe she *was* being stupid.

Either way, she didn't speak as they made their way to the docks outside another bustling town.

Oddly, she'd expected a single ferry for crossing the sea. But there were boats of all sizes lined up at the wooden docks and along the shore.

"This many people really go to Oath Island?" she asked as they dismounted.

"Not at all." Xaydin stroked his horse's nose before he headed toward the docks on foot. "No one usually ventures there."

That confused her. "Then why so many boats?"

"They're mostly for fishermen. There are only two ferries that go back and forth between then island. One stays there and one on this side. They're always manned in case an *apaswere* needs to leave or return."

As she continued to glance over all the so-called fishermen, she was even more confused by his words. "That's a lot of fishing boats."

Masakage chuckled. "Trolls and giants eat a lot of fish."

Oh...that made more sense. She should have thought of that herself.

But then she wasn't a troll, ogre or giant. She really didn't know what they ate, especially since they'd refused to allow her to purchase food.

Without a word, Xaydin led them toward the largest boat where a troll sat off by himself.

He scowled at Xaydin, then sighed heavily. "You're back."

"Always, Ferris. How are you today?"

"Too sober to be taking you across. Can't you learn to fly or capture a dragon or something?"

Xaydin tsked at him. "And miss out on your charming company? Why would I do that?"

"Because I'm getting a reputation, and my other clients are highly resentful that I ferry you to their shores. Can't you find another hobby?"

"I like this one too much. Besides, I'm on an errand for the High King. Don't you want to make him happy?"

The troll spat into the water. "Take your unicorn and shove it someplace highly uncomfortable. I got no use for the High King. Or any low king either. They can all rot for what I care. Except for your father. He was a good one. The *only* good one."

Chuckling at the surly beast, Xaydin held up a small red bag of coins. "What about your favorite hobby?"

"I do like making money."

"Then consider this hazard pay."

Ferris snorted. "I'm sure it's not enough for the danger you're putting me in." He glanced past to Xaydin to where she and Masakage stood. "They with you?"

"They are. And you'll be glad to know that the woman is here to save the *apaswere* I'm after."

Ferris arched a single brow. "She thinks she can stop you?"

He nodded.

The troll laughed uproariously. "That alone makes the journey worthwhile. I'll be hearing tales of this for years to come." He pushed himself to his feet. "Get onboard. Not like I'm expecting anyone else anyway."

Xaydin pulled the black scarf from around his neck and used it to blindfold his horse. "You might want to do the same.

It'll make getting them on board the boat a lot easier and keep them calm during the trip."

Since she wasn't that familiar with dealing with horses, she'd trust him on that. But there was just one problem. "I don't have a scarf."

"Here." Masakage handed her a long purple cloth.

Thanking him, she duplicated their actions and covered her horse's eyes. Or at least she tried to. Unlike theirs, her horse had a mind of his own.

Just as it jerked its reins from her hands, Xaydin caught its bridle. "Easy, boy. Easy."

The horse quieted.

He held his hand out for her scarf.

Sheepishly, she gave it to him.

Without a word, he blindfolded the beast, then handed the reins to her.

She blushed as she led the horse onto the boat. "Sorry. Horses and I aren't exactly friends. They've never liked me."

"It's all right. I can't ride a human horse."

Those words confused her. "Human horse? You mean unicorn?"

Xaydin shook his head. "Horses that are used to humans. Trolls, oni, fey and such have different pheromones. Unless a horse is used to the scent, they tend to be skittish of us."

That made total sense and it was something she'd never thought of before. "Oh. It's not used to my scent."

Those words caused Xaydin's eyes to darken an instant before he cleared his throat and looked away.

Gisela froze as she realized he was attracted to her.

That thought sent a wave through her that was as disturbing as it was electrical. Not because she was offended.

Far from it.

Rather, she was thrilled, and that terrified her.

Blushing profusely, she stepped back and saw that Masakage was watching them both with an amused glint in his dark eyes.

She quickly hid behind her horse as she tucked it on board.

Xaydin clicked his teeth. "C'mon, Glory."

"Glory?" she asked.

"Name of my horse. I forgot to ask about yours. Should we name him?"

She'd not thought about that. "Does Masakage's have a name?"

"Bluden. And yours is called Gellen."

Patting her horse's neck, she was confused by Masakage's words. "Gellen? How do you know?"

"Kage talks to animals. One of his many annoying gifts."

"All animals?" she asked.

Masakage nodded. "It's why X and I get along. I'm one of the few creatures who can speak his language."

Ignoring them, she scratched Gellen's neck. "So what is he thinking?"

"That he doesn't like the boat. He wants to fight, but he's too scared to try since he can't see."

"How do I know you're not making that up?"

Xaydin snorted. "He's not creative."

Ferris moved to stand next to Xaydin. "Ready?"

"Sure. Why not?" There was a note in Xaydin's tone that gave her a bit of worry.

"Why do you say it like that?" she asked.

"Because we're about to hit rough waters. I suggest you sit."

She had no idea what he meant until they traveled far enough that there was no shoreline in sight. "How do you know where we're going?" she asked Ferris.

"How does one know how to breathe? I make this journey enough that I could be as blind as your horse and still find my way." Something he proved as he effortlessly glided them over the calm sea.

Only it wasn't that calm, she realized as she saw waves in the distance.

Big ones that were heading for them.

"X?"

They both looked over to Masakage.

Scowling, Masakage studied the commotion, heading for them. "Is it me, or are those waves filled with Nereids?"

Xaydin cursed. "Worse. Mermaids."

That only confused her. "Is there a difference?"

"Little bit," he said sarcastically. "Nereids are friendly and only attack when threatened. Mermaids and mermen protect the *apaswere* and kill anyone who threatens them."

5

Xaydin turned toward Gisela. "Can you swim?"

"Not at all."

He growled low in his throat. Of course she couldn't swim. Why would this be easy on them? "Get in the center of the boat and brace."

Manifesting a bow, he nocked an arrow and took aim at the waves, waiting for one of them to show themselves. Masakage moved to stand at his side with a fireball at the ready.

Xaydin smirked. "Has anyone ever told you what happens when fire meets water? You might as well be pissing on them for all the good that'll do."

Masakage gave him an irritated smirk before he threw the fireball into the water.

It exploded, sending waves out toward the mermaids.

"You were saying, brother?"

Respect went through him. "What a fine weapon you've crafted. Really makes my bow obsolete."

Shaking his head, Masakage manifested another fireball.

Ferris pulled the rudder in and sat down near the bow.

Letting out a sigh, he glared up at Xaydin. "They're starting early. Who are you after that they're so eager for you?"

"I assumed it was just your average goblin. Nothing special."

But Ferris was right. This was a lot more intense than his usual. Normally, it was only one mer creature and it took nominal effort to bypass it.

The horses began prancing as if they could sense what was coming for them.

Masakage took a knee so as to remain steady.

Xaydin admitted he wasn't as intelligent as his brother. A wise man would do exactly as Masakage, Gisela and Ferris were doing. Steady himself on the craft.

But he wanted blood. Let them throw him overboard. He'd take a piece of them with him into eternity.

Suddenly, something struck the bottom of the boat. Hard. So hard that it knocked him from his feet.

Masakage caught him before he fell overboard, into the sea. "What was that?"

"No idea." It'd been too strong a hit to be a simple mermaid or merman.

It hit the boat again.

Ferris held on tight to the edge. "They break my boat, you're buying me a new one!"

"Sure. If you live, I'll be glad to."

The older troll didn't appreciate his humor.

Neither did Gisela nor his brother. To be honest, he wasn't exactly fond of it, either. Not with this much turbulence. They were surrounding the boat like a school of piranha.

And sadly, none were dumb enough to poke their heads above the waves to give him a target.

They're learning.

That was his thought until one of them shot out of the

waves and into the air. The merman launched his own fireballs at them.

Masakage fired back as Xaydin let fly his arrow. His mark struck true but ricocheted off the merman without leaving a wound.

What the hell?

More of them jumped from the water. One was even bold enough to land on the boat.

Xaydin traded his bow for a staff, but before he could strike, the merman fell screaming to the boards at his feet.

It was only then he saw Gisela holding a bloody sword in her hands.

"Thank you."

She nodded before she moved to go after another one who was trying to climb on board.

"Don't!" Xaydin barely had the word out before a merman reached up and yanked her into the water.

Gisela tried to scream as she sank into the sea. Choking, she couldn't see anything but water. Feel the hands of the creature that was trying its best to drag her down.

Hold your breath!

But it was impossible. The more she fought, the more she needed to breathe.

She gulped, ingesting the dark water against her will. Water that stung her eyes and lungs.

I'm going to drown if I don't turn into something that swims!

But if she used her powers, Xaydin might shoot her with his bow. Just for spite.

He hates shape shifters. Don't do it!

She tried not to panic, but how could she not? She couldn't swim in her human body, and she didn't know how to float in this nightmare. Not without pushing her companion to a murderous rage.

Just as she sank deeper, someone lifted her head above the water.

"I've got you," Xaydin said in her ear. "Don't fight me."

Her heart pounding, she closed her eyes in relief and laid her head back against his shoulder. She was so grateful that if she could, she'd kiss him for this. No one had ever saved her before.

They'd only stabbed her when she fell.

With what seemed like no effort at all, Xaydin swam them to the ferry boat, then lifted her up so that Masakage could help her back in.

Gisela turned around to reach for Xaydin to return the favor when one of the merman broke the surface.

Before she could react, the merman grabbed Xaydin from behind and pulled him under.

"No!" Gisela tried to reach him, but he was gone so fast that all she could do was cry out.

Masakage started to dive into the water, but Ferris stopped him.

"They'll tear you apart. You can't!"

Gisela heard the words, along with her common sense that reminded her she didn't know how to swim in her human body. There was nothing she could do for him without making him hate her completely.

Nothing.

And yet she couldn't sit here and watch him die. Let him fight the monsters by himself.

Before she could stop herself, she dove back into the water and turned into her real form.

"STOP STRUGGLING!"

Xaydin slammed his fist into the merman's throat.

With a fierce curse, the beast slapped him in the ribs with his fin. "Would you please stop?"

The please was what kept him from hitting the merman again. That and the fact that he realized he was somehow able to breathe underwater. "What's going on?"

"My king wishes a word with you."

Seriously? "He couldn't send an invitation like a civilized creature?"

"Would you have come?"

So the merman had a valid point. Still...

"There are better ways to get my attention."

The merman bowed to him. "Forgive us. We meant no harm or offense to you. Please, Your Highness." He actually gestured in the opposite direction where a group of his kin were carrying what looked like a giant battering ram.

That must have been what they'd used to strike the bottom of the boat. Those bastards really were getting smarter.

"Do you have a name?" Xaydin asked his attacker.

"Captain Mersin of the Ningyoan Navy."

That was interesting...although it made sense. He'd never before thought about the fact that the Ningyoans had armed forces. Since he had no way of visiting the underwater nation of Ningyo, their society and politics had held little interest to him, other than watching out for and avoiding their citizens whenever he traveled to Oath Island.

All he knew about them was the name of their king, Mardyth. And only that because it was bandied about by those who traversed the waters over Mardyth's domain.

Most of what anyone knew came from the Nereids who were amphibious. Whenever they were on land, they complained incessantly about the Ningyoans who often warred against them.

Now, he had the rare chance to meet them. He might as well see what the king needed.

"Very well, Captain. Take me to your king."

Mersin held his hand out to Xaydin. As soon as he took it, the merman pulled him through the sea to a small city not that far away. In fact, he doubted if it was more than a couple of leagues from the southern tip of Oath Island.

"Is this your capital?"

"It is. Hyteria."

Xaydin would say it was similar to one of theirs, but it was nothing like the villages, towns or cities he was used to. For one thing, the walls were made of coral and shell. Even in the dim light of the sea, they managed to glisten vibrantly. Of course, some of that came from strange-looking fish they had harnessed to the walls like living torches.

There was also something painted on the walls that glowed reminiscent of fireflies.

Truly magical. And even more so as they swam through a guarded gate toward a large tower that was surrounded by numerous buildings. He would ask how they expected to keep anything out, but there was a huge dome over the walls.

Mersin looked back and smirked. "The mirrored dome keeps earth-dwellers and mages from finding us."

A part of Xaydin wanted to look around more and even explore this place, but he didn't really want to stay under water any longer than he had to. Honestly, he found all of this rather disturbing. The fact that he could breathe...

Magic he could handle. Monsters he handled even better.

But this...this was the most unnatural thing he'd ever experienced, and he didn't like it at all.

"Why is there a giant mirror at the tower?"

Mersin paused and released his hand. "It's a divine reminder that order cannot be forced. It must be coaxed and cared for."

That made no sense to him. "How so?"

"It's part of our religion. All important buildings are marked with a mirror to pay tribute to our great sea goddess, Sanow. It's a reminder of why she left the land to dwell in the sea. Her land siblings were cruel and so she came here to be away from them. But after a while, she became lonely. So she returned to the world above. It was still chaos there. As she stepped back on land, she turned and saw her own reflection in the sea. In that reflection, she remembered the tranquility and peace that she craved. Order. Not the chaos of the land. And so she returned to the sea where she found the god, Enon. Together, they created our domain and our race."

He liked their view of things. His people believed the world had been created when Ofdan stomped his foot on the ground from the heavens and demanded all creatures bow to him. When they refused, the god slaughtered them and their blood mixed with the earth to create the trolls. Which said it all about troll culture and their mindset. They weren't a peaceful lot, by any means.

Mersin bowed to him, then gestured toward the tower's door. "Come, Highness. My king awaits."

Xaydin swam in behind Mersin, noting the brightly colored corals and shiny clam shells that decorated the inside of the building. Interesting plants swayed in the cracks, oblivious to them as they went down a long, narrow hallway that led to a large throne room. Six Ningyoan guards were there. Unlike Mersin who had a blue tail, theirs were all green.

Were their tails similar to a unicorn's horn? Or were they simply a product of birth, like eye color? He would ask them, but this didn't seem like the right time for such chit-chat.

81

King Mardyth's tail was a vibrant gold, and he didn't sit on a throne. Rather, he lay on a chaise. His chest was bare, and he had gold bands around his wrists and biceps. With gold hair and bright gold eyes, he had skin that was slightly translucent.

"Thank you, Captain Mersin. You're excused."

Mersin bowed before he quickly swam back the way they'd just come.

Xaydin quirked an eyebrow at his hasty retreat. "Hope he's not my only ride out of here."

The king laughed a lot harder than Xaydin expected. Especially since it wasn't *that* funny.

After a few minutes, he sobered and shook his head. "You're not at all what I expected, given what I've heard."

"Not sure how to take that."

Mardyth smiled. "Relax. It's a compliment. Most of the ogres and trolls we meet are those who are drowning."

"Let me guess...you help them along on their death journey?"

"Depends. If they're kind and respectful, we help them home. Those who aren't—" He sucked at his teeth. "Let's just say sharks have to eat."

"Of course, they do. We have them on land, too. Only we call them vultures."

The king scowled. "Not a compliment, given your tone."

"Not really."

The king's tail flicked.

Xaydin wasn't sure if that was irritation or just habit. Since he knew very little about the Ningyoans, he had no idea how to read their monarch.

"I'm sure you're curious as to why you're here."

He had to bite back a sarcastic retort. Clearing his throat, he nodded. "Very much so."

The king held his hand up, and a servant swam toward him

with a small box. "In case you don't know who I am, I'm King Mardyth. My family has ruled here since the day the goddess left the land and became the bride to our god. Back when the world was young." He took the box but didn't open it as his servant left. "As I'm sure you know, we don't participate in the politics of the land dwellers."

"Except to try and drown me when I visit Oath Island."

"An unfortunate history that I'm hoping you'll overlook."

Of course. Why would he think otherwise? But the real question was what game was the king playing? "Why?"

"Because my idiot son has run away from home, and I need him returned to me."

That was an interesting bit he'd never considered.

"Your idiot son?" He couldn't help repeating that. Mostly because he found it hysterical.

The king nodded. "Marstyn thinks he's in love."

"I'm assuming it's with a land dweller."

"Yes. A two-legger. Like a fool, my son made a pact with a sorcerer so that he'd be a legged beast as well." Now that tail flicked with fury. Xaydin was slowly learning to read the king's mood.

As well as the fact that the king's eyes began to glow more. "Find him, return him and I will make sure that you will have fair and easy passage for the rest of your life."

That seriously got his attention.

The king moved from the chaise to approach Xaydin. "More than that, once you finish, I'll give you this." He opened the lid to show him what appeared to be...

"A baby pacifier?"

Unamused, the king glared at him. "It will allow you to breathe underwater without having to be in the presence of one of my people."

Now that was even more helpful.

Xaydin reached for the box. "May I?"

"Please." The king held the box while Xaydin pulled the pacifier out to examine it.

Seriously, it looked like one of the objects his brother's nurse used to place in his mouth to quiet him when he'd been a baby.

But who was he to question that?

"Put it in your mouth and try it."

Xaydin obeyed the king, then realized the difference between what he'd been experiencing and the true gift the king was offering. With the pacifier in place, it was like breathing on land.

Until that moment, he hadn't realized how heavy the water was to breathe.

With this though...he'd be just another fish in the sea. No different than his host.

The king held his hand out for it.

Xaydin reluctantly handed it over. Normally, he'd fight, but since he couldn't survive underwater without their help, resisting them would be exceptionally stupid.

"All you have to do is return my son. It's that simple."

"That hard." Xaydin jerked his chin toward the pacifier in the king's hands. "I'll be back for that."

He closed the lid on the box. "I'm counting on it."

Just as Xaydin moved back in the water, he heard a terrible struggle from outside their room.

"What have you done with him! I'll have all your bloody fins!"

The sound of the shrill, belligerent voice made him laugh.

Gisela.

He'd know that outrage anywhere. And for once, it wasn't directed at him.

When two guards came in with his favorite assassin squirming between them, it was all he could do not to laugh.

Not at her, but at the effort it took her guards to keep her contained.

She was exceptional.

And the moment her gaze focused on him, she stopped her tirade against them. "Xaydin! You're alive. Thank the gods!"

For reasons unknown, that expression combined with those words touched a part of him that he'd all but forgotten existed. If he didn't know better, he'd think she cared for him.

But they barely knew each other. More than that, they were at odds.

Except in this.

She rushed toward him as if she intended to embrace him. But just as she would have been able to do so, she stopped short.

A becoming blush stained her cheeks.

Xaydin smiled. "I'm glad to see you, too."

Her cheeks darkened even more.

"I take it she's a friend of yours?" the king asked with an amused glint in his eyes.

Xaydin actually smiled. "She is, and I'm glad your soldiers didn't kill her."

"We never kill royalty. Not even bastard ones."

Those words caught his attention. Xaydin turned back toward the king. "Pardon?"

"Being friendly with the gal, surely you know. She's Queen Meara's bastard."

6

Those words shocked Xaydin to his core. Gisela was Meara's bastard...

"You're shitting me?"

Gisela swam back and would have gone farther from him had the king's guards not stopped her retreat.

Rage the likes of which he'd never known—which given his childhood said it all—descended on him. In that moment, he wanted to rip out her heart and feed it to her. To beat her until she made the same screaming sounds of every child he'd seen tortured by her mother.

Her mother.

And I actually saved her in the tavern from the same nightmare that had been so viciously given to those around me.

No, the nightmare they'd given him without any mercy. Memories he'd hidden so deep that even now he couldn't face them. He'd spent a lifetime in denial. A lifetime trying to forget.

Pain is power. Meara's sick and twisted belief. Either the pain swallowed you whole or the pain reshaped you into a stronger version of yourself. One who learned that they could overcome and be invincible.

It was a lesson he hadn't needed. A lesson he doubted anyone needed.

And this was her progeny...

A daughter Meara had sent out to die so that Meara could be free of a contract she voluntarily signed.

Xaydin paused as that thought broke through his senseless anger and returned his mind to a rational state. Meara had knowingly and intentionally sent her own child on a quest that would likely end with her death.

Typical bitchtress.

And it explained so much about Gisela's mannerisms and fear. And yet...

Meara was a centaur. Gisela wasn't.

Fuck me.

If there was anything Meara hated, it was any race not her own. Yet she'd bred with someone else.

Something else.

Had it been voluntary?

Either way, Gisela wasn't just her daughter. She was her deepest shame, and Meara would shit twice and die if she knew anyone had discovered this matter. No wonder Gisela had been so silent about her past.

So sympathetic about their experiences in her mother's court. He could only imagine how much worse her childhood must have been than any of theirs.

Meara as a mother...

He shuddered. Xaydin couldn't imagine any worse hell.

"I won't hurt you, Gisela. No one can help the family they're born into, and I won't hold your mother against you."

Gisela wanted to believe he meant those words, but it was impossible. And the worst part was that she couldn't even blame him for hating her. Her mother was a wretched, awful creature who tortured everyone.

That was Meara's idea of fun.

Yet he swam toward her slowly and raised his hand for her to take it. She held her watery space, even though she wanted to run. But running had never been in her nature. Or if it had been, her mother had beaten it out of her so young that she couldn't remember a time when she'd done so.

Her breathing ragged, she met his gaze without flinching. All she saw was sincerity. But could she trust it?

Could she trust him?

While he hadn't given her any reason not to, it still wasn't in her to give such. Not to anyone.

Hoping she wouldn't regret it, she took his hand.

He looked back toward the king he'd been conversing with when she arrived. "Are we done?"

"We are. I'll have the captain return you to your boat."

Xaydin inclined his head as a gong rang out. A few seconds later, another merman came forward. He bowed to his king before leading them from the palace.

Gisela didn't say a word as they left. In part because she was still too impressed with the city, but mostly due to the fact that she didn't know what to say to Xaydin.

"Did you fall overboard?" he asked her.

Heat suffused her cheeks so much that she wondered if they glowed in the water. "I did."

Mersin snorted. "Not what I heard. She jumped in after you, threatening anyone who harmed you, my lord."

"I did not!" she quickly snapped.

The captain smirked at Xaydin. "Did."

Xaydin was amused by their argument. But most of all, he was strangely thrilled at the prospect of her jumping into the sea to save him. "You can't swim."

"Which is how you know I didn't jump in. Who would do such?"

"Really, she did. Four of my men described it in great detail. They were quite impressed by her determination to find and free you."

Xaydin turned to look at her.

"Liars. Troublemakers. Everyone knows you can't trust a Ningyoan."

"But they were right about your mother," he reminded her.

"As I said, troublemakers."

Now, she wouldn't meet his gaze at all. Nor did she say another word until they broke the sea's surface not far away from their boat.

With a relieved breath, Masakage held his hand out to Gisela to help her on board first. Xaydin pulled himself up, then turned back to Mersin. "My thanks, Captain."

Mersin inclined his head before he vanished back under the water.

"Do I want to know?" Masakage asked.

Xaydin didn't answer. "What I want to know is why *you* didn't jump into the sea to help me?"

"After Gisela went in, I thought it best someone stay here and make sure our guide didn't leave you to a watery grave."

Ferris looked away sheepishly. "Not saying I'd have done that."

"He would have done that." Masakage gave Ferris a stern glower. "I had to threaten his life and those of every member of his family to keep him here."

Ferris muttered something under his breath.

"And you didn't stop our princess from diving in after me?"

"She moved too fast to be stopped. Besides, I knew she was going for you and that you'd both return."

Xaydin arched a brow at the arrogant tone and the fact that his brother hadn't reacted to something he'd just disclosed. "You knew she was a princess?"

"Of course. You can smell it on her. I knew the moment I met her that she was a daughter of the bitch."

Now that really made him want to beat Masakage into shoe leather. "And you didn't think it pertinent to tell me?"

"Given that you wanted to keep her with us, I thought you knew and intended to keep watch on her."

"You're such an arse."

Masakage tsked, then held his hand out and waved over Gisela who instantly dried off. Afterward, he moved to Xaydin. "Say you're sorry."

Scoffing, Xaydin shook his head. He wasn't about to offer an insincere apology. "I'd rather stay wet."

"Suffer then. Sopping suits you."

"Fuck you."

Masakage took a seat next to Gisela. "He really is a dreadful beast. But I do so enjoy his rages."

"You're not quite right, are you?" Gisela asked.

"Too much time spent with your mother. How you ended up so normal makes me wonder about your father."

She scowled at his words. "You don't know?"

He shook his head. "That is shrouded. Not sure why, but by your current form I'm guessing he was two-legged."

She fell instantly silent.

"Or was he?" Masakage asked.

Gisela wasn't about to tell him anything regarding her paternal heritage. It was something that infuriated her more than anything else. "Does it matter?"

That caused Xaydin to focus his penetrating glare on her. "Shape shifter?"

The thing he hated most.

Xaydin cursed under his breath. "A fucking shape shifter! No wonder you didn't have a horse." He glanced to Masakage.

"She didn't need one because she can be one. No wonder horses don't like her. Did you know about this?"

"I suspected."

"And said nothing?"

Masakage held his hands up in surrender. "Didn't know how you'd react to the news, as your overreaction right now is proving. Besides, with those skills, she could come in handy on your quest."

Xaydin growled in response.

Gisela swallowed hard. "If it makes you feel better, your hatred of me is only surpassed by my mother's." Her voice was barely more than a whisper.

"Why would that make me feel better?"

She shrugged. "Misery loves company. Or so I'm told."

Shaking his head, Xaydin sighed heavily. She was an Outlaw, same as them—betrayed and tortured. Broken by life. Yet she still clung to the mother who'd cruelly raised her.

He'd never understand creatures like Gisela. But then who was he to judge? He allowed his uncle to live, even though he should plunge a dagger through the bastard's head. Life was a struggle for everyone, and it spared no one from pain and grief. Didn't matter if they were princes or beggars.

Tragedy came. Sometimes he thought it took a particular sense of pleasure from going after those who were envied. Like a kind of tulpa. So many wished ill on those they thought had it better that it manifested a particular kind of harm for them. One summoned by others for no reason other than petty jealousy where they thought someone had it easier or better.

But that wasn't how life worked. Everyone had their problems no matter how enviable their situation might appear on the surface.

It was a lesson too few learned. Because that jealousy fostered all types of evil.

Such as Meara who'd turned on her own daughter because she had abilities the queen lacked.

Sickening, truly.

"I will never hold your mother against you. I'm well aware that it's not your fault that you come from her and to your credit, you're not heartless or cruel." Xaydin offered her a kind smile.

An instant later, he was dry.

Scowling, he looked at his brother.

"You're such an arse that I sometimes forget how much heart you really have." Masakage picked the rudder up with his powers and returned it to its place. He gestured for Ferris to return to his position.

"If you can do all that, why don't you just poof yourselves to the shores? Why do you need a boat?"

Xaydin snorted. "And miss your charming company? Why would we do that?"

Muttering under his breath, Ferris shook his head and resumed their journey.

"So what happened?" Masakage asked Xaydin.

"Mardyth wants me to hunt down his son and bring him home."

One finely arched brow rose. "Well, isn't your dance card getting filled?"

"Indeed." He glanced over to Gisela who remained silent. For reasons he definitely didn't understand, he wanted to comfort her.

What is wrong with me?

And yet he was unable to resist her. Pulling his waterskin out, he moved to sit beside her and offered her a drink.

She scoffed. "Really? Didn't you get enough water at their palace?"

He laughed. "It was interesting, wasn't it?"

"You think they have games like the Thassalians?"

The mention of Meara's favorite entertainment made him want to curse. Her arena was filled with fights to the death...the gorier the better. She loved it. Most of all, she loved pitting creatures against each other who were unmatched. Those who were small and weak up against much larger and accomplished opponents. Those who were more vicious against the meek.

His first fight, he'd been up against a stoneman. He still couldn't believe he'd survived the fight. It was the only time in his life that he'd really been afraid. Terrified.

How he'd failed to piss his pants, he didn't know. What Meara hadn't known then were the gifts his mother's genetics had provided. He didn't need physical strength. His telekinesis helped exponentially in fights.

Sadly, they hadn't been enough to help anyone escape. She only allowed those powers in her arena. Outside...

Meara had paid members of his mother's nation to make sure those with similar powers in her kingdom couldn't use them. It'd rendered him powerless, and to this day, he couldn't stand for his powers to fail him. It was something he had a hard time dealing with.

No one would ever imprison him again.

He'd kill himself first.

But right now, those thoughts fled under the nearness of being with Gisela.

"Is it too much to ask that next time I get pulled underwater and you can't swim that you refrain from throwing yourself in?"

"Maybe. But remember, I can turn into a fish."

He tsked. "Being your mother's hammer, I would have thought you'd be callous toward anyone in distress."

"As you are?"

One would think that, given he was every bit the assassin. And she was right, he had saved her when most of his kind wouldn't have even glanced her way. "I only kill *apasweres*."

"And I only kill the ones who need it...regardless of what Meara commands." Fury burned in her eyes as she stared at him sincerely.

She spoke the truth.

"Then we are alike, you and I."

"Indeed."

Except in this mission where she intended to protect what he was hellbent to kill.

This should be very interesting...

7

Now Gisela understood what Xaydin had been trying to tell her. The *apasweres* were not at all what she thought. At first sight, they were twisted and horrible—hard-to-look-at ugly. They had wings and strange body parts that stretched out beyond belief. The majority of them had writing all over their bodies, including their bald heads and eyelids.

And they all had bald heads. Even the children and women.

"They also tattoo inside their mouths," Masakage said as they slowly rode their horses into town.

She flinched as she imagined how much that had to hurt. "All this to keep a contract?"

He nodded. "They are the ultimate bureaucrats."

Yes, they were. But the weirdest part was that other than their garish appearance, everything else looked normal. They sat with friends, went about errands, had families.

Just like any other species she'd ever seen.

And they stood out even more than she had among the trolls and ogres. Were taller, too. There was no way for them to blend in with any other group.

Something made even more obvious by the ones who turned to stare at them as they made their way toward a rundown stable. By the glares and anger, she could tell that they knew who Xaydin was and they weren't happy about his presence in their town.

That level of hatred made the hair on her arms stand up. She didn't like being the center of attention and especially not when it was hostile.

As they neared a stable in the center of town, an *apaswere* came out to greet them. Unlike the others, he didn't have as many words on his flesh. His wrinkled face was blank, as was most of his bald head.

"You're not dead yet?" he asked Xaydin.

Xaydin snorted at the question. "Not from lack of trying."

"I'd imagine." His gaze went to her and Masakage. He studied them for a second. "Are you planning to sign a contract instead of breaking one for once?"

Xaydin gave him an amused smirk. "Not hardly. They just came along for the ride."

"Since when do you keep company with others?"

Xaydin smirked. "Since I haven't found a way to shake them off. No matter how much I abuse them, they won't leave."

The *apaswere* laughed before he took the reins of her horse. "I'm Athgar, my lady, and you are?"

"Gisela."

"Nice meeting you." He turned his attention to Masakage. "You seem familiar."

"Masakage of Tenmaru. And I have a lot of siblings. You might have run across one. Most of us travel a great deal of the time."

"Perhaps." He walked their horses into the stable so that he could tie them up and remove their saddles. "How long will you be here?"

"I'm looking for the *apaswere* who deals with Queen Meara."

Athgar screwed up his face. "That won't be easy. She has a number of us she contracts with."

Of course, she did. Why would her mother make this easy on anyone?

"This would be an older *apaswere*. Back when she made her deal with the Licordians."

Placing Masakage's saddle on a rail, Athgar let out a low whistle. "Start at the tavern. They might know. But an *apaswere* that old will take some time to find."

"Always do."

Again, Athgar laughed. "True...and I should probably let you know something."

"What?"

"There's a contract out on your life."

Gisela widened her eyes.

But those words didn't faze Xaydin at all. "What else is new?"

"Still, be careful. The High Guard is due in any moment. They'll be doing their usual sweep."

"High Guard?" she asked.

Xaydin passed her a less than pleased grimace. "They patrol the kingdom, looking for those who don't belong here."

"And if they find you?"

"They'll do their best to kill me on sight."

She nodded. "Good to know. Same for us?"

"No. They usually escort foreigners off their shores. Besides, you're here to help guard an *apaswere*, and him..." Xaydin smiled as he looked at his brother. "As I said, he's just along for the ride...like a bad canker sore."

Gisela had to bite back a laugh at the offended look on

Masakage's face. She should be appalled, but it was a very unexpected comment.

Athgar said nothing as they left him and headed down the dirt street to the largest building in town. It was four to five times bigger than any other structure.

"Why's the tavern so huge?" she asked.

"This is where most contracts are made. Some *apaswere* can be summoned, as is the case with the one we're seeking who went to Licordia to make the contract decades ago, but most stay here. So if you want a contract, you have to come to them to create it so that they don't have to risk travel."

"Really?"

"Safety in numbers. They don't like venturing out into the world where they don't blend and are easily identified. Tends to make them targets for those wanting to break a contract they might be holding. Here, it takes a skilled tracker to figure out who is who."

"Which is what you're good at, I take it?"

"Exactly. And it makes me an easy target as they will be sending word out to the demon I'm after and summoning those who want to kill me."

That made sense to her and terrified her. "So that he can go into hiding."

"No. So that he can find friends and come hunt me." He stopped and turned to face her. "You asked how I found them. I don't have to look. Athgar is sending word, right now, to the demon I seek. All we have to do is wait and they'll assault us in the tavern. Or outside it when we leave."

She wanted to say it was cheating. But given the fact that he'd just summoned *apaswere* assassins after him, how could she? It was a bold move.

"And this always works for you?"

"Not dead yet."

But that only confused her. "If that's the case, then why don't they all attack you now?"

"They're a nation of bureaucrats and lawyers. Everything to the letter. It's why they're so frustrating. In order to kill me, they have to have the proper paperwork and credentials. This isn't Thassalia or Vaskalia where anyone can kill someone they don't like. Their citizens don't start fights or break their stringent laws. The only *apaswere* who can come for me is the one I'm seeking and those he contracts with to help him eliminate his threat. The rest will stay out of his matters. It's why they're eye-balling us with hatred, but aren't moving in to stop us."

"That is so..." She couldn't find words, so she settled on, "messed up."

"Yes and no. At least here you know who your enemies are."

There was a lot to be said for that. She'd spent her entire life on high alert. Watching every shadow and waiting for the next attack.

Sadly, she could tell Xaydin had done the same. It was a hard way to live, and no one should have to go through it.

Without thinking, she took his hand.

Xaydin almost jumped at the unexpected contact. The softness of her hand was unlike anything he'd ever known. Or that he could remember.

Before he could think, he gave her hand a light squeeze and turned to smile at her.

A smile she returned bashfully as she bit her lip and quickly glanced away.

Yet her hand remained in his.

Masakage put more distance between them. *What are you doing?*

Xaydin fought the urge to glance over his shoulder at his brother. *She's reaching out.*

Maybe. Just be careful.

Always. He wasn't a young, naive fool. He more than understood what was at stake. How quickly friends turned to enemies.

Often over nothing. Petty jealousies. Imagined slights that were never intended. Creatures used those and more to justify hate so that they could tear down a friend or lover.

Xaydin would never understand it. Even now, with Gisela reaching out to him, a part of him was wary. Good things never lasted.

Bad things went on forever.

Or at least they seemed to. He hated that most of all. It was why he chose to live alone, away from the world. Away from family and friends. That way, he couldn't be hurt.

While it could be lonely, it was safe, and safety was something he'd had too little of in his life.

But as he walked with her hand in his, he knew that it was something much more than a light caress. She trusted him. That was so rare in his world that he wasn't even sure what to think about it.

And as they reached the tavern, she released his hand so that she could place it on her sword. While he was glad to see her caution, it saddened him that she had the same instincts he did.

She was a princess. She should have been sheltered and taken care of like the others of her ilk. If he hated Meara for no other reason, it would be for this.

But then who was he to talk? His mother had been just as bad. She'd birthed them and then vanished. All the years they'd been tortured in Meara's court, his mother could have come and freed them.

She'd chosen not to.

If anyone could have negotiated with the bitch-queen, his mother would have been the one.

Instead, she turned a blind eye and left them to suffer.

Pushing that out of his mind, he led them to a table in back where he could watch the door and not worry about anyone sneaking up on them.

Gisela turned her chair so that she could watch the door as well. "Want me to turn into a dormouse and see what I can find out?"

Xaydin gave her a droll stare. "Are you trying to piss me off?"

"Just trying to help. Since you know...there's no reason to hide what I can do."

"There are lots of reasons to hide." Masakage jerked his chin toward all the stares they were collecting. "Wish I could turn into a dormouse."

Xaydin tossed a handful of peanuts that had been left on the table at his brother. "You can do better than a dormouse. You can vanish."

He flashed a smile. "Very true." Then he scanned the room. "Wonder if any of them could use a fortune or two."

Before he could respond, Masakage wandered off to hustle business.

Xaydin ordered them drinks.

"You still mad at me?" Gisela asked.

"I don't know. I want to be, but I know it's not your fault. Although, that being said, you should have been the one who told me."

"Would you have told me if you were in my place?"

"Would depend on how churlish I was feeling."

She smiled at that.

And all he could really think about was her hand in his. *What is wrong with me?* That was the last thing he should be thinking about.

Their server came over with two tankards of mead and set them down with a grimace. "Two crowns."

Gisela scoffed at the amount.

Without a word, Xaydin fished the coins from his pocket and tossed them on the table.

As soon as they were alone, she gaped at him. "Why would you pay so much?"

"Should I die, I'd like to be drunk when it happens. Should I live, I'll bill this to Dash. Either way, I'm good."

Gisela shook her head at his glib tone as he downed a good portion of his mead. She sipped hers much more slowly. "You really are reconciled to death, aren't you?"

"Everyone dies at some point, my lady. Doing what I do, Theren is more likely to come for me sooner than later."

"Theren?"

"Our god of death. It's said he comes personally to claim the souls of true warriors. That's why trolls fight so fiercely. We all pray for him to escort us to our paradise where we will fight, wench and drink for eternity."

"That sounds nice. We don't have paradise."

"Centaurs?"

She nodded. "We believe that if we're worthy, we're reborn into a new family and body. If we're unworthy, we cease to exist."

He drank the last of his mead and grimaced. "What do centaurs believe makes them worthy?"

"If you're a leader, leading. If you're a follower, following. We accept our lot and don't fight it."

"Hence why you blindly follow your mother's orders?"

She nodded. "I don't know what shape shifters believe in. Do you?"

"They believe in a paradise where they live in peace with everyone."

"How do you know that?"

"Ronan. He's one of the Outlaws I grew up with. And up until you, he was the only shifter I could stomach."

For reasons she couldn't explain, those words flooded her with warmth. "Even though we're enemies?"

"My enemy's enemy is my friend." He signaled for the server to bring him more mead.

She had no idea why, but she liked the thought of being his friend.

What do you know about being anyone's friend?

That thought made her stomach ache. It was true. She'd never had a friend before. Unless she counted her sword. Which was why she'd named it Brant. A stupid name, really, but she'd been very young and it seemed like a strong name for a sword.

And while Brant had saved her life a few times, he wasn't nearly as handsome as Xaydin.

Nor as sarcastic...

As their waiter returned, the door to the tavern opened. At first, Gisela paid no attention. Not until the newcomer turned and locked the door behind him. She slid a suspicious glance toward Xaydin who had already straightened up and put his hand on the hilt of his sword.

The room went silent as the *apaswere* made his way toward their table.

Was this the *apaswere* she was supposed to protect?

By Xaydin's countenance, she'd say it was something else. He was completely tense and wary.

The *apaswere* stopped in front of them. "Xaydin of Vaskalia?"

"Who's asking?"

More than half the room stood up almost in unison and drew nearer the *apaswere*.

Fear quickened her heart as she saw their number. If Xaydin felt anything, he didn't show it. He appeared completely calm. But given the sheer number of them, this couldn't be good.

"Is this my welcoming party?" Xaydin asked.

The *apaswere*'s dark eyes narrowed dangerously. "We're done being hunted by you."

To her immediate shock, a slow insidious smile spread across Xaydin's handsome face. "Really?"

If she didn't know better, she'd swear he was salivating.

The eager note in his voice caused several of the *apaswere* to take a step back and look suddenly nervous.

And it wasn't doing much to help her own apprehension. What did Xaydin know that she didn't?

The *apaswere*'s eyes narrowed at Xaydin's nonchalance. "Do you think this is a game?"

"Given the number of lives *apaswere*s have destroyed, no. You kill without compassion, and the cold callousness of your race is what birthed me." He stood up and unsheathed his sword. "Come get some."

That defiance caused half the group to disperse with fear in their eyes as they realized what they were facing. Not a mercenary hunting for coin. A battle-tested warrior craving vengeance.

Those who remained...

Attacked at once.

Without thinking, she turned into the dormouse she'd been joking about. But only long enough to get clear of the group before she returned to her human body and unsheathed her own sword so that she could help.

Not that it really mattered.

*Apaswere*s were being thrown about like ragdolls as Xaydin took out his vengeance against them. It was so potent that she wasn't even sure if she should join the fray. For someone so terribly outnumbered, he appeared jubilant.

Never had she seen anyone so happy in a fight.

Masakage was driving the group around him back with green magic fire.

Grabbing the *apaswere* nearest her, she engaged him with her sword. He turned on her with a vengeance, and as he did so, his body elongated so that he towered over her. His wings expanded.

Big mistake. The one thing Gisela couldn't stand was whenever someone tried to physically intimidate her. Too many years under her mother's thumb had left her raw over such actions.

She wasn't a little girl anymore. She was a battle-tested warrior in her own right.

Growling in her throat, she quickly turned into a stonewoman and knocked the *apaswere* flying.

Those around her backed away. Her temper flaring, she headed toward the one that was still fighting Xaydin, intending to guard his back.

Just as she reached him, Xaydin turned around.

When their gazes met, she saw his surprise. Then amusement before he stepped around her to counter a sword strike.

Xaydin wanted to be angry. He really did. But the sight of Gisela filling the room all the way to the ceiling was laughable. She was a gigantic piece of rock. One that was impervious to the *apaswere* around them.

His first thought was that he wouldn't have to worry about her, until one of the *apaswere*s launched a fierce fireball at her. It landed on her shoulder with such force that it knocked her off her feet and left a nasty burn in her rocky flesh.

Now, he was furious. "Hey, punk!" He returned the hit with his own fireball. Then another in quick succession.

Screeching, the *apaswere* fell back and ran from the tavern. Several others followed after him.

Xaydin put himself between Gisela and the others, waiting to see what they were planning to do next.

The *apaswere* who started it came forward. "We are not your prey any longer. And you are no longer welcome here. Take your friends and get out."

Xaydin wanted to argue. But they were drastically outnumbered. While he had all confidence that he could take a large portion of them in a fight, he didn't want to chance Masakage or Gisela in a drawn-out battle.

Alone, he might have continued.

But he would never risk anyone else.

His gaze went past the *apaswere* to where Masakage stood near the door. His brother still had a glowing green ball in his palm while he eyed the *apaswere* around him as if debating which one he wanted to launch a fireball at next.

Xaydin bit back a smile at the defiant stance from the one person he could always count on. And he'd never allow Masakage to be hurt. Not if he could help it.

With a deep breath, Xaydin turned to the *apaswere* in charge. "We're going. But I'm not the only one who'll be after your friend. King Dash wants a head, and I will deliver it to him. One way or another, I will clash with the demon. Either now or when the bastard goes for Dash."

The *apaswere*'s gaze narrowed.

It didn't faze Xaydin at all as he sheathed his sword.

Gisela returned to her human form. She had her left hand over her right shoulder where she'd been hit. Blood oozed between her fingers and for that alone, he wanted to finish this.

Finish them.

The fact they had made her bleed... He wanted to return the favor with interest.

But first he had to get them to safety.

Holding his hand out toward her, he waited for her to take it with her right one. Keeping his eyes on their enemies, he carefully led her from the tavern.

Still holding a green fireball, Masakage stepped in behind them, covering their exit to make sure none of their enemies went for their backs. It was unnerving to have that many pairs of eyes watching them. As an assassin, Gisela was used to working in the shadows and never standing out.

This...this she didn't like in the least. How Xaydin could stand it, she had no idea.

As they left the building, a group of *apaswere* followed them outside to watch them make their way across the street.

None of them spoke as they drew near the stable. Instead, they kept their attention on the group gathered to wish them dead and be prepared in case they decided to act on that impulse.

Only when they opened the stable door and stepped inside it did Xaydin take his hand off the hilt of his sword and let go of Gisela.

Masakage gave him a grim smile. "Well, that was fun. What should we try next? Diving into a piranha-infested stream?"

"I'm up for it. But only if you go in first."

Masakage shook his head.

Gisela snickered. At least someone appreciated his humor.

"How do we find the *apaswere* now?" she asked.

"I still have my ways, but first I need to deal with an annoyance..."

"Athgar?"

Xaydin nodded at her. "I'm not real happy with the beast who has a big mouth." Those words were barely spoken before he found said beast with the big mouth in the stable where they'd left him.

As soon as Athgar saw them, his eyes widened and he began to sweat. "I didn't do anything wrong." He spoke hastily before Xaydin said or did anything to wring them from the *apaswere*, which told him just how guilty Athgar was.

And the *apaswere* knew it.

"Athgar... Athgar... Athgar...Why don't I believe you?"

"Because he's lying. I don't even need my powers to know that." Masakage manifested his staff out of thin air. The stone at the tip of it shone a deep, dark purple that lit up the stable and bathed them in a soft amethyst glow.

"I didn't know what they had planned or what the contract on your life said. I was told to notify Sigurd whenever you showed up again. I had no idea they were going to attack you."

Xaydin rolled his eyes. "What did you think he planned? A birthday celebration?"

Masakage tsked. "He knew what they would most likely do."

Athgar glared at him. "What are you? A fucking mind reader?"

"Yes."

That made the *apaswere* go pale as he turned toward Gisela.

But she wasn't swayed by his pleas any more than the men were. "I don't have to read your mind. Guilt is written on your face more plainly than the contracts on your body." She met Xaydin's gaze. "You don't really have to kill him to break the contract, do you? Can't you just cut off the limb where it's written?"

"Never considered that before. Killing them was just too much fun. Guess we could start dissecting Athgar and see what happens."

Athgar turned to run, then froze as if an invisible hand had caught him and held him in place.

Gisela arched a brow as she looked at Masakage. "You?"

He smiled. "One of my more favorite abilities."

"I have the best friends." Xaydin narrowed the distance between him and Athgar who kept struggling against Masakage's powers. "You're wasting your time. I've been where you are, and it's annoying as shit. That being said, I do know the one and only way to break free of that unholy grasp. Bet you wish I'd share it."

That only made Athgar more nervous. "What are you going to do with me?"

Xaydin met his brother's gaze. "What do you think?"

An instant later, Athgar vanished...at least in his *apaswere* form. Where he'd been standing, a mouse stood frozen in the straw.

Gisela gaped. "Is that..."

"Athgar. Yes." Masakage snapped his fingers and the mouse ran off.

Xaydin shook his head. "That makes questioning him more difficult."

Masakage laughed.

Gisela wasn't so easily amused. "Anyone have a clue about what happens to his contracts now?"

Xaydin scratched at his cheek. "Good question. Did that nullify them?"

Masakage shrugged. "Why ask me? I have no idea. You're the *apaswere* expert."

"Not on this, I'm not." Xaydin sighed heavily. "Oh well. Maybe he'll get caught in a trap, and that'll end them for sure."

While Gisela understood the sentiment, it did make her a bit wary. Xaydin had no remorse or compassion for what they'd just done. Not that Athgar didn't deserve it for his betrayal.

Still, it made her uncomfortable. It was too close to the injustice her mother meted out on whims. Having suffered under that cruelty for the whole of her life, she wasn't keen on dealing it to anyone else.

You're an assassin. What do you care?

She shouldn't. And it made no sense for her to care. She was the first to admit that. But at least it allowed her to know that she hadn't lost her soul. While her mother had taken most everything else from her, she hadn't lost all her humanity.

Grateful for that small mercy, she watched as Xaydin retrieved his saddle. "What's our plan now?"

He pulled one of Candara's bottles from his saddlebag, then glanced about. "What should we put this on?"

Masakage created a glowing ball. "How's this?"

"That'll work."

She had no idea what they were planning. Not until Xaydin broke the wax seal on the bottle, then poured the thick green liquid over the glowing ball. That caused it to turn even brighter. Their saddles vanished from their perches and then appeared on their horses.

Gisela shivered at their use of magic. "Isn't there supposed to be a cost for magical powers?"

"Not this." He indicated the saddles. "These are parlor tricks." Xaydin handed her the reins of her horse. "Candara's potion...is another story. Those are unpredictable. I have no idea what the payment might be."

"But you're using it anyway?"

"I'm stupid like that." Effortlessly, he mounted his horse.

Masakage snorted. "At least my brother knows his fallacies."

True. It was actually quite refreshing given the dandies she met at court who thought themselves superlative in every way. The idea of being self-deprecating never occurred to them. They were always too busy preening and bragging.

"You're not like any prince I've ever met," she said as she mounted her own horse.

"You should get out more. Most of the kings and princes I know are decent...enough."

It was the enough part that concerned her.

And as soon as Masakage was situated on his mount, the ball began to hum. It swam in a circle in the middle of the air between them before it darted out of the stable.

"Hyah!" Xaydin kicked his mount forward, rushing to catch the ball.

She waited for Masakage to go next, then she rode in the rear. Mostly because she didn't like for anyone to be at her back. This felt safer. Not that she thought they'd do anything. She was becoming more accustomed to them.

Especially Xaydin, and she didn't know why.

Well, that wasn't exactly true. Even now, she saw the way he'd moved in to protect her. No one had ever done that for her before.

While she didn't need it, it was refreshing to have someone care.

He doesn't care, you idiot.

She swore that was her mother's voice in her head. The same voice that had told her, her entire life that she wasn't good enough. Smart enough. That she didn't deserve love.

Or even kindness.

Xaydin wasn't like that. He had a soul inside him. One that was warm, and it drew her in despite her fears and reservations.

And now we're chasing after a ball...

Truth be told, she felt a little ridiculous. Would this even work?

"How does it know where to go?"

Masakage looked at her over his shoulder. "No idea."

"Then why are we trusting it?"

Xaydin smiled at her. "Candara's potions are flawless. They never fail."

Until they did. There was always a first time.

"I heard that," Masakage said to her.

Heat suffused her cheeks at Masakage's playful retort. "Sorry. I was born negative."

"With your mother, I can't blame you." He slowed down a bit so that he could ride beside her. "So who's your father?"

She quickly forced her mind to go blank. That was the one secret she'd never let out. Mostly because she had no idea how they'd react to it.

How anyone would react. The one thing her mother had impressed upon her most was that she was never to breathe one single word about her father. The only reason she knew was because her mother had slipped up and told her during one of Meara's more stellar tantrums.

Even now, she could see the shock on her mother's face as it'd slipped out.

Eyes wide, Meara had stormed at her with so much rage that she'd been sure she was going to die.

Her mother had grabbed her by the neck and slapped her hand over Gisela's mouth. The pressure had been so intense that she'd feared her mother would suffocate her. "Tell no one! You ever repeat that name and the gods as my witness, I'll cut out your tongue, nail it to your forehead and have you skinned alive. Do you understand?"

Gisela had nodded while the name spun through her head with shock and alarm.

In that moment, she'd known what her mother had. No one ever needed to know who had sired her. No good could ever come from it.

So she glanced over to Masakage. "Does it matter?"

"You're hiding a lot of pain from me."

Interesting bit he just confessed. "Does that mean I can block you from my thoughts?"

"Of course. X blocks me constantly. And I've never been able to read Candara."

Good to know. She didn't like the thought of someone digging through her mind.

"Kage!" Xaydin snapped. "It's turning blue."

"What's that mean?" she asked.

"We found him."

8

They slowed down as the glowing ball left the road and headed into the woods on their right. They'd barely moved into the woods when the brush and trees became so thick that they were forced to dismount and leave their horses behind.

Gisela cursed as she ran through spider webs.

Pulling her to a stop, Xaydin helped her wipe them away.

"I hate these things!" She shivered in revulsion.

"Not as much as you should."

She scowled at his odd words. "Meaning?"

"They're enchanted to let someone know we're here."

Her stomach sank. "Wait? What? Seriously?"

Xaydin nodded. "They're a unique species that only lives on this island. It's one of the reasons the *apaswere* claimed this place as their own. Their webs form a conduit and the *apaswere* can monitor it."

"Couldn't they find something better as a warning? Like an infectious disease?"

He snorted. "Given everything I've learned about you so far, I wouldn't have taken you for an arachnophobe."

She should probably be offended, but she recognized the fact he was teasing. "We all have our secrets," she said flippantly. "And our *rational* fears. Spiders are evil things best left far away."

There was an amused glint in his eyes that warmed her a lot more than it should. He was such a handsome beast. Terribly so.

And that thought had barely gone through her head before an arrow went whizzing past her face. One so close that it barely missed hitting her.

To her even greater shock, Xaydin caught it and turned quickly in the direction it'd come from.

"Show yourself," he growled.

Another arrow flew at them. Xaydin used his powers to create a large wood shield to catch it. The arrow landed in the center of the shield with a loud twang. He handed the shield to her, then put his hands together and made a pushing movement. The moment he did, she felt the air around them shift.

A few seconds later someone cried out.

Xaydin rushed toward the sound with her and Masakage hot on his heels. She wasn't sure what they'd find until they broke through the thick growth to see an *apaswere* writhing on the ground.

Completely bald like the others she'd seen, the *apaswere* was at least seven feet tall with giant, bat-like wings. Writing covered every single inch of his body, including his eyelids and tongue.

He gave Xaydin a harsh, accusatory glare. "What did you do to me?"

"Returned your fire."

The *apaswere* was indignant. "I shot arrows at you! This is far more painful!"

Xaydin snorted as he created a bow and nocked an arrow.

"Shall we compare the two and how much pain each one causes?"

"No!" The *apaswere* held his hands up to shield his face. "I'm in enough pain. I'll take your word for the rest."

Just as Gisela expected Xaydin to fire an arrow anyway, he lowered his bow with a frown.

She was just about to ask him why when he spoke. "How old are you, boy?"

The *apaswere* froze at his question. With a panicked expression, he glanced about their group. "What does that have to do with anything?"

Xaydin let out a long, exaggerated sigh. "I don't kill children."

Gisela scowled. "What do you mean?"

He jerked his chin toward the *apaswere*. "He's a kid. Fifteen, maybe sixteen years old. Far too young to be the one we're seeking."

With a gape, she turned toward the *apaswere*. "Is he right? Are you that young?"

"I'm old enough to have contracts!"

"But you don't." Masakage snapped his fingers and all the words disappeared from his flesh. "They're all fake."

"No!" the *apaswere* cried. "Put them back! They're mine!"

She exchanged a shocked stare with Masakage. "How is this possible?"

He shrugged.

Xaydin wasn't so kind. "It's baby school magic. They occasionally masquerade as each other to protect themselves or others. Who told you to duplicate the contract between King Dash and Queen Meara?"

The young *apaswere* stared at him sullenly.

Using his powers, Xaydin lifted him up from the ground. "Do I really have to slam you down until you bleed? I'm really not into child abuse, but if the occasion calls for it, I can rise up when needed."

The *apaswere* squirmed and growled in frustration as he realized that he was at Xaydin's mercy. With one last glare, he whimpered, then stopped fighting. "Fine. Saress did it. I'm old enough and I *can* make my own!" Spoken in the tone of a surly teen.

Xaydin smirked. "And have you?"

The boy actually pouted. "They keep telling me I'm too young, but I know I could do it. If only someone would give me a chance. Saress gave me copies to shut me up. But I'm old enough. I know I am!"

Sighing, Xaydin shook his head. "Take your time growing up before you start courting someone like me who will most likely end your life because someone contracted with another to get their back scratched."

That only made him angry again. "I know how to fight."

Xaydin gave him a droll stare. "Ambushing someone isn't fighting."

Growling, the youth charged at the invisible wall that held him.

"Rage doesn't win battles, my young *apaswere*." He turned toward Masakage. "Release him."

Masakage hesitated. "He knows where Saress is."

That got Xaydin's attention. "You sure?"

Masakage nodded.

The *apaswere* backed away from the invisible wall, but he couldn't go far before he hit the one behind him that kept him in place. Realizing he couldn't escape, he paused and became brave before their eyes. "I'll take you to him...on one condition."

By the look on Xaydin's face, she could tell he was tired of bargaining. "And that is?"

"Each of you has to make a contract with me."

120

"Hell no." Xaydin's tone was flat, but his eyes blazed with anger.

Gisela wasn't so fast to dismiss his earnest request. "What makes a contract? How precise does it have to be?"

The boy shrugged. "It could be anything. A promise that you won't insult each other to..." He shrugged. "Anything really."

"That doesn't seem so hard," she said to Xaydin. "Why not do it?"

"Because if you contract to eat vegetables every day and you don't, little guy over there will hunt you down and kill you."

That left her with one major question. "How does he know if you don't abide by it?"

It was the *apaswere* who answered. "It's a spell. When it's broken, my skin burns and the signature of the party violating the contract lights up. It's actually quite painful and it won't stop burning me until I kill the offending party. The longer it takes, the more the contract burns."

Oh. That sounded awful. Much worse than the problems she dealt with. "Then why do you want a contract so badly?"

"I'm an *apaswere*," he said simply. "If you don't bear contracts, you're an outcast. I want to be respected by my people. The youngest *apaswere* to bear a contract was only nine years old. I'm fifteen. If I don't have my own contracts by the time I turn eighteen, I'll be driven off our island."

"That seems harsh." And reminded her far too much of how her own mother had treated her.

Earn your keep with me or go beg or whore in the street. Make a choice. I don't care which you pick. But I won't keep you up for free.

The saddest part? Her mother had meant that.

No, her mother still meant that. It was a harsh reality when you had nowhere to turn, and that made her heart ache for the boy in front of her.

The last thing she wanted was to see him hurt.

"Can't we help him?"

Masakage shook his head. "I never make deals with other wizards. It doesn't turn out well to mix magic. Things tend to explode...in more ways than one."

"Then I'll make two." Xaydin's offer shocked her.

The *apaswere* was giddy. "What are they?"

"I swear I won't kill my brother. No matter how much he annoys me."

Masakage rolled his eyes.

The *apaswere* tsked. "You have to make a contract with someone for it to involve us. Those are the terms."

He looked at her. "I promise not to kill Gisela so long as she swears not to kill my brother."

"Nothing for yourself?" the *apaswere* asked.

"Don't care about me. I only want to make sure my brother survives this."

Nodding, he turned to Gisela. "And you, my lady? Do you agree?"

"Agreed. I promise not to kill Masakage. Not that I had any intention of harming him."

Xaydin gave her a hard stare. "Today. But things change. Sadly, so do people and their intentions."

Spoken like a man who knew the same betrayals she did. No one should be brutalized by those who were supposed to protect them. And she hated that he knew her pain.

Trying not to think about it, she turned to the boy. "So what do we need to do?"

Still excited, he pulled a medallion from his pocket. Gold and silver, it held an intricate pattern in the center unlike anything she'd ever seen before. Lines intersected and were surrounded by what she assumed were words in an alphabet she couldn't read.

The most interesting part was the very center raised slightly to a sharp point.

He held the medallion out toward Xaydin. "Repeat your oath."

Grimacing, Xaydin made a low growl in his throat before he spoke. "I promise not to intentionally kill Gisela so long as she swears not to intentionally kill my brother Masakage."

The boy pressed Xaydin's finger against the point until a drop of blood ran down, across the medallion.

Then, he turned to Gisela. "Now repeat your vow."

"I promise not to intentionally kill Masakage."

He pressed her finger against the point.

"Ow!" she hissed as pain went through her entire body.

The boy didn't react as he watched.

Once their blood mingled on the medallion, it turned a deep, dark purple. As it did so, the blood rushed from the medallion to his finger and then words began to appear on the boy's flesh.

He hissed in pain, but a slow, delighted smile curved his lips. Elated, he touched the words on his forearm. "Finally!" His eyes shining, he all but jumped in his bliss. "Thank you! Both of you!"

Gisela started to remind him that he'd bargained for another contract from them, but he was so excited that she didn't want to dampen it with details. Let him bask in this moment. Happiness like that was all too rare in the world.

And sadly, too many enjoyed stealing it from others. She wasn't one of them. If she could, she'd preserve that happiness and make sure everyone had as much of it as they could tolerate for the whole of their lives.

Xaydin cocked his head. "Are you all right?"

"Light-headed from the blood loss," she quipped. "You?"

He turned back to their *apaswere*. "I still want information. Where's Saress?"

"Not far. On the north shore. For one more contract, I'll show you to his home, personally."

Masakage leaned toward Xaydin so that he could whisper loudly in his ear. "We have the tracking potion. Do we really need him?"

Xaydin seemed to consider it. Until his gaze went to the boy. "We'll use our *apaswere* guide."

"You're too soft-hearted. I hope we don't regret this."

She caught the glint in Xaydin's eyes that said he agreed, and yet he ignored his brother's warning.

"What's your name, lad?" Xaydin asked.

"Fenrys."

"Then lead us to the North Shore. But be warned. If this is a trap..."

"Understood." Humming to himself, Fenrys spread his wings, then took flight. He circled above them before he headed off in what she assumed was the correct direction.

Gisela wanted to change into her preferred mode of transportation, until she remembered that Xaydin hated shifters and if he ever saw her true form...

Who knew how he'd react?

They walked in silence for a couple of minutes with Fenrys flying just above them. In her mind, she considered what it would take to look like an *apaswere*. It wouldn't be hard. She even had the power to mimic the contract words written on their flesh.

A grand illusion.

One that made her curious about Xaydin.

"Why do you hate shape shifters so much?" The question was out before she could stop it.

His face emotionless, Xaydin slowed to ride beside her. "What?"

"I was just wondering what you have against..." She barely caught herself before she said *me*. "Shape shifters."

He didn't hesitate with the answer. "One killed my father, and others of their ilk used to spy on us for your mother when we were in captivity. Were you one of them?"

"No!" She was insulted that he'd even ask. But to be fair, it made sense that he would. She was her mother's daughter, and she knew firsthand that her mother resorted to those tactics.

And worse. Her mother loved using such information against others, as well as allowing it to stoke her into a furious rage so that she felt justified in abusing those she targeted as enemies.

How many times had her mother used her for a scapegoat? Or beaten an innocent servant who made the mistake of being in a room when her mother received bad news.

Why?

Because her mother believed everyone was scheming against her. She couldn't enjoy a single moment for fear of what was being plotted.

Gisela couldn't imagine living that way. She was suspicious enough, but she didn't believe every single person in the world was out to cause her harm.

Maybe you should have treated people better, Mum. Honestly, she believed it was the guilt of her mother's actions that had made the queen insane. Because at the end of the day, Meara had to know that she brutalized others, which fostered the hatred she was trying to stamp out.

"I'm well aware of the fact that my mother has no soul and will do whatever she must to maintain her throne. I'm sorry for what happened to you and your friends."

Xaydin had to stop his jaw from going slack. No one had

ever apologized for what had happened to them. Not even his father. He was completely speechless. Especially given the fact that it was obvious she meant those words.

Truly meant them. He'd never expected sincerity from anyone and especially not from the daughter of a bitch-queen.

Damn.

Clearing her throat, she gave him a hard stare. "I understand, Xaydin. We can never trust each other. It's the only way to guard against betrayal."

Those words cut through him. Not just because they were true, but because he understood her need to protect herself. It was why he preferred solitude. Since he couldn't reach his back to put a dagger in it, he didn't have to watch himself all the time.

With others...

He couldn't help his suspicious mind. He'd spent too many years bleeding internally because of troublemakers whose only pleasure came from hurting others. Or worse, those who sought scapegoats to distract them from their own dubious actions. He'd never been able to decide which group deserved an eternity in hell the most.

But as he looked at her, he wanted to believe that she wasn't related to her mother. That maybe, just maybe there was someone who was decent.

Someone who had a soul.

His past said it wasn't likely. Experience laughed at him for even thinking it. Yet there was some tiny little ember deep inside that sparked whenever she was near.

It made no sense. The troll in his blood scoffed at the thought of ever being with a shifter who had a human base form. They were fragile and weak. But even as that thought went through him, he knew there was nothing weak about her. She had a core of steel.

One that allowed her to stand up to him even in her weakest

form. Maybe because she knew she could transform into something larger.

Yet she didn't. Now that he thought about it, she didn't shift like the others of her ilk. The shifters he knew thought nothing of switching forms whenever it suited them.

Gisela kept herself weak, even when she shouldn't.

Interesting...

And it made him wonder why. Did she hate that part of herself? That would make sense.

"You don't shift much, do you?"

Her eyes turned dark.

"Sorry if I overstepped. It was just an observation."

She shook her head. "Maybe you did, but that wasn't what made me flinch. I don't shift forms much because it makes my mother furious. She's always hated her equine body. Though she'd never say that to anyone else."

"It's why she hates the Licordians."

Gisela nodded. "They can be human or unicorns. They aren't trapped between the two species."

"It's sad to hate yourself. Hate what you can't change. I'd feel sorry for her if she wasn't such a..." He caught himself before he insulted her mother.

"Insane bitch?"

He arched a brow.

She smiled at him. "Don't worry. You can't hurt my feelings or make me angry by insulting her. I'm intimately aware of all her faults."

"I suppose you are." Oddly enough, he wanted to reach out and soothe her. Something completely out of character for him. The idea of comforting someone else normally repulsed him. But with Gisela...

He cherished the thought of soothing her. Of making her smile and even laugh.

She was very different. If only he knew why.

And with that thought came another... "That's why you appear human, isn't it?"

She scowled. "I don't follow."

"You choose to be human to rile your mother."

Blushing, she looked away.

Xaydin laughed at her act of supreme rebellion. She wasn't perfect, but she was perfectly charming. What better way to get back at her mother than to be the one thing Meara would sell her soul to become?

Masakage slowed down until he was on the other side of Xaydin. He passed a droll stare to his brother. "What?"

Tsking, Masakage passed a stare between them. "Just wondering what you two were conspiring about. You looked all intense until the laughter. I'm starting to worry."

"Nothing to fear. Just learning more about our charming companion."

"That scares me even more," he muttered under his breath.

Xaydin would have asked him about it had their guide not chosen that moment to land near them.

"What is it?"

Fenrys jerked his chin toward the north. "His cottage is just over there. You can't miss it. But I don't want to be seen. I shouldn't be helping you. I could get into a lot of trouble for it."

"Because you want contracts more." Xaydin tsked.

"No one else would help me get them." He rubbed his hand over his bare arm. "Ready to write the next one?"

"After I make sure this is the right *apaswere*. As you said, you're breaking protocol. I want to make sure you haven't lied to us."

Fenrys appeared insulted by his words. At least for a few seconds. "Fine. I guess some mistrust is warranted." He went over to a large rock and sat down. "I'll wait here."

Xaydin started to chide him but decided to withhold his teasing. The boy was actually afraid. It was soul-aching when duty clashed with lifelong dreams. In some, it inspired to great acts of sacrifice, and in others...

They betrayed their beliefs to get what they wanted. Something hard to live with. Neither decision was easy.

Xaydin dismounted. "Chin up, Fenrys. This won't take long."

The boy didn't speak.

Xaydin led his companions the short distance to the cottage that was set on a small, intimate beach. What a strange setting for an *apaswere*. They normally preferred homes in the mountains or in the open where they could watch for those seeking them. As a rule, they had greater trust issues than he did.

But not in this case. The small cottage faced the sea so that the occupants could take in and appreciate the beautiful view.

Xaydin put his hand on his sword as he slowly approached the door.

To his shock, Gisela placed her hand over his. "You know I can't let you kill the *apaswere*."

He paused to look down at her. "I don't want to fight you, Gisela. Don't make it come to that."

"You know I have no choice."

"Yes, you do. You don't have to go back to your queen. She can't touch you here."

Gisela's heart stopped at something she'd never considered before.

In that moment, she felt stupid for the fact she'd never thought of it.

But he was right. She didn't have to go back. She was free. Her mother couldn't touch her here.

Terror filled her. The thought of giving up what she knew... living among strangers...

You have no friends at home. No real family.

True. Her mother had killed her own brother and Gisela's half-brother. Meara had no attachment to anyone other than herself.

Only Brant held her loyalty, and he didn't care what place they called home.

So, why was she doing this? To curry favor with a mother who barely spoke to her? It wasn't like this would suddenly cause Meara to grow a conscience or motherly love.

Most likely, she wouldn't even say thanks or good job.

Masakage shook his head. "You've stunned and confused her, brother."

Xaydin couldn't agree more. Her eyes betrayed her inner war.

Wanting to ease it, he turned toward her. "You are fearless. Brave. Intrepid. Throw off the chains Meara has used to cripple you. For once in your life, live."

How simple he made it seem.

But was it that simple? The Thirteen Kingdoms were vast. She could easily hide, and she had the skills to make sure no one ever dragged her back to Thassalia.

How horrible that the thought of walking into an unknown future was more frightening than returning to the misery she knew awaited her at home.

Did everyone feel this way?

Xaydin gently lifted her chin until she stared into his dark eyes. "I have all faith in you. Change your destiny, Gisela. It's not easy. But better for you to change it yourself than allow someone else to take control and force it upon you. Think about it. You could be free of Meara forever."

He was right. And it was terrifying.

"Meara promised me my freedom if I protected him."

"And you believe her? You really think once you return home she'll just let you go?"

She wanted to say yes. But he was right.

Gisela knew her mother better than anyone. Meara wasn't a creature anyone could trust. The only reason she hadn't broken her alliance with Dash was because of this contract.

Even then, she'd actually tried. While Dash had been out, seeking his sister's murderer, Meara had "invaded" his lands by saying he'd assisted the rebels who'd been trying to overthrow her. A technicality that she was lucky hadn't already called down the wrath of an *apaswere* on her.

"Let's see this *apaswere*, and then I'll let you know my decision." That was the best she could do at present.

Changing one's destiny wasn't an easy thing, and it shouldn't be decided on a whim. And definitely not under pressure.

Xaydin inclined his head before he headed toward the cottage.

Stunned, she exchanged a panicked look with Masakage. "Is that it? We just walk right in?"

He shrugged. "It would appear so."

Very well, then. Though to be honest, she would have expected something a little more incognito. 'Course, given the huge size of Xaydin, his sexy swagger, and the fact he had the chiseled features of an angel, she supposed incognito was impossible for him. He tended to leave a memorable mark.

"Has he always been like this?" she asked.

Masakage just nodded.

Sighing heavily, she trailed after him, hoping she could do something. She had no idea what. It was futile. As skilled a warrior as she was, she knew she'd be no match for him. Not physically. His reach was too great, and he was too massive in size. While she might be quicker, he was much, much stronger.

Granted, she could fight in her alternate forms, but she wasn't as skilled at that. Nor as agile. Shape shifting took a lot of effort, and it wasn't easy to fight in the skin of someone else. If she were injured in another form, she'd immediately revert back and that could be even more dangerous for her.

Besides, there was only one form she was as adept at using as her human body.

The one that pissed off her mother to no end. That form was kept as buried as the secret of her father.

Gisela quickened her steps as Xaydin approached the cottage stoop.

Before he reached it, the door opened to show an *apaswere* who appeared around the same age as Fenrys.

"Are you here to see my father?"

By the expression on Xaydin's face, she could tell he was as stunned at that question as she was.

"Saress?"

The *apaswere* nodded. "My father. Are you friends of his?"

Now they were all exchanging bemused stares. What was going on?

Xaydin was the first to recover from shock. "Not friends, per se. Why?"

"If you wish to say goodbye to him, there's not much time. The doctor said he'll be gone within the hour." He opened the door to admit them into the modest dwelling.

Once inside the small cottage, Gisela pulled up short in the room she assumed was also the kitchen, given the size of the hearth and the large pot set over the fire. But instead of a table and chairs, they'd placed a bed there. One that looked out on the sea.

The kitchen chairs lined the walls where five other *apasweres* sat in tears. A female *apaswere* was at the side of the bed, holding the hand of a male who lay dying.

132

Tears filled her eyes at the sight of their grieving. Granted she was a fierce warrior who normally suppressed her own emotions, but it made her vulnerable whenever she saw others feeling them. It was one thing to kill someone quickly, it was another to watch them suffer. That had never been her goal. She didn't like pain. Not her own and definitely not that of others.

The female looked up at Xaydin. "Welcome, friends. I'm glad you made it in time."

Saress shook his head at her words. "They're not friends, Asla. Do you not recognize him for who he is?"

She scowled as she looked at all three of them. "No."

Saress laughed bitterly, then coughed and wheezed. Once he was able to breathe again, he jerked his chin toward Xaydin. "Behold the legendary Oathbreaker. I'm sure he's here to collect my head."

The five who were seated stood immediately, ready to fight.

"Hold," Saress said in a weakened tone. "I don't want my last memory to be the sight of my family bleeding or fighting for the likes of me. I'm done with this world. What difference does it make on how I leave it?"

Asla began weeping harder.

To her shock, Xaydin held up his hands. "Forgive me, my lord. I didn't realize you were ill, and I mean no one in this room any harm."

A bitter laugh rattled in Saress's chest. "You vowed to see all *apasweres* dead. Are we really supposed to believe you're here for any other reason?"

Xaydin flinched at that questions. Because he was right. He'd spent years tracking down *apasweres*. Taking pride in killing them and watching their contracts fade away with their lives.

But this was the first time he'd seen one of them surrounded by family, dying of natural causes. While he'd known they had families and lived similar lives to others, it was completely different when confronted by it.

And as much as he hated their species, he respected the *apaswere*'s right to pass peacefully today.

But he did have one question. "What's wrong with you?" Because it was obvious that the *apaswere* wasn't elderly. Just in a lot of pain.

"Ersi," Asla said with a catch in her throat.

"What is that?" Gisela asked softly.

Asla drew a ragged breath. "It's a horrible disease that afflicts us far too often."

"Caused by taking on too many contracts." Saress passed a meaningful look toward Xaydin. "The magic speeds up our internal aging. On the surface I might appear to be middle-aged, internally, I'm ancient."

Xaydin scowled. "I've never heard of this."

"We don't talk about it," his son said. "If word got out, some might think twice about using us for their deals."

Saress took his son's hand. "Although most of us pass the contracts on to our heirs before we go."

"What do you mean?" Gisela looked at him. "They can do that? It's not like what we saw earlier with the fake contracts?"

Xaydin sighed heavily. "No. They're not the same. But I've heard of this. They can make binding copies of contracts appear on others, but those aren't enforceable by the recipient until the original *apaswere* passes on."

"Which is what makes your friend so deadly." Saress gave her a wan smile. "Prince Xaydin is exceptionally talented at ensuring we don't have time to make copies before he ends us." He met Xaydin's gaze. "Or if there are copies, that he finds them and ends them too."

For reasons Xaydin couldn't begin to fathom, he felt a vicious wave of guilt go through him.

"May I ask you, Prince, which of my contracts has brought you to my door?"

"The one for Queen Meara and King Cratus that King Dash inherited."

"Good."

"Good?" Masakage asked.

"I feared it would be one of the marriage contracts. I'd hate to think that one of the couples I helped unite hated one another enough to kill me for my part in their union."

Xaydin shook his head. "I would never take a life for something of that nature."

Asla scoffed. "What do you care? You've assassinated us without hesitation."

"Not true, my lady. I don't care about the lesser contracts as most will never break them. It's the contracts forced on others that I execute with extreme bloodshed. Those that have caused another to be killed or sacrificed needlessly."

Saress placed his hand over Asla's. "Don't be so harsh, my love. The prince's father was executed over something that shouldn't have been enforced. I understand his fury at us and so do you."

"We're not all honorable," Asla finally confirmed. "Some of us can be bought off. I'm sorry you were hurt, Highness."

And he was seriously regretting his decision to intrude on their last moments together. "I'll leave your family in peace. Forgive our intrusion."

As he started for the door, Saress called out to him.

Pausing, he turned back toward the ailing *apaswere*.

"Is it necessary to take my head to your king?"

"No. Dash will accept my word that the deed is done."

"Thank you for that mercy."

It wasn't mercy. It was decency.

Xaydin led them outside, but before they could go far, Masakage pulled him to a stop.

"I can heal him."

Xaydin was surprised by his brother's words. "How so?"

"I have the means to spare his life, if you want."

With a side glance to Gisela, he hoped he was wrong about his brother's intentions. "We'd have to take a life to spare his." That was the common price for such magic.

Masakage screwed his face up in protest. "I'm not talking about dark magic, idiot. I can heal him with herbs."

Gisela's face lit up. "How so?"

"It's a poison that's making him sick. All poisons have antidotes that don't require magic."

"Not all poisons," Xaydin reminded him.

"Most poisons have antidotes that don't require magic. This is one of them."

"And you can do this for them?" Gisela asked.

"Rather sure I can."

Xaydin cursed his brother silently. Of course, he could. Anything to make his life more difficult. "So you want me to kill him?"

Masakage gave him a droll stare. "No. I'm proposing an exchange. He releases the contract for his life."

Just as Xaydin warmed to the proposition, Gisela's happiness faded. "Wait a second. You still intend to break the contract?"

He rubbed his jaw as he considered it. "Void the contract, not break it."

"Semantics."

Xaydin nodded at her hostile word. "And the most important semantics for you is that you will have fulfilled your orders. The *apaswere* you were sent to protect will live. Semantically, you will have done what you were ordered to do."

Gisela considered that. He was technically correct. In good conscience, if the *apaswere* was alive, she would have fulfilled her mother's orders. But that wasn't the intent. Her mother wanted the contract preserved.

"Dash will kill my mother." And while she had issues with her, she didn't want her mother dead, per se. Maybe because she kept hoping her mother would do better.

Be better.

So long as her mother was alive, she had hope that they could rectify their broken relationship. And hope was so important.

"That would be up to your mother. Unlike me, Dash doesn't kill indiscriminately."

He said that, but she hadn't seen him kill anyone haphazardly. Indeed, if it were true he'd have slaughtered Saress on his deathbed and not cared.

No, there was more to Xaydin than his terrifying, callous reputation.

A lot more.

"Shall we talk to him?" Masakage asked Xaydin.

He nodded. "Let's see how badly he wants to live."

Masakage left their group and went back to knock on the door.

She frowned. "Should we go with him?"

"My presence would only make them nervous. If they weren't grieving, they'd have normally attacked me." He squinted toward the cottage. "Grief does strange things to people. Even the *apaswere*."

"I've never known grief. It's as foreign to me as happiness." Her honesty surprised even her. She wasn't sure why she made such a confession. But it was true.

"You've never lost anyone?"

She laughed bitterly. "Never had anyone to lose."

SHERRILY KENYON

Xaydin flinched at those heartfelt words. But he understood. He was a loner himself. Loved ones made him vulnerable, and he knew it.

Because he knew the pain of loss. Of watching those he cared about suffer and die, he kept to himself so that he wouldn't have to live through that pain again.

To not know it...

Xaydin couldn't decide if she was lucky or cursed. Cursed because it meant that she'd never known friendship or family. That awakened a horrible feeling inside him.

He cared. And he hated the part of him that was touched by her honesty.

Touched by the beauty of her unusual features.

Stop it!

He couldn't afford any tenderness for her. So he decided to focus on what he knew would end these feelings. "How many shapes can you shift into?"

She gave him a stern frown. "Pardon?"

"You're a shifter. What I know about your breed is that you have forms you take easily and some are harder. I'm just curious what forms you usually take. Besides human, what's your preferred form?"

If he didn't know better, he'd think she was shamed by his question...which had not been his intent. He hadn't meant to hurt her, only protect himself.

"You said you took one form to get to the town where we met. What was it?"

Gisela felt the heat rush to her cheeks. *Don't you dare tell him. Don't do it.*

It was a secret she'd been keeping the whole of her life. Letting it go wasn't easy. It was impossible.

"I don't want to anger you."

He gave her a confused stare. "Why the reticence? I won't get angry."

"You hate shifters."

"True, but I don't hate you."

Those words wrenched a sob from her. How awful that it was the kindest thing anyone had ever said to her. The closest statement to love that she'd ever received.

I am pathetic.

Because those words touched her. They made her ache for a normal life.

It was so hard to live at court and listen to the petty concerns of those who thought their lives were hard. They had no idea how lucky they were. No appreciation for the love that was thrown at them.

Not the ones like her mother who dealt with falsity and lies. Everyone claimed they loved their queen, but Meara knew the truth as well as Gisela.

No one loved her mother. Not even her daughter. It was what had turned her mother into such a horrible beast.

With her mother's power and position came such paranoia that Meara had long ago convinced herself no one could be sincere. She'd expected Gisela to hate her and so, by her own actions, Meara had guaranteed that outcome.

As a child, she'd done her best to love her mother.

But cruelty had crushed that love beneath her iron hooves.

And so Gisela had learned to keep her head low and care for no one.

Now...

She wanted the world to see her and more than that, she wanted some of what she'd seen. Did that make her greedy? To want a friend?

Someone to treat her with kindness?

"I do have one form I prefer over the others." The truth was out before she could stop it.

"That is?" he asked.

Gisela shook her head, then did what she'd never done around anyone else.

She shifted into her birth form.

Xaydin gaped as he saw the black unicorn before him. As shocking as that was, it was the horn that held his attention most.

Red, but tipped with black. Never had he seen or heard of such.

A unicorn's character and skills were always evident to those around them as their horn colors changed as their bearers did. White horns belonged mostly to children. Those who bore them were innocent and pure. Orange came from those who encouraged and passionately led others. Blue horns meant the unicorn was calm and tranquil. They were the unicorns who mediated between others or were found in administrative jobs and tasks.

Unicorn healers held green horns, while yellow signified those who were driven and creative. Purple horns were their clergy or those who held high levels of intuition or magic.

Silver horns usually came with age. It showed wisdom and sacrifice. Great leadership.

Then there were the gray horns who were indecisive and deceptive. Ostracized within Licordia as the bearers couldn't be trusted. They were renowned for their selfish pettiness and jealousy.

But there were three colors in particular to note, with two of them being exceptionally rare.

The first of those colors was the black horns. Those who'd mastered their powers to such an extent they were to be feared by any who crossed their path.

King Dash had been such a beast for most of his life. His red horn had turned black after he killed his own father and took the Licordian throne. By that infamous black horn, everyone had known the power he wielded and the temperament to make his enemies pay dearly.

His deceased sister's horn had been gold. Pure of heart, those who bore gold were altruistic...willing to sacrifice themselves for others. For centuries, Dash's sister had been the only unicorn to bear a gold horn.

To his knowledge, no one since Queen Amandine.

Until Dash had been killed by his enemies. When he returned to life, he did so with something no one had ever seen before...

A black horn that was edged by gold. His dark powers were tempered by his willingness to die for those he loved. To sacrifice himself for his kingdom.

And then lastly were the red horns. While not uncommon, they were still a minority in Licordia as they belonged to those who were angry and aggressive. Those willing to fight to the death.

With the exception of Dash, Xaydin had never heard of any unicorn possessing a mixed color.

Black and red meant she was powerful.

And furious.

Yet there was more to it than that.

"You're not just a shape shifter," he said with a tsk as he realized she'd been lying to them.

"How do you mean?"

"Shifters can't duplicate unicorns. Not without telltale signs that betray them, such as two horns instead of one. It was a curse placed upon their blood long ago by the great Queen Amandine. Only a unicorn can be a unicorn. The rest are just cheap copies that are easily identified... Is Meara really your mother?"

She turned back into her human body and quickly picked up her cloak to shield her nudity. The shock on her face further proved his point. A born shape shifter knew they couldn't mimic unicorns, and they would never have attempted such. Never mind claim it as the first choice of form.

No, she was a unicorn by birth. And she could take other forms.

"Is Meara your mother?" he asked again, giving her his back so that she could redress in her clothes. Now, it was imperative that he know the answer.

"Yes."

Xaydin cursed. If that was true, then he knew Gisela's father, and it explained so much about why Meara hated unicorns as much as she did. Especially given Gisela's age.

This woman was King Dash's sister.

9

Xaydin was still reeling from his newfound discovery. "You're a daughter of Cratus."

Fuck me. He didn't want to believe it, but...

"You can turn around now. I'm dressed."

She still hadn't answered his question and he had to know. "How long have you known?"

"Most of my life. My mother accidentally confessed it one night when she was in the midst of a tirade."

"And you never thought to reach out to your brothers or sister?"

She scoffed at his question. "You think they'd believe me?"

"Again, only a unicorn can be a unicorn. The moment they saw you, they'd have known the truth." And now that he knew who she was, it was obvious how much she favored her father. And brother. She was definitely the feminine version of Dash. How he'd missed it, he had no idea. "They wouldn't have questioned it."

Gisela let those words sink in. Her mother had convinced her that they would have all killed her. Her father for tying him to her mother.

145

Her brother because she could have contested his inheritance.

And her other siblings just for spite.

The last thing that bastard wants is anyone knowing how intimate we were. You are my guarantee that the unicorns won't dare invade. The daughter of two equine races, you are the rightful heir to their throne!

She'd always wondered what had made her mother so positive they'd know her.

Now she understood. It was the alternate form her mother had forbidden her from taking. Her mother must have known that only unicorns could be unicorns.

You are centaur! Damn you for not showing my blood!

When Gisela had been born as a unicorn, her mother had slaughtered everyone who had witnessed her birth.

Everyone. All to safeguard her mother's illicit secret that she'd slept with King Cratus of Licordia.

Gisela had been born in blood, and but for her mother's politics that wanted to use her, she'd have been slaughtered, too. As it was, she'd been kept completely sequestered until she'd been able to turn human.

Released only so long as she swore to her mother that she'd never turn into her birth form.

Never be the unicorn she'd been born to be.

As if it were Gisela's fault that her mother's centaur genes hadn't fought any harder to show themselves in her blood. Her mother had acted as if Gisela had done it on purpose to anger her.

No one had a choice as to what they were born.

Only who they'd become.

"I never wanted to be an assassin," she whispered in a confession that caught her off guard. "I just wanted my mother to acknowledge me."

To her shock, Xaydin pulled her against his chest and held her. "I know it hurts and I'm sorry. Every child should feel wanted and loved."

How would she know? Neither of her parents had held an ounce of parental concern. Her father had handed her brothers over to be brutalized. He'd separated Dash and Ryper to be raised separately. What kind of monster divided twins?

It made her wonder how Xaydin's mother had felt about her children. She was still alive and they didn't know her...

Gisela couldn't imagine being like that. She'd never be able to let a child go. Not for anything.

But here they were. The unwanted.

And yet standing this close to Xaydin...

She didn't feel unwanted at all.

We're enemies.

Weren't they?

Why did she have this overwhelming urge to trust him? To seek him out? It wasn't like her at all, but she had learned to enjoy their company. Enjoy having someone at her back.

But dare she be that stupid?

MASAKAGE COULD FEEL the hatred from the *apasweres* around him. It hung heavy in the air, like humidity in the atmosphere right before a mighty storm. They begrudged his presence, just as they'd ached to attack Xaydin earlier.

He'd give them credit, they knew restraint. How to hold themselves back even when they were filled with fury and a need for vengeance.

Masakage respected that. Holding his hands out to show

them that he meant no harm, he gestured toward the bed where Saress coughed and tried to breathe. "I can save him."

His eldest son scoffed. "For what price, wizard? One of us must die?"

Normally, they'd be right. The usual price was a life for a life. But there was something he'd sensed earlier. And it was something he didn't want to let Xaydin know.

"The ink used for Meara's contract was bespelled. I can smell it. Let me take it from you and you'll see."

Saress scoffed. "Lies."

"No. Deep inside, you know it, too. You felt it the moment you began carrying that contract. Something wasn't right. But your pride kept you from correcting it or saying anything. This isn't the usual illness some of you get. This one is special. A built-in safeguard to make sure the queen wouldn't always have to abide by her word."

Saress sat up.

Masakage approached the bed slowly. "Admit it. You haven't been right since the moment you took that contract on."

Saress started to argue but then caught himself. He looked to his wife, then back to Masakage. "How did you know that?"

Because wizards knew their own kind. They could smell magic no matter how little. It literally sizzled on their skin when they came near it. Not even the most skilled of their ilk could mask the unique sensation.

"The how isn't important. What matters is that I can cure it."

"For a price."

"Magic always comes with a price." A price usually paid by the one wanting the magic enacted.

"And that price?"

"We transfer it to another course, and you never speak of the contract again."

"What difference would that make?"

"You would no longer be poisoned by the ink, and you have no reason to enforce it." Because without it on his skin, he would never know if or when the contract was broken.

Saress narrowed his gaze on him. "What do you get out of it?"

"That's no never mind to you. Just do as I say and you'll live a long, happy life as will Fenrys...your son." The boy who'd led them here had wanted his father put out of his suffering, and he was carrying a grudge because his father wanted to give contracts to his brothers, but not him.

All because Saress didn't want his youngest son hunted.

Masakage manifested the medium he intended to put the contract on. "Are you ready to be healed?"

Asla nodded. "Do it, my love. We'll tell no one."

Saress cupped her cheek in his hand. He waited for so long that Masakage was sure he'd turn the bargain down.

But after several minutes, he nodded. "Do what you must, wizard. I want to be with my family for as long as the gods will allow."

Masakage inclined his head, then used his powers to pull the ink from the *apaswere*'s skin to the document in his hand. Word by word, the ink floated from his skin to the parchment until the tainted contract was transferred.

Satisfied, Masakage rolled it up and smiled.

It was done.

Now the question was who would pay the highest fee for this...

King Dash or Queen Meara.

10

"How did it go?" Xaydin asked as Masakage rejoined them.

"Taken care of. Gisela has achieved her goal and so have you. The *apaswere* will live and the contract is gone."

Xaydin smirked at Gisela. "Guess diplomacy can work. Don't ever tell Dash. I don't want him to get cocky...er."

Gisela rolled her eyes. "But you don't have a head to deliver to your evil overlord."

"Dash is neither evil nor my over anything, least of all my lord."

"'Cause you answer to no one," she teased.

"Exactly." Xaydin sighed. "But I have to admit that it feels weird to achieve my objective and have no head to show for it. Rather anticlimactic, if you ask me."

Masakage shrugged. "Guess you could always take another *apaswere* head. Dash wouldn't know the difference."

"I don't kill the innocent." Even when they were *apaswere*. There were plenty of them like Fenrys who had easy contracts and who didn't ruin the lives of others. He only wanted the ones who were like the greedy bastard who'd murdered his father. Those who refused to exercise humanity and reason to see who was innocent and who wasn't.

Xaydin only wanted the corrupt *apaswere*. The rest had nothing to fear from him.

"Shall we retrieve our horses and get home?" Masakage asked.

"Let's. You lead the way."

Masakage headed back to where they'd left Fenrys.

Xaydin held Gisela back.

She looked up at him with a frown. "Something wrong?"

He turned around to walk backwards while facing Gisela so that he could mouth the words, "My brother never calls Dash... Dash." Being raised with the Tenmaruns, Masakage was more formal than that. Unlike Xaydin, Masakage wasn't really friends with the king.

No. Masakage either called him king or by his full name, King Deciel.

And now that he thought about it, Masakage had said and done several things that didn't ring true.

Every part of him was on alert now, and in case he was right, he wanted Gisela to be wary, too.

She cut a suspicious glance to his brother before meeting Xaydin's stare. "What do I do?" she whispered.

"Act naturally. Watch him." He turned around and quickened his steps. "Kage!"

His "brother" slowed to allow him to catch up. "Yes?"

"Did you leave a coin with the *apaswere*?"

"Why would I leave coin with him? He didn't charge me for the service."

Right...

Xaydin silently cursed. This definitely wasn't Masakage.

How had he missed that? Masakage would have offered one of his fortune coins to Fenrys and Saress.

Why hadn't he realized that sooner? That annoying habit of handing out coins was one Masakage couldn't stop himself from doing. It was compulsive.

Damn it!

Which begged the question, who was with them? They'd started this quest with Masakage.

Was his brother still alive?

Grinding his teeth, he cursed himself for being distracted. This was his fault. Had Gisela not been with them, he would have realized the masquerade sooner. Too much of his attention had been on her and not what he should have been focused on.

If his brother was hurt, he'd never forgive himself.

What if they killed him?

Not possible. Masakage was too powerful for that. He refused to believe that his brother could be killed by some two-bit animal who was playing this game with them.

Which was the real question. Why do this? If they wanted to stop him or Gisela, why not just attack?

Who hired them?

It definitely wasn't Dash. The king would have never called in someone else after telling Xaydin to do this. While Dash was as suspicious as anyone Xaydin had ever known, Xaydin was one of the exceptionally few Dash trusted.

No, something else was going on here.

Something sinister, and he would find his brother, then kill this bastard.

Forced to stay calm, Xaydin didn't say anything as they made their way back to Fenrys who looked completely crestfallen.

"Did you kill him?" the boy asked with a catch in his voice. "Was he in pain?"

Xaydin knelt down by where he sat on a rock, waiting. "You wanted to spare him pain, didn't you?"

Fenrys refused to look at him.

"Don't worry. Your father's no longer suffering."

The boy sobbed.

"No!" Xaydin added quickly. "I mean, he's still alive. And he's no longer suffering."

He caught the last sob in his throat. "What?"

"We didn't kill him. We healed him."

Fenrys blinked in disbelief. "How?"

"Your father was poisoned and Masakage—" he almost choked saying the name, "—cured him. He's all better now."

The boy drew a ragged breath. "He's been in so much pain for so long. You have no idea."

Actually, he did. He'd seen more than his fair share of such deaths while in captivity. Poison had been a preferred method of murder for those who'd been thrown to Meara's care. The twisted queen had taken great pleasure watching others suffer a prolonged, painful death.

The memories of all those needless deaths haunted him eternally.

Fenrys reached out and hugged Xaydin. "How can I ever repay you? I know! I'll cancel your contract!"

"It's all right. Keep the contract and go see your father. I'm sure he'll be delighted."

Squealing, Fenrys released him and flew off.

Gisela glanced away from Xaydin's sheepish grin as he watched the boy leave. Her giant troll would die if he knew how adorable that made him appear.

He had a much bigger heart than he wanted anyone to know. But she saw it, and she was touched.

Biting her lip, she turned her attention to Masakage. Was

Xaydin right? Could he really be an imposter? Had the real Masakage ever been with them?

She wished she knew him better so that she could help Xaydin find out the truth. It had to be driving him crazy to think that someone had taken over his brother's place.

Which meant whoever was pretending to be Masakage was a shifter...

No wonder he hated them so much. It was frustrating to know that such a creature could step in at any time and "replace" someone you thought you knew.

Someone you cared about.

It was why her mother loved them so. In fact, her mother even paid some to masquerade as her from time to time. Most of those fools ended up dying from an assassination. Poor things to not see that end coming.

Unlike unicorns, any shifter could pretend to be a centaur. The only way to identify her mother was a unique mark that existed underneath her mother's tongue.

A mark only three people knew about.

Gisela, her mother, and the poor, now tongueless man who'd placed it there. He was kept alive to identify the mark should there ever be any question of someone trying to impersonate her and remove her from power. Not that Gisela had ever met or even seen him. Her mother had told her about it, just in case.

While Gisela knew the mark was there, she didn't know what the mark was or even what it looked like.

You'll know if you ever see it. I'm not like any other and neither is my mark.

Which had always made her curious as to what it could be, but not so much that she'd risk her life to find out. Her mother would have her head if she dared such an affront.

But that had also made her curious if all shape shifters had such a mark so that they could tell each other apart.

One thing was certain, she had no idea that Masakage wasn't Masakage.

Or was Xaydin so paranoid that he was suspicious without cause?

She could drive herself mad trying to reason this out.

What was the truth?

Xaydin led them back through the woods until they reached the waiting horses. "Shall we go tell Dash the good news?"

"Sure." And with that, another thought hit her.

Rushing to catch up to Xaydin, she pulled his head down to hers. Shock registered on his face as she pressed her lips against his ear. "You said you knew a shape shifter?" she whispered.

He nodded.

"Can you send for him?"

Scowling, he looked down at her.

"Trust me." And with that she kissed his lips.

It was supposed to be a meaningless thing. Nothing more than a friend might give a friend or a child to its mother. An act to keep the imposter thinking they were being intimate and that she wasn't scheming.

Yet the moment her lips touched his, electricity went through her. Not just because they were softer than she'd ever imagined, but because the spicy masculine scent of him hit her at the same time.

More than that, he pulled her against him with a heated passion the likes of which she'd never experienced. His tongue swept against her lips. Instinctively, she opened them and welcomed him with every part of her.

Xaydin couldn't breathe as he tasted innocence and passion. Never in his life had he ever been kissed like this. She fisted her hands in his hair and held him close.

A part of him wondered if he were dreaming or if she were trying to bespell him. Something that should be impossible, and yet he had no resistance to her. Especially not at this moment.

Holding her close, all he could do was imagine what it would be like to lose himself inside her. To make love to her until they were both sweaty and spent.

Had she ever been really and thoroughly loved?

Sadly, neither had he. But that truth had never bothered him. As a prince, he knew he was nothing but a trophy to the fairer sex. He'd never expected to be loved by anyone.

Not really. His own mother couldn't stand to be around him. Why should anyone else?

And he'd been content with that all his life. Yet now...

He wanted something more. Something impossible.

The touch of a loving hand...

A dream he knew would never come.

"Umm..." Masakage began coughing. "Do I need find a water bucket? I was debating a bolt of lightning, but that might cause permanent harm."

Xaydin cursed the bastard as Gisela pulled away and ducked her face behind her hand.

"Sorry."

He hated the sound of her embarrassment. If that had been his brother, Masakage would have vanished and not interrupted. Of all people, his brother would have known how rare an event this was. That he didn't just reach out and molest any woman near him.

No, Masakage would have respected what he saw and made himself scarce.

The temptation to slug the imposter was even greater than before.

Which reminded him of what had led to that kiss.

Ronan.

Rubbing his thumb across his bottom lip that still tingled with the memory of her kiss, he inclined his head to her. *I'll take care of summoning my friend.*

She gasped as he sent that thought to her.

The fact that Masakage wasn't in his head, asking him what he'd said only confirmed what he knew.

His brother wasn't here.

And that infuriated him. But at least he knew Masakage was a survivor. They might have him for a moment...

Gods help them when he regained his feet. His brother didn't go down without a massively brutal fight.

Which made him wonder what sick game this was. What shifter would dare impersonate Masakage?

And why?

Not that it mattered. He would find his brother, and he would skin this imposter alive.

With that thought in mind, he headed for his horse and pulled out one of Candara's potions and the small whistle he'd been given years ago.

The whistle was part of a relay set up for him specifically by Ronan.

Unlike the others, I know you won't use this unless you really need to.

Because Ronan understood that it physically hurt for Xaydin to reach out to others for help. The only reason he was doing this now was for his brother.

For Gisela.

"What are you doing?" the imposter asked.

Masakage would have known the answer. "I'm letting Dash know that we're on our way," he lied.

He locked gazes with Gisela who inclined her head to him to let him know that she was in agreement with whatever he sought to do.

They were united in this.

Whatever was going on, they'd get to the bottom of it.

Discreetly, he blew the whistle, knowing that even here it'd travel to whatever fowl creature heard it and they would relay the call to Ronan who'd find him.

In the meantime...

He pulled out one of Candara's strongest potions. The purple liquid swirled. This would taste disgusting. Why she couldn't make an appetizing potion was beyond him. Sometimes he wondered if she took pleasure in making them as nasty as possible.

Shivering at the thought of tasting it, he steeled his taste buds and took a drink of it.

As expected, it was akin to drinking sludge shat out of the back end of something dying.

It took everything he had not to gag.

You owe me, brother.

While he knew it would be powerful, what he didn't expect was the way it would slam into his stomach like a fist and cause him to fall to his knees.

Thankfully, his horse was used to such. But Gisela rushed to his side.

"Are you all right?"

He couldn't answer. His consciousness was being stripped from his body and sent out toward Masakage's.

Xaydin gasped as he found himself in...

Tenmaru?

It was the only place he knew that held such peaceful gardens. Luminescent butterflies shimmered in the daylight as they danced over a variety of flowers. The sun held a peculiar cast to it as it highlighted Masakage sitting in the middle of the garden with his legs tucked beneath him.

"Meditating? Really?"

Masakage opened one eye to look up at him. "About time you realized I wasn't with you." Ironically, there was no judgment or emotion whatsoever in that tone. He merely spoke fact.

"What happened to you?"

"Your irritating little ferryman. While you were under the sea, I was ambushed."

Bloody figured. He should have checked for that. Should have realized he couldn't trust anyone. "Where are you?"

"Being held by King Mardyth in his palace, under the sea. He wants to make sure you bring home his son as he doesn't trust you to abide by your word."

Xaydin walked a small circle around him. "And who's this new asshole I'm having to deal with who pretends to be you?"

He smirked at Xaydin's choice of words. "A spy hired by the king. You should be familiar with such."

Xaydin ground his teeth in frustration. "Are you in any danger?"

"No. King Mardyth is treating me like a guest. He just doesn't trust you to take care of his son without added—"

"Stress?"

"Incentive is the word the king used. Since I'm underwater, he knows I can't leave without their assistance."

Of course not. "And he sent a fucking shape shifter to babysit me?"

"I tried to warn him how you'd react if you discovered his ruse. Sadly, he thought me a liar."

"Let the fish know that I'm not happy about this."

"Already accomplished."

He could just imagine. Though he was quite certain

Masakage had been much more polite in conveying Xaydin's displeasure. His brother was terribly irritating that way.

"Can you reach me, if you need me?"

Masakage gave him that infamous droll stare. "I don't think that's nearly as much a problem as you reaching me."

Valid point. "I will get you out of this."

"I have all faith in you." Could he have sounded more sarcastic?

Not that it mattered. Mardyth had no idea what forces he was playing with and Xaydin didn't care for games like this. It was one of the reasons why he didn't seek his father's throne. He didn't want to play nice with those he couldn't stand. Be cordial to enemies. It was bad enough he had to stomach the mongrel masquerading as his brother.

How anyone such as Dash could do this full time...

He shivered more than when he'd drunk his sister's concoction.

"I'll be back for you, Kage."

"I know. Just be careful. I don't trust the king's man he sent to watch you. And neither should you."

"You know I don't."

"What's wrong with him?"

Gisela scowled at the Masakage imposter. "I don't know." Xaydin seemed to be in a trance. She'd barely been able to guide his massive body to the ground before he'd succumbed to whatever spell had him enthralled.

At least she assumed it was a spell. She could have sworn she saw him take a drink of a potion before he'd gone down. But at this point...

She wasn't sure of anything other than how large a beast he was. His head was cradled in her lap while she stroked his cheek. Nothing could wake him. For all intents and purposes, he appeared to be asleep.

Or dead.

"What did you do?" she whispered, anxious to know if this was planned or not.

He'd given her a knowing look right before he'd gone down. Had she misread it? Maybe it'd been a look begging for help.

She almost laughed out loud at the thought of Xaydin asking for help.

No, he'd never do that. He'd rather die.

So what exactly was happening? Why didn't she have some of Masakage's abilities?

Anything?

Instead, she was helpless as she sat on the ground, holding the head of a virtual stranger. She'd laugh if it didn't hurt so much. She despised this helplessness. It reminded her too much of her childhood. Of having no sovereignty over herself. Of being powerless against others.

It was what had made her such a vicious warrior. That fury that refused to be at the mercy of others.

No more!

But she couldn't control this.

"Speak to me, X. Say something."

He took in a deep breath before he opened his eyes and met her gaze.

An unbelievable wave of relief tore through her. She hadn't realized until then that she'd been holding her breath. Not until she met those gorgeous eyes that captivated her.

"Hello."

Grimacing, he blinked. "Hi."

She laughed at his confusion. "You had me worried. Where did you go?"

"No place. I would say I fainted, but I think the potion's fumes grabbed me."

"What potion?"

Xaydin cursed as he realized the imposter was standing near them. Damn it!

His attention had been captivated fully by Gisela and the fact that his head rested in her lap. He'd never had so comfortable a pillow before.

But now he had something much less pleasant to contend with.

Growling low in his throat, he rolled out of her lap and stood to face the irritating look-alike. "What have I missed?"

"Nothing."

Xaydin dusted himself off and sighed. "Well then, let's get off this damnable island and be about our business. Shall we?"

The imposter nodded. "What's our first order?"

"I'll summon an Outlaw to let Dash know that we've taken care of the contract. While we wait for our contact, we'll head after Mardyth's son."

"You're really planning to do that?" the imposter asked with enough sincerity that Xaydin could almost believe him.

"Gave my word. Not something I renege on." He exchanged an amused smile with Gisela who shook her head at him.

But it wasn't really amusing. His brother's life hung in the balance, and he needed to get Masakage out of that watery tomb where he was being held.

Hopefully, word would reach Ronan within a day, possibly two and then Ronan would find his way to them.

In the meantime, he had to make sure that the imposter or another didn't plunge a dagger into their backs.

II

FOUR DAYS LATER

R onan Diffydd, so-called for being renowned as faithless, wasn't one to cater to anyone's whims. He hated most creatures and none as much as the dead centaur spy in front of him.

"You can't get any news for Dash if you keep killing every spy we find."

He grimaced at Dubhdara, an elfin by-blow and friend. Almost even in height to him, Dove had blond hair and a set of piercing blue eyes. Women often said they were celestial, unlike Ronan's that were a deep stormy gray.

"Why are you here, Dove?"

"To annoy you and to remind you that we're trying to find useful information. Hard for the dead to give us that information when they can't speak." He sighed heavily as he swept a meaningful gaze over the corpse of the spy.

"Not that hard." He pulled the small vial from his pocket and dribbled the potion onto the lips of the centaur. "Dead-speak does wonders for those who want to take their secrets to the grave."

Dove actually looked impressed.

Ronan knelt down beside the spy. "Why are you in Licordia?"

"To find the rebels who want to bring down King Dash."

Made sense. They'd be easy for Meara to turn and use to harm his friend. "Is your queen getting ready to invade?"

"No."

Dove sighed. "Is this necessary?"

"No." The centaur returned to death.

"Are you fucking kidding me?" Ronan rose to his feet to stare at Dove. "You know I only have three questions I can ask."

"Sorry. I didn't think he'd answer it. It was directed at you."

Rolling his eyes, Ronan wanted to beat the shit out of him. Even if it was an honest mistake. Hell, even he'd made it in the past.

Still...

"Are you a toddler?"

"No. I'm an idiot. You know that." Dove's unexpected admission took the fury from him.

"At least you know it."

Dove flashed him a grin. It was hard to hate anyone with that amount of charisma.

But Ronan really wanted to at the moment.

"So are we burning the body or digging a really big hole?"

A twinge of guilt went through him. Maybe he shouldn't have been so rough, but given the fact that the centaur had almost gutted him...

"I can't dig at the moment." He lifted his shirt to show the nasty stab wound to Dove. "You missed the prelude to this."

"Apparently. Damn. You still have any internal organs left inside you?"

It didn't feel like it. "I'll be fine." He hoped.

Sighing, Dove used his powers to start a fire.

Ronan moved downwind. Ever since their childhood, he'd never been able to stomach the smell of burning flesh. It brought back too many years of their suffering.

But he was grateful that part of their past didn't seem to faze Dove at all.

He moved over to the side to sit on a rock when he heard a hawk's cry.

Dove paused to look up. "What's that?"

Ronan called out to the bird.

The large brown hawk circled before it landed on the ground beside him. *I have a message for you, my lord.*

"From?"

Xaydin. He needs you.

Dove turned to watch them. "What's going on?"

"He says that Xaydin needs me."

That had the same effect on Dove that it had on him. Xaydin never asked for assistance. Not in all the years they'd known each other. It wasn't in him.

So if he reached out, it wasn't on a whim and it meant something dire.

"What's happened?" Dove asked the hawk,

"He doesn't know. He's not the first messenger. All he knows is that Xaydin sent word to find me and go to him."

"Dear gods...he's dying."

That was the most likely outcome for this. Ronan couldn't think of any other reason for Xaydin to send such a message. It wasn't like the beast needed help of any kind.

"Should we tell Dash?" Ronan asked.

"I'll go tell him. You get to Xaydin. I'll only slow you down."

Dove was right about that. It'd be a lot faster for him to

search as a hawk than have to worry about a land-based tagalong.

Ronan stroked the hawk's back feathers. "I'll send word as soon as I know something."

"Rendezvous later."

Ronan inclined his head before he switched forms and flew off with his messenger. This was a day none of them thought would ever come.

Xaydin asking for help.

Panicking, he headed off in the direction the hawk sent him, praying he wouldn't be too late. For all he knew, this could be a trap.

Not that it mattered. If one Outlaw was in trouble, they all were. Because the one oath they'd sworn to each other was that no member of their family would ever be left out on their own.

The world might have failed them when they were young, but they would never fail each other.

I'm coming, brother.

He just hoped he wasn't coming too late.

XAYDIN LITERALLY JUMPED as someone slammed a tankard down by his arm. His heart settled as he realized it was only Gisela trying to get his attention.

"Was that necessary?"

"You told me to let you know when you were giving yourself away." She glanced over to where the imposter sat, hustling fortunes, then gave him a pointed glare. "You're being obvious in your glower and staring."

That had always been a problem for him. He wasn't one to hide his emotions well. Especially not his fury.

"It bothers me that he's all happy in his role while thinking we're idiots."

She nudged the tankard toward him. "Keep drinking, butterbean."

"Butterbean?" He deepened his scowl.

"Form of endearment. You look like you could use one."

He grunted as she took a seat next to him. It should bother him how comfortable he'd become with her. Normally, he'd be more than ready to ride off and find solitude after this many days spent in the company of another.

She didn't invoke his desire to run.

Rather, he liked conversing with her. She was funny and observant.

If it wasn't for her lethality, he might even call her sweet. Shame really. But for her mother, she'd have made a perfect lady.

And that was what she should have been. A woman wrapped in protection who knew nothing of how ugly life could be. How vicious others were.

But was that really a benefit? Those who didn't know were prey for those like her mother.

Like his uncle.

They didn't constantly sweep their gaze at the door, watching every creature who came and went. They didn't make sure to keep their backs unexposed.

But it made him feel good that she currently had her back to him while she scanned the room.

Somehow, she'd learned to trust him. Yet what scared him most was the fact that he was beginning to trust her, too. Something about sharing their secret over the fake Masakage had bonded them. It was that need for comradery in suffering that allowed them to understand each other.

Rely on the other even when they knew it wasn't wise. But what choice did they have?

All they had was each other.

The true test would come once the threat was eliminated.

Sighing, Xaydin motioned for a server.

The ogress took one look at Gisela and curled her lip.

"Don't," he warned, pulling out gold coins. "Bring us some pork and porridge. Extra if you can find honey cake."

Her eyes widened appreciatively on the amount he was offering. "Yes, my lord. Is there anything else you need?"

A bed would be nice.

One to share, even nicer.

But he wouldn't push his luck. "That'll do for now."

She scurried off.

Gisela turned toward him with an arched brow. "You certainly know how to handle others."

Whenever she said things like that, he suspected it was to get a rise from him...in more ways than one.

It had to be. She wasn't *that* innocent.

Little did she know, one of the rises happened almost every time she drew near him.

Sighing in unspent irritation, he downed his ale. "Did you find out anything interesting in your sweep of the room?"

"Only that we're a day and a half out from reaching Cryxa. The docks there are where we'll supposedly find Marauder ships in port."

So nothing he didn't already know. But he wasn't about to tell her that. She didn't like it when she didn't feel useful.

"Our information better be right." It seemed a little pat for a merman to be in love with a Marauder. But then it made sense. Who better to fall in love with a fish than a human who spent most of their life on a boat?

Pat or not, it made logical sense.

She sat beside him and leaned in close. "Have you spoken anymore with your real brother?"

He shook his head. "I don't want the other one to get suspicious." He cut a meaningful glance toward the Masakage in the corner, laying out cards. Something his Masakage didn't do. He read coins and tea leaves.

Masakage had always claimed the cards took a price he wasn't willing to pay.

While Xaydin had been curious about that, he hadn't been curious enough to pursue a more definitive answer. Not that he was even sure Masakage would answer under torture. His brother cherished secrets.

She took a sip of her ale. "Do you think word has reached Ronan yet?"

He shrugged. "I won't know until he appears."

"That's unfortunate. One would think with all the magic that there was an easier way to stay in touch."

"There are other ways."

That surprised her. "Such as?"

"I can use a mirror to talk to Candara anytime I choose."

"Really?"

He nodded. "Or any shiny object, really."

"How would you do that?"

The hairs on the back of his neck rose. But that was just his suspicious nature. He doubted if she'd ever use the information against him.

Then again, that was the point of betrayal. It always came from a trusted hand. The one you'd never believe would do such a godawful thing.

Gisela offered him a kind smile. "I understand. I wouldn't trust me either. It was a thoughtless thing to ask. I was just curious is all."

And that only made him want to trust her more. Because she understood and backed off without his having to explain it.

She was a rarity in this world, and he was jaded enough to appreciate her unique insights.

Stifling a yawn, Gisela drank the last of her ale. "I'm going up to rest...provided I don't get stopped again by some awful-meaning ogre or troll telling me I don't belong here. No offense, but I can't wait to get out of Vaskalia."

"Noted. If they give you lip, send them my way. I need someone to beat on tonight." Anything to get rid of this pent-up...

Well, he'd go with frustration. It covered a lot of what was wrong with him at present.

Sighing, he glanced back to his fake brother. He never really realized how much Masakage had meant to him until the last few days of dealing with someone pretending to be him. It also reminded him of what Dash had always said—Xaydin was hard to get along with.

Yes, I am.

Yet Masakage had rarely gotten on his nerves.

Oddly enough, Gisela, so far, had yet to get on his nerves.

That latter statement was a rarity he was grateful for.

Maybe I'll get lucky and someone will knife the bastard for us.

If only he was that lucky. But it'd never happen.

With a sigh, he downed the rest of his drink and tossed coins on the table as a tip for their waiter. Then, he headed off for the stairs to get some well-needed sleep so that he'd have enough patience on the morrow to deal with his fake brother.

GISELA SIGHED as she rinsed her hair. She missed having warm baths. The one thing about Meara's court that was nice...

Her mother's bathing room. Even now she could feel the warm water as she sank below it.

Of course, she could only use it in the wee hours of the night when she was certain her mother was asleep. Even though she had permission to use it, her mother would fly into a fit of rage if Gisela dared be in it should her mother want to bathe.

Her jaw currently ached from being clenched tight to keep from chattering. She'd always hated taking frigid baths.

It is what it is.

Suddenly, the door behind her opened.

She turned with a gasp to catch Xaydin there with an equally shocked expression. Before she could gather her wits, he quickly shut the door and gave her his back.

"Sorry! I had no idea you'd be bathing."

She grabbed her clothes and quickly threw them on. "Freezing more than bathing...I didn't think you'd come up so soon." Normally, he stayed downstairs for at least an hour before coming to bed. "You can turn around. I'm covered...and thank you."

"For what?"

She clutched her shirt tight against her neck. "Not shaming me or recoiling from my scars."

"I didn't see any scars."

Then he must not have really looked at her. They were impossible to miss. It was one of the reasons why she'd never wear a dress or anything that didn't conceal her entire body. She hated the sight of them.

They were everywhere.

Especially on her soul.

She picked up her towel from the floor and returned to drying her hair.

His eyes twinkled as he glanced at her before making his pallet on the floor. "I wondered how you managed to smell so fresh every day."

Gisela had to press her lips together to keep from saying something insulting. She didn't want to go there, but it did make her curious about one thing. "I've noticed you don't have the same thick cloud of horse enveloping you that our imposter does."

"I bathe in the morning...outside."

That was what she figured. "Isn't it even colder than this?" She gestured at the basin and pitcher she'd been using.

"Cold as the dead. But it drives away all sleepiness and puts me into fighting shape."

That made sense, but she'd rather be less of a fighter than combat the morning chill. Just the thought of it sent a shiver over her.

From the corner of her eye, she watched him.

He was a spectacular specimen. Gorgeous and gruff, yet kind when it came to her. She'd never been around anyone like him before.

Never spent this much time alone with any man.

Or woman for that matter.

"You don't wench much, do you?"

His jaw went slack. "Pardon?"

"No insult. Just an observation. You watch those around you for potential threats. Not for bedmates."

"As do you."

"Exactly. That's how I know you're not much for wenching. I find that very curious."

"Why?" he asked.

Sitting on the bed, she shrugged. "You're a handsome one. A prince, even. I see the way women look at you...and sometimes the men, too."

"So do I. Like a prized stallion up for auction."

She caught the irritated note in his voice. Though whether it came from her questions or the truth, she wasn't sure. "I thought all men wanted to be studs for whatever broodmare would shelter them."

He scoffed as he pulled off his boots. "Not those of us with bounties on our heads. No wench is worth a knife in my throat because I couldn't hold my lust."

He had a point. Seducing a man was an easy way to end him. She'd used that tactic herself.

"Most men aren't so reserved."

He gave her a dry stare. "Most people are stupid."

"Fair enough." But even so, she imagined that he'd had more than his share of women. He carried himself with confidence and it made her wonder about him. "So, what catches your attention?"

"How do you mean?"

"I've not seen you take notice of anyone for a bedmate." Which was unusual for a man of normal looks and swagger. For one of his ilk, it was unheard of. "What does it take for you to go there?"

Xaydin was absolutely stunned by her unexpected question. One that seemed completely out of character for her. "Why do you ask?"

Her eyes widened as if she suddenly realized what she was asking. "I...uh...I didn't mean *that*! It's not... Forget it!" She quickly turned her back to him.

Amused, he unbuckled his weapons and laid them on the floor, within reach. "If you must know, my lady, I look for those who aren't trying to get my attention. I like a good challenge in all things."

And she was definitely challenging.

Sitting on the edge of the bed, she gently combed her wet hair.

A hundred thoughts and images went through him. None of them appropriate.

Put her out of your mind.

Definitely easier said than done. She was thoroughly captivating as she ran her hands through her hair. He could imagine doing the same while he buried his face against the nape of her neck and just inhaled her soft, rosy scent. He didn't know how she managed it, but she always smelled divine. Even after an entire day of riding.

The woman held her own unique magic. He wouldn't have thought anything could be stronger than the magic Candara brewed in her cauldron.

He was wrong.

And he wasn't about to pressure her or anyone else. His life was screwed up enough. The last thing he wanted was to screw up someone else's.

GISELA TUCKED the comb away in her saddlebag and took a quick glance toward Xaydin. He lay on the floor, with his back to her.

How strange that she'd become accustomed to his presence. She no longer slept fretfully at night.

I've begun to trust.

And that terrified her more than anything else she'd ever experienced.

She trusted someone. Trusted them enough to sleep in their presence.

Why? She had no idea. There was no guarantee he

wouldn't turn on her. No reason to think he wouldn't become a monster hell-bent on her utter destruction.

Her mother could kiss the cheek of a lover one minute and then watch them be gutted in front of her, minutes later. Little to no reason on most days.

That capriciousness had always left her on edge. The feeling that whomever she was with would pop off and start attacking for no reason.

She hadn't seen anything to make her think Xaydin was one of them.

Still...

Regret was a hard thing to live with. She knew because she regretted much of her life.

And what will I regret tomorrow?

That question had barely gone through her mind before she knew one thing she'd definitely regret.

Xaydin.

He was within arm's reach.

But did he feel anything for her? That was the other important question. He was as guarded as she was. Impossible to tell what he felt or thought.

There's only one way to find out...

It was terrifying. Just like he was.

Mostly because she'd never been with a man before. Not that she hadn't had a chance to or that some hadn't tried to force themselves on her, but because she'd never been interested in them.

At all.

Xaydin changed that.

He made her want to take something for herself. To know what it would be like to lay with a man. It was something she hadn't thought about in years. Back when she'd been young, she'd tried to imagine what sort would interest her.

As a woman…

No one came to mind. Not until Xaydin had slammed into her life.

For that alone, she should thank her mother.

Don't.

That single word hovered in her mind. If she did this, it would change her forever. She might even conceive his child.

A pregnant assassin. Her mother would definitely throw her out.

Or have her executed. Most likely executed. After all, her mother was nothing if not a hypocrite.

But in the end, it was her curiosity and desire that got the better of her. Her mother had always said it would lead her to her damnation.

Tonight, that led her straight toward the arms of a man who should be her enemy. Yet this was where she wanted to be.

"Make love to me, Xaydin."

12

Xaydin was stunned by Gisela's unexpected words. This was a woman who'd come here to kill him. One he still wasn't sure wouldn't try if he gave her a chance.

Granted, the last few days had been...

Special wasn't quite the right word. Different, but that didn't sound right either.

There wasn't really a word for what they'd shared.

So, he stared at her in disbelief. "I'm not sure how to respond to that."

Her cheeks turned bright pink. "I'm sorry. Forget I said anything."

As she started away, he caught her hand.

"Gisela—"

"It's fine, Xaydin. I wasn't serious."

He didn't need his brother's mind reading abilities to know that was a lie. She'd definitely meant it, and she was currently pissed off at him.

"I'm not saying no, my lady. You just caught me off guard."

Gisela wanted to be angry. More than that, she wanted to strike out at him.

SHERRILY KENYON

But he was right. From his perspective, her request had come out of nowhere. She'd given him no indication that she felt like this about him. Or that she was the least bit interested in him.

In truth, she'd rebuffed him and been quite standoffish, one kiss notwithstanding.

Xaydin rose slowly from his pallet so that he could face her. "Is this really what you want?"

Honestly, she wasn't sure. A part of her salivated for him, but another part was terrified.

Would it change her? That seemed stupid, but she didn't know for certain. She'd seen plenty of men and women who were wanton. Lust controlled them. She didn't want to be like them. A pawn driven by hormones.

But at the same time, she did want to experience it at least once. Preferably with someone she liked.

"Is it pleasurable?" She felt stupid even for asking.

An adorable grin curved his lips. "It can be. If done right."

Mortified, she covered her face with her hands. "Forget I said anything."

He approached her slowly. Even though she couldn't see him with her eyes closed, she felt every inch of him. He gently pulled her hands from her eyes and cupped her face in his hands. Tilting her chin, he bent down to whisper in her ear. "Look at me, Gisela."

She did.

"This is up to you. You're a beautiful woman and I would be honored to be with you, but I would never impose or encroach."

And that was why she adored him. He was so different from anyone she'd met.

For all she knew, she could die tomorrow. Her own mother could order her killed. Anything could happen. Regrets were part of her life.

But the one regret she didn't want to have was this man...

"I want to know." The words were barely more than a whisper as she stared up at him. "I want you, Xaydin."

Xaydin's heart pounded. A decent man would most likely pull away from her.

But he wasn't decent. Not tonight and not after that invitation. He was feral and hard.

A part of him was skittish. He'd never let his passion rule him. Too many had fallen victim to their lust. In the back of his mind, he knew how vulnerable it made him. How easy it would be to lose his life over his hormones.

He'd never been that kind of man. Just as he'd never been one for seductive words. Now, he wished he knew how to tell her how much this moment meant.

How much *she* meant to him.

He'd been so long without the comfort of a woman's body. So long without the warmth of a tender caress that he could barely remember it. Even then, he'd had no attachment to the woman. Just a physical ache to be sated.

Gisela meant something to him. They weren't strangers who'd part ways as soon as it was done.

She would be here on the morrow.

Don't do this.

It was all kinds of folly.

Yet how could he not? The taste of her kiss was still branded on his tongue. The silken heaven of her mouth was more than he could resist.

He was a mere mortal, not some saint who lived to suffer.

His thoughts racing, Xaydin traced the curve of her lips with his fingertip, before he parted her lips and kissed her deeply.

He closed his eyes and inhaled the sweetness of her breath.

The feel of her supple body pressed against his while he loosened the stays for her top.

"Are you sure, Gisela?" he asked one final time, giving them both a chance before they did something stupid.

She nodded before she pulled his lips back to hers. "I will never regret you."

He felt the same way. "Then no regrets for either of us."

Gisela's heart fluttered as he offered her a real smile. It was unexpected and breathtaking.

His dark eyes were hungry and feral as his heat surrounded her. Never had she felt anything like this as he swept her up in his arms and carried her toward the bed where she'd intended to sleep alone. The heat and strength of him surrounded her.

And she wanted more.

He laid her down before he joined her on a bed that seemed to shrink in size. While she'd known how large he was, he seemed even more massive now.

But all that fled as he returned to her lips to kiss her. She actually purred. Never once had she been touched like this. Never had she thought a mere kiss could be so incredible.

And when his warm, callused hand closed around her breast, she jumped in nervous excitement. Pain and pleasure stabbed through her body as heat pooled itself between her legs.

What was this burning in her body? This strange ache that craved him? She'd thought in the past that she knew lust, but this was an entirely different sensation.

Much more intense.

Much more terrifying.

She didn't understand these confusing sensations. How could her body feel like this?

Xaydin left her lips to kiss a trail down her throat to the breast he cupped.

Trembling, Gisela swallowed at the sight of his dark head at her breast, at the feel of his tongue teasing her taut nipple. His tongue was rough and hot, his lips soothing and tender.

She cupped his head to her and reveled in the sensation of his dark curls teasing her fingers.

He was so beautiful there, tasting her, teasing her. His incredibly handsome face showed the pleasure he received just from touching her.

Gisela sighed in contentment and let the incredible earthy sensations sweep her away until she was nothing but an extension of the man holding her.

Tonight, she would be his without reservation or fear. Biting her lip, she whispered his name.

Xaydin had never tasted anything like her body. She was so warm, so inviting. More so because he knew she was sharing with him what she had shared with no one else.

He was her first. As incredulous as that seemed. She was so worldly in some manners.

But not in this.

Why she chose a creature like him, he couldn't imagine. He was so unworthy of what she offered.

But then they were like creatures. Born of brutality and sorrow.

Something that hit hard as he exposed more of her skin and saw that she held as many scars as he did. Without thinking, he traced a vicious mark that had almost pierced her heart.

The moment she realized what he was looking at, she tried to cover it. Her eyes flared with shame, igniting a fury deep in his soul.

"I'm sorry," she whispered. "I know they're hideous."

He pulled her hand away and stared hard into her eyes. "Our scars are the story of our pasts that made us who we are. Never hide yours, my lady. They are beautiful and so are you for having survived them."

Gisela couldn't breathe as she heard the sincerity in his voice. In that moment, she wasn't ashamed.

She felt beautiful. Something that she'd never felt before. "Thank you."

"For what?"

For seeing her when no one ever had. "For being you." And for being more wonderful than she could have ever imagined. Especially given his reputation. She'd have never guessed that such a beast would have a heart like his.

Because until he'd found her, she'd never had one herself. Never cared about anyone. She'd believed the lies of others. That she was frigid and emotionless.

No, not emotionless. Lost to her pain. Lost to those scars that had cut much deeper than her flesh. They had seared themselves into her soul and left her cold and angry.

But not tonight. Tonight, she felt reborn by his kindness.

And she was glad that tonight, for this one moment and for whatever reason, she was with him.

Gisela tugged at his black tunic.

Eager to oblige her, he pulled it off.

She gasped audibly as she ran her hands over his tense, muscular arms. He was exquisite, and she reveled at the softness of his skin over the steely feel of his body.

Xaydin clenched his teeth as his head reeled from pleasure.

The things her touch did to him...

It was incredible. Invigorating. It made him feel virile and wild. He was hard and aching. Most of all, he felt vulnerable to her in a way he'd never felt before.

Even so, he couldn't pull back. Her touch was addictive and he craved every inch of her body.

And he wanted more of her...

Gisela felt a moment of panic as he removed her chemise from her. She was suddenly exposed to him.

It was scary and strangely erotic. She couldn't recall ever being naked in front of another person. Mostly because of her scars and her fear of how they'd sneer at her for having them. Especially the lash marks she'd been given as a girl. Marks that proved how bad she'd been at everything.

No one knew what she looked like bare.

Except Xaydin. He had just as many scars on him, if not more. But in his case, she suspected they weren't because he was bad at something.

Rather because he'd chosen to break rules and fight hard. That was who he was.

Unlike her, he probably hadn't cried, but rather dared them to hit him again.

And harder.

He was defiant, and she loved that most.

Without a word, he withdrew from her and removed the rest of his clothes. Gisela wanted to look away but couldn't bring herself to do so. He was resplendent.

Yet as she stared at the large size of him, she tried to imagine what it would feel like to take him into her body. Surely, it wouldn't be possible.

Would it?

"Will you hurt me?" she asked hesitantly.

His eyes warm, he stroked her cheek with his fingers. "That is not my intention."

She smiled up at him, trusting him completely even though she wasn't too sure he spoke honestly. How could *that* not hurt? It was huge.

He lay down on top of her and gathered her into his arms as he buried his face against her neck. Her thoughts scattered at the glorious feeling of his skin against hers. Of his heavy weight that felt good instead of oppressive.

Xaydin took her hand into his and guided it back to him. "Don't be afraid to touch me, Gisela," he whispered.

She ran her hand down his shaft to the tip of it. It didn't seem quite so terrifying now.

Xaydin watched her exploring him. "If you want to stop, we can."

She smiled up at him, knowing most men would never offer her that. It made her even more tender toward him. "I'm here to the end."

He laughed at her words. "You don't have to make it sound so dour."

"Sorry. I didn't mean it that way."

Shaking his head, he kissed her again, then drove himself deep inside her.

She tensed at the burning pain of him filling her.

Xaydin whispered sweet encouragements in her ear while he used his tongue to toy with the tender flesh of her neck.

She panted against the pain and tried to relax as he coaxed her. She'd never imagined a man would feel like this, but she was glad it was Xaydin who was inside her. Thrilled she'd had a say in who was her first.

There had been a number of times when she'd had to fight hard to keep one away from her. Times when she'd feared she'd be taken.

This was hers to give, and she couldn't imagine anyone better than Xaydin.

And she was glad for the strength of his arms around her and the sound of his deep voice in her ear.

Gisela wrapped her arms around his shoulders and buried her face against his muscled neck and inhaled the warm scent of him. She wanted this more than she'd ever wanted anything.

Xaydin ached with want as he forced himself not to thrust even deeper into her. But it was hard.

He wanted her in a way unimaginable. She surrounded him with heat and her breath against his neck sent a thousand chills over him.

She felt wonderful, and he never wanted to let her go.

"Relax, my lady," he said gently.

He waited until her hold on him loosened. She looked up at him, her face trusting. That was a look he'd never forget because he knew that trust came no easier to her than it did to him.

That was as much a gift as her sharing her body. Because trust broken could never be regained. And creatures like them didn't just randomly toss it about.

They guarded their trust like the sacred treasure it was. Having been betrayed so viciously, he'd never do that to anyone else.

And he savored this moment of her lying under him, her body bare and joined to his. It was the most incredible thing he'd ever experienced. A wave of fierce possession tore through him then.

She was his and she now owned a part of him that no one else had ever claimed.

Smiling up at him, she brushed the hair back from his face. "You feel so strange inside me."

Xaydin returned her smile. "How do I feel?"

"Full and deep. I can feel you all the way to my core."

He sucked his breath in at her words and the image they created. "Can you now?"

She nodded.

He pulled back, then thrust his hips against hers. They moaned in unison. Xaydin moved slowly against her, driving himself in as deep as he dared.

"You are an incredible beast," she growled.

It was the first time in his life that he could recall being referred to as a beast where it didn't insult him. "And you are a beautiful woman."

Those words embarrassed her and it infuriated a part of him because he knew she'd never heard that enough. A woman this special should have been told that.

A lot.

He cursed everyone who'd hurt her. No heart should be trampled so callously. Rather, they should be cherished.

Xaydin rolled over with them still joined. He sat her on top of him and watched her in the candlelight.

Her eyes widened even more. "This is interesting..."

He actually laughed at that. "Do you like it?"

She bit her lip and nodded enthusiastically.

Xaydin showed her how to ride him slow and easy. He ran his hands down her thighs and watched the way the candlelight cut across her pale skin. His mind was dazed from the feel of her naked body sliding against his.

She wiggled her bottom against him. "What am I supposed to do?"

He lifted his hips up, driving himself deeper into her. "Whatever you want to do."

She ground herself against him in a way so sublime that he groaned in satisfaction.

Gisela felt so strangely free with him. She ran her hands over the hard muscles of his chest and abdomen. It was so odd to see him lying there, under her.

He held her hips in his hands and guided her movements. But what held her transfixed was the ecstasy on his face. His cheeks were flushed, his eyes dark and unfocused.

She moaned as he ran his hands from her hips to her breasts where he toyed with them.

She'd never thought anything could feel like this. Never

considered she would want to sit on a man like this and enjoy it. Yet she loved the sensation of his thick hardness inside her.

"What do I feel like to you, Xaydin?"

"Wet and soft."

She supposed that was a good thing. Though it didn't sound like it to her.

And it left her wondering something. "Have you been with many women?"

He stopped moving. "Why do you ask?"

"I want this to be special between us. I don't want to be just another in a long line of lovers for you."

Xaydin cupped her face in his hands. "You are nothing like any woman I've ever known. Believe me, no one compares to you, and you could never be just another anything. You are uniquely beautiful." He pulled her down and kissed her fiercely.

Gisela trembled at the passion she tasted, and at the way he teased her lips with his. His muscles flexed under her hands, making her tremble.

Xaydin pulled back from the kiss, then rolled over with her and took control of their passion.

Gisela arched her back as he moved faster. Every stroke brought more pleasure. Every kiss and touch reverberated through her.

"Make me yours, Xaydin."

But in her heart, she knew he already had. No one would ever have the part of her that he did. Somehow, he'd slid his way past every defense she'd erected. Every trap she'd laid.

She was his and she wouldn't have it any other way.

He claimed her lips again as he slammed himself into her even deeper than he'd been before.

She wrapped her legs around his hips and let his passion sweep her away.

He lowered his head to her shoulder and released himself inside her with a fierce growl.

Gisela drew a ragged breath as he collapsed on top of her and held her tight.

"Thank you, Gisela," he whispered in her ear as he panted fiercely. Then, he kissed her lips again in a tender caress that sent chills through her.

Slowly, he withdrew from her and rolled over onto his back and pulled her against his side.

She assumed he was through with her so it surprised her when he spread her legs and touched the most private place of her body.

Stunned, she stared at him. "What are you doing?"

"Giving you your pleasure."

She didn't understand what he was talking about. "I already had it."

He smiled wickedly at that. "No, sweetheart. You haven't."

Confused, she had no idea what he meant by that. But as his long, lean fingers delved deep into her body, she began to realize that there was more than what she'd already experienced.

Xaydin pulled the blanket to him and used it to wipe between her legs. She blushed at his actions.

"What are you doing?"

His eyes were warm. "Trust me. I promise you'll like this." He laid his body between her legs and spread her thighs wide.

Gisela felt heat explode over her cheeks as she realized he was staring at the center of her body.

He ran his finger down her cleft. She shivered. Then, he used his fingers to spread her open and dipped his head down.

Gisela jerked as his mouth covered her. Every nerve ending in her body sizzled as she cried out in surprise. He stroked her with his tongue and lips.

She hissed and moaned as she cupped his head to her. No

longer able to speak, all she could do was feel each and every luscious lick he gave her.

Who could have imagined? His breath was hot against her bared flesh, and when he slid a finger deep inside her and rotated it, she thought she would die.

She looked down to see him staring up at her while he tormented her with ecstasy.

He pulled back but left his finger inside her. A strange sensation of intimacy that overwhelmed her.

"Don't be embarrassed, my lady," he whispered, then he returned to taunt her with his mouth.

With a mind of its own, her body writhed to his touch and kisses. And as he continued, she found herself unable to speak anymore. Unable to do anything other than feel him. Feel his tongue sliding around her, his finger swirling.

Her pleasure built to an unimaginable height. Until she was sure that she would explode with the weight of it.

Then, in the span of one heartbeat, she did explode. Her body splintered apart and she cried out.

Even so, Xaydin didn't stop. He stayed there, licking and teasing until she'd come for him twice more.

When he seemed content to tease her more, she begged him for mercy. "Stop! Enough!" she whimpered. "If I do that one more time, I might die from it."

He chuckled at her plea, then turned his face to suckle the tender flesh of her thigh.

Gisela lay there, completely spent and weak. She breathed raggedly as Xaydin gathered her into his arms and held her close.

"I had no idea *that* existed."

He kissed her brow and cradled her head with his hands. "Neither did I," he whispered softly.

Gisela smiled and snuggled against him, wanting to be as close as she could.

Her breathing ragged, she was so grateful for this night. It'd been the single best one of her life.

Tomorrow might divide them forever, but here for a moment she'd been really happy. She finally understood why some were willing to die for this intimacy.

So many things made sense now.

She would treasure this always.

Xaydin listened to Gisela's breathing as she fell back asleep. He covered them with the blanket and ran his hands through her hair. He had nothing to offer her. All he knew was what he felt when he held her like this.

Possessive and protective.

It really didn't make much sense. He'd been with plenty of women in his life. But none of them had ever touched him the way Gisela did.

Overwhelmed by the depth of what he felt for her, he traced her scars in the candlelight. It was obvious that Meara hadn't spared her daughter her cruelty any more than she'd spared him and his friends.

The bitch is going to pay.

Whatever it took, he was going to help Dash remove that bitch from her throne. He didn't care who sat upon it. But he wanted justice for what Gisela had been put through.

Somehow, he was going to make this right for her.

13

"Do you have it?"

Garyn cringed at the question from the troll in front of him. Glancing around the crowded inn, he only relaxed once he realized that Xaydin wasn't in the room. "Are you trying to get me killed?"

The huge, green-fleshed beast glared at him. "Do you think me stupid? I waited until they were both gone. Been gone, in fact. No sign of either returning."

That only disturbed him more. Normally, he kept a tight eye on Gisela and Xaydin. It bothered him that he'd become so caught up with his hustling the other patrons that they'd slipped away without his noticing.

Such a mistake could get him killed.

"So how's your guest?"

The troll shape shifter shrugged. "Keeps making threats. He's not happy that we liberated him from the fish king. I'm thinking we should kill him rather than let him go."

Made sense. Masakage wasn't known for his mercy. His reputation as a wizard was well known throughout the kingdoms.

And well feared.

Maybe they *should* kill him. But only if they could kill Xaydin first. The last thing he wanted was to be hunted down by the pissed off Oathbreaker. No one had ever survived a fight with Xaydin. At least no one he knew of.

And while he considered himself among the best swordsmen in the Thirteen Kingdoms, he wasn't stupid enough to think he could best Xaydin.

Not in a fair fight, anyway.

Which returned his thoughts to the *troll* in front of him. "Why are you here?"

"I got your message that said the contract was taken care of. Do you want me to notify the queen?"

"Not yet."

Diflyn arched a heavy brow at that. "Why?"

Because it wasn't taken care of the way Meara wanted it to be. Before the fish king had hired him, Meara had sent him out to make sure the *apaswere* died...preferably by Dash's sword and not hers. This was about public perception. She wanted the other kingdoms to blame Dash...

Fear him and learn to be suspicious of his intentions. If the High King broke the contract, then she could cry foul to the other rulers and hopefully gain enough support from their fear to overthrow Dash.

It was why she'd sent her "best" assassin out to protect the *apaswere*.

Meanwhile, she'd told him—the real mercenary assassin she relied on for such matters—to make sure the *apaswere* didn't survive this excursion.

He'd started out following Gisela in any manner of ways... such as being a flea on her while she traveled as a unicorn.

Everything had been fine until they were on board the boat.

Even though he was disguised as a fly, Masakage had

captured him after the other two had vanished under the waves. "Why are you following us?"

Garyn had seen the fury in the wizard's eyes as Garyn had used his powers to change into his human form and pin Masakage against the side of the boat while the scared ferryman had looked on. "I mean you no harm."

That had only angered Masakage more. "And I mean you all manner of harm. Answer my question."

So he'd done what he always did...lied his way out of it. "I'm here to protect the princess. Make sure no harm befalls her."

The fact that Masakage hadn't reacted to the news meant he'd already learned the secret no one, especially not the queen, knew Garyn had uncovered years before.

He'd always wondered why Meara tolerated Gisela's impertinence when the queen would have gutted anyone else.

Until the night he'd been spying on Meara and had heard the truth from the queen's own lips.

Garyn had known then that one day that secret might save his life.

Or end it.

That was the problem when one dealt in secrets. They could either help or kill.

With Masakage, the lie had rung true. Best of all, it'd caused the wizard to lower his guard just enough that he'd been able capture Masakage.

Not an easy feat, given the wizard's powers. But thankfully, his club had settled most matters and had rendered Masakage unconscious.

Which had been flawless until the fish king had sent in warriors to capture the unconscious Masakage from the ferry.

Which had given him the idea to pretend to be Masakage, especially when they'd offered Garyn money to keep Xaydin from learning they'd taken his brother.

Even so, it'd been an awful mess until his partner, Diflyn, had reclaimed their prisoner and removed him from the Ningyoan kingdom to the holding cell they had for him.

Something that hadn't set well with Masakage, who apparently had issues with their hospitality.

Asshole.

Now, the trick would be releasing the beast without Masakage killing them both in retaliation.

Garyn hadn't quite figured out how to let Masakage loose.

Killing him would make things a lot easier.

He smiled at Diflyn. "We're in a bit of a sticky situation right now. But I'll think of something. Run along and make sure the wizard doesn't find his freedom on his own." If he did, they'd pay for it.

Diflyn gave him a cold, hard stare before he nodded and left the inn.

Garyn checked his bag to make sure the contract was still there. While it was no longer guaranteed by an *apaswere*, it was still binding.

A contract was a contract, regardless of the medium it was written on. The question he needed answered was who would pay the most for it?

King Dash or Queen Meara?

If he sold it to Dash, Meara would still be able to cry foul and attack Dash.

After all, it'd technically been Dash's own man he'd sent for the contract who'd transferred it.

At least that was what the *apaswere* and his family would testify to. They believed him to be the Oathbreaker's brother. All objectives met, including his own that would enrich his coffers. He liked that.

I just have to survive. Something much easier said than

done, especially with an angry wizard wanting a piece of him. But he was nothing if not an aggressive survivor.

No. Opportunist. He would rise above this, and he'd make sure that in the end, he would be the richer for it.

As for his witnesses...

If his was the only viewpoint, then it would be the truth. He'd just have to make sure that Gisela, Xaydin and Masakage all met with an unfortunate accident. Then he could take the money from Meara and the fish king, and go on with his life.

14

Gisela came awake surrounded by warmth. It took her a moment to remember what had happened the night before and to realize that Xaydin was still wrapped around her.

Heat scalded her cheeks.

"Awake, princess?" That deep voice next to her ear sent shivers over her.

"Barely." She glanced over her shoulder to find him grinning at her.

Then she realized something. "Did Masakage stay out all night?"

His grin widened.

"What did you do?"

"Masakage isn't the only one who can spell a door and keep others out."

"Impressive, but isn't he likely to be upset?"

His warm hand cupped her breast. "Do you think I care?"

Obviously not. "Don't we have to get going this morning?"

"It can wait."

Biting her lip, she groaned as he moved his hand lower to tease her. "Can it?" she breathed.

He laughed in her ear. "Do you really want me to stop?"

No. Even though she knew how important their mission was, would an hour make that much difference?

Or two?

"Is that a no, princess?"

She ground herself against his fingers as they teased her. "Don't you dare stop."

Laughing, he laved the nape of her neck.

Chills ran the length of her entire body. Last night had been miraculous, but this was even more so.

His breathing turned ragged in her ear and then, he was filling her from behind.

Gisela gasped at the fullness of him inside her, especially when he began to thrust. Reaching over her head, she burrowed her hand in his soft, wavy dark locks. Her heart pounded as he quickened his strokes while his hand continued to tease and torment her with pleasure.

Xaydin growled in her ear at the incredible sensation of her in his arms. She was right, they did need to be on their way. But...

How could he resist her? She was exquisite. Delectable. And her taste, feel and scent had branded him hers. He'd never felt like this before.

And when she came in his arms with a fierce cry, he felt a satisfaction that was indescribable. No one else had ever made her feel this way, and he took pride in the fact that he was able to give her something no one else had. That she trusted him when she, like him, never trusted anyone.

This was special, and he treasured it as such.

Burying his face against her neck, he growled as he found his own release.

Gisela smiled as he tightened his hold on her. She felt enveloped by his body. Every inch of her was pressed against him. It was both overwhelming and yet thrilling.

Running her hand down his forearm, she closed her eyes and sighed. She should feel trapped or even oppressed by a hold like this. In the past, she'd hated being constricted in any way. But there was something comforting in his embrace.

She didn't feel trapped, she felt...

Loved. Wanted.

It was so intimate that she wasn't quite sure what to think or make of this. Did it mean he cared about her?

Don't be ridiculous.

How could he? This was just basic lust.

But not to her. She knew a wall inside her had fallen down, and it'd left her vulnerable.

What am I going to do? This had changed her, and she wasn't stupid enough to pretend otherwise. She cared about him. She who had never cared about anyone before now valued someone else.

And she wanted to do this again with him.

And again.

Oh my God! I'm wanton!

Horrified, she felt her eyes widen at the knowledge. For the first time in her life, she understood her mother's insatiable hunger for men.

Only she didn't want just any man. She only wanted to be with Xaydin.

Suddenly, someone pounded at their door.

Xaydin's growl of frustration brought a smile to her lips. "Bastard," he whispered in her ear, making her laugh. "Yes, Masakage," he said louder.

"Will you let me in?"

He sighed heavily. "What do you think? Should I lower the ward and let our demon bother us?"

"I don't know...I guess he's been banned long enough."

He laughed again at the feigned angst in her tone. "I'll take care of him. Take your time getting ready."

Withdrawing from her, he rolled out of bed, dressed and barely opened the door enough that he could step into the hallway.

Grateful for his thoughtfulness, she got out of bed more slowly.

Until she saw what Xaydin had done...

There was a full-sized tub with steaming water waiting at the foot of the bed.

"Oh my God! I love you!" Those words actually startled her, and she was grateful he wasn't here to hear them because she feared she might actually mean them.

Something she'd think about later. For now, all she wanted to concentrate on was that precious gift.

And it wasn't until she'd sunk her body into the luxurious waters that it occurred to her just how much power he had that he could create this for her. It was miraculous.

More than that, it was terrifying. Just how much magic was he capable of?

Given his gargantuan size, it was easy to let his physical prowess and strength intimidate. So much so that she hadn't even really considered how much magic he wielded. Her thoughts there had been for Masakage.

But Xaydin downplayed his abilities and skills. Strange how she hadn't really thought about that before.

Now...

She realized how pompous and stupid she'd been when she first confronted him. He could have laid her low with little effort.

I need to be more careful. But it was easy to get cocky when not confronted. To think that her abilities were superlative, which in most cases they were. But no matter how strong and capable someone was, there was always someone stronger and more capable.

Closing her eyes, she knew how lucky she'd been. How grateful that so far, they weren't enemies.

Her only hope was that they'd continue to be friends and not turn sour.

That thought made her stomach cramp. Nothing ever lasted forever.

Not the bad.

Not the good.

And nothing ever ended well. Tears pricked at her eyes as she thought about the truth. All things came to an end.

Just how bad would their ending be?

"Am I banned from the room?"

Xaydin just stared at the fake Masakage. "For now. Yes."

"You know I slept outside in the alley last night, right?"

Blinking slowly, Xaydin just stared at him. Masakage would never have complained about resting in an alley as he'd made his bed there on many occasions. Instead, he would have been teasing him because Kage would have known exactly what Xaydin had been doing and why he was banned from the room. "And?"

Shaking his head, the imposter crossed his arms over his chest. "There's a royal contingent that just came in. Should we be concerned by it?"

"Not really."

"You seem rather nonchalant for someone wanted dead by the crown."

Masakage would know and understand. There was a difference between them wanting him dead and being dumb enough to actually try.

But Xaydin wouldn't give him the satisfaction of an answer. Instead, he shrugged and walked past his nuisance, toward the inn so that he could get them something to eat.

As he walked down the stairs and entered the main part, a strange sensation came over him. One he knew intimately.

Ronan.

His presence washed over him with a slight jolt. Few creatures commanded the amount of power Ronan did. When they'd been captives in Meara's court, the two of them had been inseparable. Of course, that was back before Xaydin learned to hate shape shifters.

'Course, Ronan had been infuriated as Meara had used an enchanted cuff to keep him from being able to change forms. It'd been its own kind of torture for Ronan who'd been forced to live as a human.

There were no words for having powers bound against someone's will. It was like having a vice placed on your lungs. Or like losing a limb. Nothing hurt more than having abilities taken away for no good reason.

Some could cope. Most became bitter and angry, especially the longer they were withheld. Not that he blamed them. He couldn't stand being bound in any manner or not having authority over his own life. It was why he'd never want to be king.

That kind of power came with restrictions he'd rather die than suffer. Nothing was worse than losing autonomy.

And as he scanned the mostly empty room, he caught sight of the beast he sought.

Sort of.

Ronan wasn't Ronan. Rather he was disguised as a troll. Light green skin and flaming red hair. But the eyes were the same.

Stormy, dark gray.

Jerking his chin, he acknowledged Ronan's presence.

Ronan cut a glance sideways.

Xaydin looked over to see the contingent of guards the imposter had mentioned.

"Are you fucking kidding me," he uttered under his breath. Further proof that wasn't Masakage. Not that he needed it confirmed.

And before he could move, the captain of the group headed straight for him.

Xaydin placed his hand over the hilt of his sword, tempted to unsheathe it and relieve the world of this particular breed of pestilence.

Don't do it.

It'd be all kinds of stupid. But it was so tempting.

"Xaydin!" Robslin grabbed him into a tight hug.

It took everything he had not to protest or shove the huge troll beast away from him. With jet-black hair and dark skin that held a hint of green, Robslin was almost as tall as he was.

"Cousin." Xaydin pounded him on the back hard enough that it finally caused the shorter troll to release him. "What are you doing here?"

"We were passing by when we caught word there were humans about. Wanted to see who dared such. Should have known it was you, but this isn't your usual haunt."

True. He stayed up north, unless he was traveling to Oath Island and even then, he stayed in the east. He rarely ever ventured to the west.

"Now you can set your mind at ease. No humans for you to chase or expel."

Laughing, Rob hit him so hard on the arm that it actually hurt.

Xaydin grimaced, then forced a smile so as not to offend his cousin. Rob wasn't trying to be an ass. He simply wasn't the brightest spark in the fire. Rather his bundle was shy a few logs.

"Won't you join us for a drink?" Rob asked.

I would rather have my eyes gouged out and eaten.

Sighing, he offered his cousin a smile. "Of course."

He followed Rob over to where twelve uniformed trolls sat. Dressed in the red-and-green armor of the royal guard, they were remarkably subdued.

That set his nerves on edge. It wasn't like a group of trolls to be so quiet. Especially not a royal patrol.

"What's going on?" he asked Rob as they sat down at the head of the table.

Rob shook his head. "Guess you haven't heard."

"Heard what?"

"My father's ill."

Xaydin wasn't sure how to handle that news. On the one hand, he felt bad for his cousin. But this was the bastard who'd helped kill his father and who ruled their people through his idiot brother. "How bad is it?"

Rob glanced over to his second in command. "They don't think he'll live."

He grimaced at the news. While he hated his uncle, he didn't really wish him dead. Before Gregun had decided to kill Xaydin's father, he'd loved his uncle. That was why the betrayal had cut so deep.

All his personal feelings aside, he wished he knew the words to comfort his cousin. "Sorry."

"Thank you." Rob leaned back as a server brought them two

tankards of ale. "And I should probably let you know that your brother wants you taken into custody."

That was completely unexpected. "Wait...what?"

He nodded. "Zagrun's afraid you'll be after the throne once my father dies."

Xaydin rolled his eyes. "If I wanted the throne, I wouldn't have to wait for your father or my brother to die. I'd take it and kick their asses into a dungeon."

"I tried to tell them. No one listens to me."

Xaydin folded his arms over his chest. "Is that why you're here?"

"God, no. This really was a happy accident while we were traveling through to the capital. As far as we're all concerned, we didn't see anything. Did we, boys?"

One by one, they shook their heads.

Rob smiled. "You know trolls. Hand us some ale and mead, and we're all good."

Xaydin wasn't sure if he should trust that or not, but normally they would follow Rob's lead. The question was if this was a trap. Was his cousin trying to lull him into thinking he was safe?

Rob's brothers wouldn't hesitate to trick him. They were all sneaky bastards, but Rob could go either way. Sometimes he was decent.

Others...

Knife in the spine.

Problem was that you never knew which way he'd turn until it was too late.

Do you need help with that group?

He glanced toward Ronan and gave him a subtle shake of his head to let him know that he could handle this.

Taking the tankard, he drained it in one gulp.

Rob laughed. "You haven't changed a bit."

"Why would I?" He slammed the tankard on the table and clapped his cousin on the back. "Good seeing you."

Xaydin rose slowly, waiting for betrayal. Rob and his soldiers stayed put. Even so, he didn't take an easy breath until he was outside the inn, in the alley where he assumed the imposter had spent the night.

Ronan followed him out, then shifted into his normal appearance of a muscular man who stood head and shoulders over almost all human males. With long, dark brown hair and stormy gray eyes, he could easily intimidate most...but Xaydin wasn't most. "Well, that in there made me shit my pants. How 'bout you?"

Xaydin laughed. "Not even close. My cousin knows better than to start shit with me with that few a number of men to protect him." At least outright.

Behind his back...

That was when Rob was most lethal.

"Glad you think that, X. I hope and pray that you're always right." Ronan grinned so sarcastically that he wanted to punch him. "Well, you're not in jail or near death. Should I be scared or honored that you rang my bell?"

"Probably both, but it's not as bad as you think."

Ronan glanced about. "Oh, I don't know about that. You know my mind runs on inappropriate thoughts of all kinds. Bad to worse is what I excel at."

That was very true. No one wanted to give Ronan too much time to think. It never boded well, as his thoughts went to interesting and always wrong places. "Fine. I have a new traveling companion."

"Imaginary friends, huh? Love it. I always thought you'd be the first of us to lose his mind. I should have made a bet for it."

He rolled his eyes. "Tolerating the lot of you, it's a wonder I have any sanity left."

"I would be offended by that if it wasn't true...so it's an actual travel companion and not a figment?"

"Scary, right?"

"More than you know. I thought you hated people."

Ronan had no idea.

Xaydin smirked. "Gets better."

That caused one brow to shoot north. "How so?"

"She's a shifter."

Ronan stood there for several minutes as those words echoed through his head.

She's. A. Shifter.

That entire sentence terrified him. Mostly because he really couldn't process it. Not in any context that included Xaydin. Because he knew his friend better than anyone.

"She...she's a shifter..."

"That's what I said."

"And you're fine with this?"

He shoved at Ronan. "Hell no. I'm not fine with this. Why do you think I sent for you?"

"No idea. The thoughts in my head aren't making the least bit of sense. First, it's a woman. I honestly thought you weren't into them."

Xaydin scowled at him. "Excuse me?"

"Don't get pissed. I wasn't thinking *that*. Mostly, I figured you were celibate or...you know. A eunuch."

By the offended look on Xaydin's face, he knew he was about to get punched. "Don't get pissed," he repeated. He stepped back, hopefully out of range. "You have to admit that most of what you do is sit in the back of a pub, eyeing everyone for target practice. I've never seen you look at anyone or anything with an interest of *that* nature. I didn't know what all Meara did to you when we were captives, but..." He gestured awkwardly at Xaydin's crotch. "For all we knew, she could have cut something off. I figured it was why you were always so eager to kill."

"You're such an ass."

He wasn't wrong, but this really wasn't Ronan's fault. Who could blame him for thinking Xaydin had no desires at all?

"Secondly, when have you started tolerating anyone around you?"

Xaydin wanted to respond snidely to that question. He really did, but what could he say to the truth?

"Anyway," he said to get Ronan off a subject that was irritating him, "She's the reason I sent for you."

That appeared to shock him. "Why?" he asked slowly.

He shoved at Ronan. "Get your mind out of there. She's a shifter."

"I still don't know how to react to that."

Xaydin growled. "Stop it."

Ronan shook his head. "Me stop it? Me? I'm sorry, I'm just having a hard time with something that refutes absolutely everything I know to be true about you. Since when can you stomach a shifter? Hell, you barely tolerate me and I've saved your life."

All true. "I know. But she's different. She hasn't been around her kind...ever."

That seemed to get his attention. "How do you know she's a shifter, then?"

"I've seen her shift. But she has a lot of questions about it that I can't answer. You being a shifter, I figured you could help her better than I could."

"No kidding. That would be like me trying to teach someone to be a troll."

"And..." Xaydin let his voice trail off.

"There's an *and*? How can there be an *and*?"

Xaydin gave him a droll stare. "There's not just an and, there's a holy shit."

214

Ronan rubbed at his eyebrow. "There can't be anything more to this. I'm not sure my brain can take it."

"Then you might want to sit."

Ronan looked around the empty alley.

After a second of figuring out there wasn't a chair nearby, he sat down on the ground and looked up with a hint of fear in his stormy eyes. "I'm scared to ask."

"She's Meara's daughter."

Ronan was glad that he'd taken Xaydin at his word and sat down. Because honestly, he would have fallen over had he still been on his feet.

Indeed, he was actually dizzy from it.

When he spoke, he enunciated each word carefully. "Let me make sure that I have this straight. You are traveling with Meara's daughter who happens to be a shape shifter?"

Xaydin nodded slowly.

Ronan let those words seep into his own brain as he repeated them silently. "Just for my benefit, is there any part of that sentence that doesn't fly in the face of everything I know about you?"

"Probably not."

"Then can you show me your tongue?" He stood up.

Xaydin's eyes flared. "Pardon?"

"I have to make sure that you're you and that you're not a shifter, too. Because none of this makes any logical sense to me."

Xaydin would have been more offended if he wasn't dealing with a shifter already posing as a family member. "Can you really tell?"

"Yeah." Ronan lifted his tongue to the roof of his mouth so that Xaydin could see beneath it. There, toward the back on the left, was a peculiar black symbol. It was tiny and yet it was obvious that it was some sort of unique mark. "What is that?"

"Each of us is born with a unique mark and no matter what

form we're in, you can find it. It's usually under a tongue, but if you don't have a tongue for some reason, it'll be somewhere else."

"Really?"

He nodded. "All shifters have it, and the symbol is unique to each of us. No one has the same symbol, and we have no ability to change or hide the mark. It's how we can identify each other."

"And you never thought to tell me about this before?"

Ronan snorted. "Why would I? It's not something you need to know, and given your unnatural hatred of us...why would I give you fodder for your fire? Or a reason to effectively find us."

"Xaydin?"

He cursed at the sound of the imposter calling him from the street. He was just about to tell Ronan that was the other reason he'd sent for him...to deal with the fake Masakage.

As the imposter rounded the corner, Ronan vanished. Xaydin glanced around the alley, making sure he didn't accidentally step on his friend who could be a spider or some other crawly creature.

The imposter drew up short. "What are you doing out here?"

Xaydin shrugged. "Thought I saw something, and I wanted to investigate it. What do you need?"

"The captain and his crew just left the inn. I thought you'd like to know."

Not really.

But the less the imposter knew about his business, the better.

"Thank you." Xaydin started back toward the inn.

The imposter glanced about the alley as if he detected something amiss.

Could shifters sense each other?

He'd never thought about that before.

After a few seconds, he clapped Xaydin on the back. "When are we leaving?"

He shrugged the imposter's touch away. "As soon as Gisela's ready."

"Good."

Xaydin took a step forward. And the moment he did, he felt a fierce sharp pain in his side. An instant later, he felt another one.

It wasn't until the third pain that he realized he was being stabbed.

Staggering back, he coughed and gasped. Just as the imposter went to stab him a fourth time, a fierce screech sounded.

Xaydin barely recognized Gisela before she turned into a giant ogre and rushed them. She grabbed the imposter. One moment, he was standing over Xaydin and the next, he was rebounding off the wall across from him.

He wanted to help and to defend her, but the pain was overwhelming. More than that, it caused a fierce buzzing in his ears. One so bad that he could barely hear anything.

Unable to stand it, he tried to step toward her.

Instead, he fell.

Then everything went dark.

15

Gisela's heart pounded as she saw Xaydin fall. Fury unlike anything she'd ever experienced before rushed through her. She wanted to run to him, but first she had to take care of the bastard who'd tried to kill him.

Wanting blood, she lunged for the imposter. But before she could reach him, he vanished.

Or at least that was what she thought until he reappeared beside her, along with a man she didn't recognize.

Before she could react, the imposter turned into a rat and the man had the imposter trapped inside a cage.

Grateful the matter was taken care of for the moment, she ran toward Xaydin who was on the ground, bleeding.

Biting her lip, she tried to think of what she could do. While she'd seen others bleed like this, she'd never tried to stop it. Mostly because she'd been the reason they were bleeding in the first place, and she'd wanted them to die.

Now...

How did she stop it?

The unknown man cursed as he knelt beside her. He pulled off his shirt and ripped a strip of cloth from it and balled it up.

"Hold this." He showed her how to put pressure on the wound in Xaydin's side.

"Who are you?" she asked.

"Ronan. I'm a friend of Xaydin's."

Her breath caught at a name she recognized from her mother. "You're an Outlaw."

He nodded. "You must be Gisela. Xaydin was just telling me you were traveling with him."

That confirmed the fact that he wasn't lying. "Please help me save him."

"I will. Keep the pressure on that wound."

While she did so, he ran off.

What the hell? Stunned, she was tempted to go after him and would have had he not come back within a few seconds.

It wasn't until he sat down across from her that she realized he had Xaydin's saddlebags in his hands.

"What are you doing?" she asked.

"Oh come on!" He started pulling out potions from the bags. "Are you kidding me! There's not a single healing potion in here? Why, Xaydin? Why?"

Gisela winced as she realized that was one potion no one had thought to grab. "He picked others instead."

Ronan looked as sick as she felt. "Why?" he repeated. That tone would have been comical if this wasn't such a serious matter.

"Failure to think ahead. Why didn't I get one?" She could kill herself for her idiocy.

Ronan gave her a dry stare. "Because no one thinks they're going to be fatally stabbed until they are."

Those words shocked her. More than that, they horrified her. "He's not fatally wounded!" How could he say that?

Without a word, he went over to the cage where he'd trapped their imposter as a rat. "You better pray he survives.

Because if he doesn't, I'm locking you in that body and feeding you to a playful cat."

The rat actually screamed as it tried to get out the cage.

Gisela grabbed the cage and shook it. "If he dies, you better pray he feeds you to a cat before I get my hands on you." Because she wouldn't be nearly as merciful.

"What is this?"

Gisela looked up as what appeared to be a group of royal guards came rushing toward them. When she started to unsheathe her sword, Ronan stopped her.

Holding his hands up, he rose slowly to his feet. "We're trying to help the prince."

Color drained from the captain's face as he rushed forward. As soon as he reached Xaydin, he cursed.

"Who did this!"

They both pointed to the small cage. The imposter actually shrank back from the bars.

Ronan curled his lip. "That's right, asshole, you can't go any smaller. The cage is enchanted so you can't shift."

The captain's eyes widened. "A shape shifter did this?"

Ronan nodded. "He ambushed the prince."

The captain snapped his fingers at his men. "Get him back to the inn. Fetch a surgeon. The best they have in this tiny place."

As they moved to help Xaydin, the captain eyed Ronan and her warily. "Make sure those two don't go anywhere."

Gisela went straight to Xaydin's side. "I'm going wherever Xaydin goes. You will not keep me from him. Anyone who tries needs to arm themselves."

That seemed to catch the men off guard, but she didn't care. She wasn't about to let him out of her sight. Not after someone almost killed him. She didn't know anyone here, and if Xaydin was awake, she was sure he wouldn't trust any of them, either.

So why should she?

But she would give credit that the soldiers picked him up with care before they gently took him back to the troll inn that was mostly empty this time of day.

"Where's he staying?" the leader asked once they neared the stairs.

"Follow me." She rushed past them so that she could lead them up the stairs to the room they shared.

Gisela winced as she opened the door and silently cursed. The day had started out so wonderfully. As Xaydin had suggested when she awoke, she'd taken her time getting ready.

If I hadn't done that, I could have helped him.

Guilt tore her apart. This was all her fault. Why had she taken so long to dress? She should have been with him when he was attacked.

Five minutes sooner and none of this would have happened. The pain inside her was indescribable.

Five minutes. That was all.

Had she not rinsed her hair twice, she'd have been there in time to stop it.

Five fucking minutes.

Stop it!

No need in dwelling on what had happened or her part in it. That wouldn't fix or improve the situation or heal his wounds. The only thing that mattered right now was saving Xaydin.

What surprised her most was the care and regard the soldiers were using as they placed him on the bed and stepped back respectfully. While they might not know him, they appeared to at least respect him.

The captain came forward. "What's taking so long on that surgeon? Galenorn!" he shouted at the one nearest her who had carried Xaydin in. "Go and check on it. Bring me someone fast or I'll have all your balls!"

Galenorn took off at a run.

Once he was gone, the captain sent the other trolls outside to guard the door. Then, he turned back toward her. "Are you his woman?"

The question shocked her. How should she answer? It seemed presumptuous and yet it was what she wanted to say about their relationship.

Ronan cleared his throat to get the captain's attention, then nodded. "She is...everything to him."

She sank down on the bed by Xaydin's feet in total stupefaction. It was a good thing Xaydin was unconscious, because she could only imagine the fury on his face had he heard that declaration.

But being called his woman wasn't nearly as terrifying as it ought to be. Rather, she liked the thought of being his. Because after last night... He had claimed her in a way she'd never thought possible. She was his, and she wanted everyone to know it.

Except for the fact that it was causing the two men in the room to stare at her strangely.

Honestly, she wasn't sure how to take it.

Part of her wanted to run and hide and the other part wanted to smile and tell them that she was proud to be with him.

Especially when the captain came forward and gave her a formal court bow. "My cousin is a good and honorable troll. For too long, he's been alone. I pray you'll take good care of him. He deserves someone who can appreciate him and love him for who he is."

She wasn't sure what to say to that. Not to mention the fact that they were watching her way too intensely. She felt like she'd been put on display against her will.

And she didn't like this feeling at all.

Getting up quickly, she directed her attention to Xaydin and trying to stanch the flow of blood as best she could. She removed his shirt and winced at the jagged wounds left behind. How could she stop this?

As Ronan had shown her, she attempted to keep cloth against the three wounds. And by the time the surgeon arrived, she was covered in his blood.

The surgeon elbowed her away and took her place at Xaydin's side. "What have the lot of you done to this poor creature with your inexperience?"

Ronan looked as offended as she felt.

"We kept him alive while you tottered," she said between clenched teeth. "And you should be grateful. Because your life hinges on his. He dies and I'll cut you from gullet to throat."

"With the full backing of the king," the captain added. "Prince Xaydin is highly valued."

Ronan glanced away with an amused twinkle in his eyes that said that probably wasn't true. But it was enough to get the surgeon's attention.

"Nothing will happen to him in my care. I rarely lose patients."

Rarely? Was he serious? That wasn't what she wanted to hear. "And I'm an assassin who has *never* lost or failed to kill a target."

The surgeon paled, then immediately set to work.

She moved to the corner where Ronan stood with the captain and the small cage that contained their imposter.

The captain took her blood-soaked hand and placed a respectful kiss across her knuckles. "I'm his cousin, Rob. Pleased to meet you, my lady."

"Princess," Ronan corrected.

That caught his attention. "Really?"

"Technically," she corrected. "Members of my family are less than thrilled that I hold the title."

"Understood." Rob kept his gaze locked on the surgeon. "Should we summon his sister and brother?"

Ronan passed a frown toward her before he answered. "I'm assuming you mean Candara and Masakage. I don't think any of the others would care."

Again, she was puzzled by that. "Exactly how many siblings does he have?"

Ronan shrugged. "Honestly, I don't really know. Do you?" he asked Rob.

He duplicated the shrug. "At least a dozen half-siblings from his father, but I don't know if we know all of them or not. With his mother...no telling. Not even sure if he knows them all."

Wow. Her mother had four children. Her three half-brothers were centaurs from various fathers who were no longer living because the queen had grown tired of them.

Ferox was the heir, but to be honest, she wasn't even sure if he was still alive given his screw up with King Dash where he'd been captured.

Her mother had been so angry over it that Ferox was persona non grata at court and anyone who mentioned his name risked a homicidal rage from Meara.

Then again, she risked a homicidal rage from her mother for nothing more than entering a room at an inopportune moment.

As did most beings.

"What are we going to do with that one?" She jerked her chin toward the mouse in the cage. "He's holding Masakage. Or killed him."

The color faded from Ronan's cheeks at those words.

Then a dark fury descended over his face. He met Rob's gaze. "There a place I can freely interrogate the bastard?"

Rob nodded slowly. "Let's string him up and see what we can learn."

Gisela took a moment to step near the surgeon again. "Remember...life for a life. Don't let us down."

He nodded as he continued to close the wounds. "He will live."

Xaydin better. Because the one thing she was best at... ending lives. And those were ones she didn't have a personal grudge against.

One who harmed someone she cared about...

The surgeon would meet with an awful ending.

16

Candara froze as she heard a voice beside her. At first, it was a quiet whisper that was barely audible.

Then it became louder as she focused on the accented voice she knew so well.

Masakage.

It wasn't like him to reach out to her like this. They normally conversed through mirrors and even then, rarely.

"Where are you, brother?" She waved her hand over her scrying mirror so that they could speak.

She gasped at the sight of her immaculate Masakage, filthy and bleeding. "What happened?"

There was a locked, metal gag around his mouth that kept him from speaking. He jerked his head to the left.

On the wall next to him, he'd used her native alphabet to write the location in his own blood.

Clever boy. Even so, it infuriated her that he'd been put in this position.

How dare they!

"On my way. Hold tight."

And with that, she sealed the door to her shop and gathered a quick travel pack as fast as she could.

Masakage needed her, and she would never disappoint him or Xaydin. They were the only family she had, and she was loyal to both of them.

No one would tear down her brothers!

"Hit him again. Harder!"

Both Ronan and Rob turned to stare at her with horrified expressions.

That only made Gisela angrier. "Oh, for the gods' sakes." She grabbed a stick from the floor of the stable where they'd secured Garyn in his human form so that they could torture him.

When she went to hit him, Ronan caught the stick and gave her a stunned scowl. "Princess Bloodlust, he's had enough. Anymore and we'll kill him."

"Fine with me." She held her hand out. "Let me have my stick."

Scratching at the tip of his nose, Ronan turned back toward Garyn and refused to give her the stick. "If I were you, I think I'd answer everything she wants to know. Not sure how long we can hold her back. She's pretty spry."

"And terribly pissed off," Rob added. "She scares even me."

Ronan nodded in agreement.

Garyn tried again to fight against the ropes that held him. They'd both learned that trolls were better at knot tying than Marauders, and that said a lot, given that all Marauders were sailors and pirates.

"I've told you everything."

"Where's Masakage?" Gisela growled.

"If I tell you, you'll kill me."

She shoved at him. "If you don't tell me, I can guarantee that outcome. The only hope you have is if you help us find him."

"Then you better summon an *apaswere* and make a contract because that's the only way I'll trust any of you."

She reached up and pressed her thumbnail into the corner of his eye socket. "Did you know that you can pop your eye out? It's quite painful and you can still see with only one eye." She pressed harder.

He screamed. "Stop her!"

Ronan crossed his arms over his chest. "Honestly, I'd rather she gouge out your eye than one of ours. 'Cause no offense, that looks really painful." He turned his back to them. "I can't watch. I saw a soldier lose an eye in battle. It's disgusting."

Rob nodded. "Been made to poke out a few. You never quite forget that pop." He shivered in obvious revulsion.

Gisela pursed her lips. "Really? I find it rather satisfying. Not the feel so much as the sound. It's rather like uncorking a bottle."

Garyn screamed even more.

You are terrible. Ronan smirked.

Of course she was. Xaydin was wounded and his brother was missing. She was more than willing to pluck off as many body parts as she needed to get the information that would help them.

"Why did you take the contract from the *apaswere*?" She pressed harder against his eye.

He refused to answer.

She went deeper with her fingernail. "Any second we'll have that satisfying pop."

"Stop!" he screamed. "I'll tell you."

She let up but kept some pressure there. Just to remind him that she didn't mind doing this to him. "Start talking."

"Your mother sent me in case you needed me."

Those words caught her off guard. "You lie. My mother would never have done that." She applied more pressure.

"Stop! Stop! She didn't send me to watch over you..."

No kidding. That would require a level of care her mother didn't possess. "Then why are you here?"

"To finish it," he screamed.

Ronan cursed as he pulled her away from Garyn. "Don't you see? He's here to kill the *apaswere*."

That made no sense. "What?"

"Your mother wants everyone to think that she's a victim. It's how she's always been. If she sends you out to protect an *apaswere* who ends up dead..."

Gisela winced at an explanation that made way too much sense. *I knew it was bullshit.* The moment her mother had told her to protect the *apaswere*, it'd sounded wrong.

Now she knew why.

Her mother wasn't about protecting anyone other than herself. This was to cover her ass when she went after Dash. Or to force the High King to do something so she could fight back without consequences.

That bitch!

She was so tired of being lied to. She doubted if her mother had ever once told her the truth.

About anything. For all she knew, her father was a lie, too.

And she was done with it. The temptation to kill the assassin was almost beyond her abilities to resist. There was only one thing that kept him alive.

"Where's Masakage?" she demanded.

He shook his head slowly. "I'm not stupid. I know the only

thing keeping me alive is the fact that you know if you kill me, you'll never see him again."

Damn him for being right.

"Not telling us will just cost you body parts." She went for his eye again.

Screaming, he tried to pull away. "Wait! We can figure this out. We don't need to be violent."

"I'd rather cause you pain."

This time, Ronan caught her. "Maybe he's right and we ought to work something out."

"Rather not. He hurt Xaydin and kidnapped Masakage. I vote we torture him just on principle."

"My bloodthirsty princess...what am I to do with you?"

Gasping, she turned to look behind her to find Xaydin leaning heavily against the door of the stable.

Without thinking, she ran to him and threw herself into his arms.

He grunted hard, then smiled as he enveloped her in a warm hug.

She pulled back so that she could look up into those startled eyes that stared down at her.

He quirked an amused grin. "I'm assuming you didn't think I'd live."

"Don't you ever scare me like that again. I was terrified." She growled at him. "If you weren't hurt, I'd beat you."

He smoothed the worry from her brow. "Always remember... I'm hard to kill."

And she'd never been more grateful for anything in her life. Except for the fact that she did notice something. "You still look..." She didn't want to say bad, not just because it was rude. But because he could never look terrible.

"Piqued?"

She smiled. "I'll go with that." But to be honest, he looked as if he needed to be back in bed.

He wrapped his arms around her again, and she took a moment to savor the sound of his fierce heartbeat under her cheek. That and the warmth of his embrace that went much deeper than a physical touch. She felt safe. Something she'd never known before.

I am his.

Those three words should terrify her more than anything, and yet she reveled in them. It felt wonderful to be part of something more than herself. To know she had someone at her back. Someone she could depend on.

Don't be stupid. You know better.

Maybe, but he'd given her no reason to doubt him. No reason to think he was anything other than a bold lover who'd be there for her.

"You've got quite the woman there, cuz. Not many women are willing to gouge out an eyeball for you."

Xaydin laughed. "I'm sure she'd do even worse." He released her so that he could approach the shifter. "You..."

Garyn actually wet himself at Xaydin's approach.

Xaydin grimaced in distaste. "You should be afraid. I tend to take it personally when someone slides a blade between my ribs while they're pretending to be my brother."

"I—"

"If you're about to say you meant no harm, you might want to rethink those words. They will move me into a homicidal rage that I'm rather sure you won't survive."

"And they'll make me..." Ronan paused as he swept a gaze over Xaydin's massive, intimidating form. "Well, I would say homicidal too, but let's face it, as massive as I am, I pale in comparison to the troll. Suffice it to say, I shall be quite put out."

He was right. Had he been alone, Ronan was intimidating.

But when standing next to Xaydin, he reminded her of a little boy in his father's armor.

Adorable. Nowhere near as fierce. And she admired the fact that he not only realized it, but that he had fun with it.

Xaydin let out a slow breath. "So how do we use this bastard to find my brother?"

"Which brother did you lose now?"

Gisela gasped at the familiar voice that came from behind them.

As did Xaydin.

Masakage stood in the doorway where Xaydin had been, along with Candara who had a frown on her face as she surveyed their small group.

"He doesn't look as dead now, does he?" she asked.

"Not even a little." Masakage jerked his chin toward their prisoner. "That one, however, looks a little worse for the wear. I hope you beat the hell out of him for me."

Rob snorted. "His woman more than the rest of us."

Masakage arched one brow. "Well, I've missed a lot."

Xaydin wrinkled his nose at the condition Masakage was in. "Including a bath."

He laughed, then groaned. "Looks like we both owe your captive an ass beating." Masakage turned his attention to Rob. "Be careful. He wasn't working alone. There's another shifter around who helped him capture me from Mardyth's kingdom. He goes by the name Diflyn. I've seen him as a merman, human and troll. I have no idea what his main form is."

Ronan let out a feral sound. "Open up. Let me see under everyone's tongues."

Rob stepped back. "I beg your pardon."

"You'll beg more than that if you're a shifter. Open wide and let me look."

With one more fierce scowl, Rob obliged.

"You're clear." He went to Xaydin who arched a brow at him. "And we'll clear you on principle."

Masakage snorted before he opened his mouth and lifted his tongue.

Candara pursed her lips. "And you wonder why everyone hates a shifter." She exposed the underside of her tongue.

"Oh, I know why we're hated. Don't blame you a bit. Shifters don't like shifters either. It destroys your ability to trust anyone or anything. It's why we don't have our own country. You'd never know if your ruler was the actual ruler...and anyone could pretend to be them. It's really unnerving when there are a bunch of us together."

It was also why there weren't that many of them. Most had been hunted down and executed by the other races. Those who remained, kept to themselves and lived remotely. Or like her, were assassins or mercenaries.

She'd never considered before how lonely it must be for them. "You really don't have a community?"

"We implode whenever we try to live together. For whatever reason, shifters just can't get along."

How awful. Even the undead had their own country.

"Have you any siblings?" she asked him.

He inclined his head to Xaydin. "The Outlaws are my family."

"Ronan's mother was the last queen of Lygaria."

Gisela winced at Candara's words. Lygaria had fallen while Ronan would have been in captivity.

The Fourteenth Kingdom. It'd been located in the southeastern tip of Sagaria, the southwestern tip of Dythnal and the northwestern part of her mother's kingdom.

When the queen's army had fallen to the Sagarians, their kingdom had been absorbed by all three. Gisela wasn't sure why or how.

She only remembered her mother's jubilance over it. Mostly because Meara had hated the shifters so much. And even though it'd been the fey kingdom that defeated them, her mother had taken the largest share of Lygaria's land.

"I'm sorry, Ronan."

"Thank you." Clearing his throat, he went back to their prisoner. "I'll keep watch on him while you take Xaydin back to bed and let him rest."

Xaydin started to protest.

"Don't even," Ronan snapped. "You look like shite and you need to heal. Don't go troll on me when I know you better. Rest for a day and you can pummel whatever tomorrow." His gaze went to Masakage. "You as well."

Rob led them toward the door. "We'll stay the night to make sure none of you are disturbed." He smirked at Masakage. "And to make sure they rent a room to you."

Which was easier said than done. The innkeeper wasn't happy at all when Rob demanded a room for Masakage and Candara. But after a show of coin and a little bit of force, he acquiesced.

Gisela returned to the room she shared with Xaydin and made sure he went straight to bed.

"I can't stand to lie about. There's too much we need to do."

"And you won't be of any use to us if you fall...because none of us are strong enough to pick you up."

Xaydin rolled his eyes at her attempt at humor. "Candara can pick me up with her pinkie."

"What?"

"Her magic's that strong. A sneeze and she can portal me anywhere."

"I doubt your sister would portal you in your current condition. Now lay down and go to sleep."

He pouted. "Can't sleep in my clothes."

Gisela caught the note in his voice. "You're incorrigible."

"No. I'm encourageable." He sat on the bed and cast the most adorable look at her that she'd ever seen. "And I like being encouraged."

Which he was doing as he opened the neck of his shirt and gave her a puppy look that begged for assistance.

"I stand by what I said. You're awful." Forcing herself to show no emotions, she pulled the shirt over his head.

Then she had to bite her lip at how scrumptious he appeared. He was far too handsome for his own good.

And for hers.

What was she going to do with him?

Well, she knew what she wanted to do with him...if he were able. But there was a paleness to his skin that told her how much pain he was in.

He might be willing, but there was no way she'd put that strain on him.

"You rest and I'll rest with you."

The hope in his eyes was quite charming and at odds with his stern demeanor.

She continued to strip the clothes from him. "Be a good boy."

"I'm yours to command."

Sure, he was. She doubted if anyone had ever really commanded him. Indeed, the scars on his body told the story of just how rebellious her proud troll could be. She pulled off the last stitch of clothing. "Lie down."

Xaydin did as she bade him. And he was instantly awarded with the sight of her slowly removing her own clothes. "Are you trying to torture me?"

An insidious smile curved her lips. "Maybe..."

No maybe to it. She was in rare, tortuous form as she bared her flesh, piece by slow, excruciating piece.

Damn, he'd never realized before how many layers of clothing she wore. Eternity seemed to have passed before she stood naked before him.

He let out a slow breath in silent appreciation for the soft curves of her body. Especially when she slid that body beneath the covers and pressed it up against his uninjured side.

Letting out a sigh, she placed her head on his shoulder and gently brushed her hand over his ribs, above the stab wounds. "You'll have new scars now."

"Not like they'll stand out."

Gisela winced at the truth. Like her, he was covered with them. The scars from wounds were horrible. But the ones that wrung her heart were from lashes.

Because she understood how much those cost in terms of his soul. There was no greater pain than to be tied down and unable to defend yourself. To be at the mercy of those who lacked any whatsoever.

Physical pain was easy to counter. Mental anguish left scars that no one could see. Scars that burned long after the injuries healed.

She ached for everything he'd been put through.

Wanting to make it better, she lifted herself up to kiss one particular nasty lash mark that ran from his arm across his stomach.

"You keep doing that, princess, and I will not sleep."

"Sorry." But she wasn't even a little bit.

She moved her hand only to have him capture it in his. He brought it to his lips to place a sweet kiss across her knuckles before he placed their entwined hands over his heart.

Gisela couldn't breathe as she felt his heart beating and felt that strong grip on her hand. For this one moment, she felt loved.

No...

She felt cherished.

And if she could, she'd will herself to death in this moment because she was terrified it wouldn't last. If she died right now, at least she'd know what it felt like to be with someone.

It can't last.

Nothing ever did and she didn't want to be here when he broke her heart.

She'd had enough pain in her life. Enough of her mother and others lamenting all her shortcomings.

I don't want to be here anymore.

It was an anguished cry her soul made because she was so tired of fighting. Tired of being alone.

Tired of everything.

"How do you do it?" The question was out of her mouth before she could stop it.

"Do what?"

"Keep going through all the pain?"

His grip tightened on her hand. "I don't think about it."

"Ever?"

"I'd be lying if I said my demons didn't roost at times. But I won't let them defeat me. I had no say in the past, only in my future. The way I look at it, princess, is that we have two options. Either we let the pain of our past drag us under or we keep our gaze on the horizon and what we're after. I'm too stubborn a bastard to let anyone win, including the past. Or my demons."

She liked the way he saw things. "I wish I was that strong."

"Lady, you're stronger than you know." He stroked her fingers with his. "I've never met anyone with your courage or heart. Never let anyone tell you differently."

"I love the lies you believe about me."

He shook his head. "I wish you could see the beauty I do.

One day, you'll learn your true nature. Not the daughter of an awful queen, but a great lady who outshines all others."

She pushed herself up to look down at him. "Did that really come from you?"

"I'm not always a brooding jackass."

"Apparently." She gave him a light kiss.

"You are determined to keep me awake, aren't you?"

She laughed. "No. Sleep! Rest. Or else I'll leave."

Xaydin immediately closed his eyes.

Gisela returned to her spot and forced herself not to stroke or bother him. But it was exceptionally difficult.

Instead, she took a moment to savor the quiet.

Don't break my heart. It was a silent prayer she wanted the courage to speak out loud.

So much had happened in such a short time. Her mother wanted a war.

For the first time in her life, Gisela wanted peace. She wanted a future.

And she wanted Xaydin to be part of it.

You're an idiot.

It was an impossible dream. He would never give up his cause. And in spite of what her mother said, she knew Meara wouldn't let her go.

She'd kill her first.

But here for a moment, she had the peace she craved. She was living a dream, and her only hope was to enjoy these fleeting heartbeats. Because every one signaled the coming end she could feel in her bones.

17

Masakage entered the stable where Garyn was still being held.

The shifter's guard looked up in startled alarm. "My lord, what brings you here?"

Masakage kept his gaze on his target. "Might I have a few moments with your charge?"

The troll guard looked about sheepishly. "I don't know. I'm not supposed to leave him."

"Believe me, I won't let him escape. No one will know about this except the two of us."

Still, the troll hesitated. "I guess if I stay outside, it should be all right."

Masakage didn't speak until after the troll had left and he was alone with Garyn.

Garyn's eyes widened at his approach. "What do you want?"

"Peace among the kingdoms. Meara's head in my saddlebags and for you to tell me where your friend is."

"I don't have any friends."

"Your lover, then. Whatever it is that Diflyn is to you. Where has the bastard gone?"

Garyn glanced up at the shackles that held him in place. "How would I know? He doesn't report to me."

"Not the impression I had when you kidnapped me." Masakage used his powers to squeeze a certain piece of Garyn's anatomy until he cried out in agony. Let the bastard be impotent after this. It was the best for the kingdoms and for whatever poor child that didn't need this shite for a father. "Returning the favor, Shifter. You should have shown me better hospitality."

Gasping, Garyn narrowed a hate-filled glare on him. "We should have killed you."

"Yes. You should have. Why did you refrain?"

"We didn't want you dead. Just held so that I could watch over Gisela without interruption."

The bastard omitted another primary target. "And my brother."

Garyn looked away, confirming his suspicions.

Masakage pulled the contract out from his sleeve and held it up for Garyn to see. "And what of this?"

His eyes flared as he realized what Masakage was showing him. "Where did you get that?"

"Does it matter? You used magic to extract Meara's contract from its *apaswere*. Why?"

"Why does anyone do anything?"

Really? He was trying to be philosophical?

Bad move considering his mood.

"I'm not asking why you chose to eat porridge in the morning. I'm asking why you'd do something of this nature. I know you didn't care whether the *apaswere* lived or died. So why would you transfer it?"

"Safe keeping."

Masakage laughed. "On a sheet of..." His voice trailed off as he realized it couldn't possibly be written on the back of a regular piece of parchment.

How did I miss this?

Of course, it was enchanted. Indestructible.

Cursing, he blasted the beast with a fireball.

Garyn screamed.

Masakage really wanted to kill him. But it wouldn't do any good. It might even make it worse. "What magic binds this?"

"You don't know?"

Growling, Masakage punched him, but it did nothing to alleviate his agitation.

With a grimace of distaste, he left the beast and headed out. "He's all yours," he told the guard as he made his way toward the inn and the room he shared with Candara.

CANDARA LOOKED up as the door to her spartan room was thrown open with force. At first, she feared it might be an enemy. Until she saw the fury in Masakage's dark eyes. "What's happened?"

He shoved a document at her.

Frowning, she glanced over it. "It's a contract?"

"I know. The parchment's enchanted. Can you tell by what?"

Of course she could. There was no magic in existence that she didn't know.

Closing her eyes, she took a deep breath. The tangy sweet scent was unmistakable. "Fey magic printed on the skin of an elf."

He curled his lip. "What? Why?"

"Elves have magic encoded in every part of their being. Like

245

the fey. Parchment from their skin enhances any spell placed on it...rather like an *apaswere*. Only this is more potent."

"Would the same be true of the fey?"

"Probably." She handed the paper back to him. "But I've not heard of anyone skinning a fairy and walking away. Not that it was easy to do that to an elf."

It was rather like taking a unicorn horn while it was still attached. There were creatures dumb enough to try. And sadly, unicorn horns were a treasured magical item that held a lot of power within them.

As did the flesh of creatures born from magic.

She didn't even want to know what her own skin would be worth. Relic Hunters were a terrible thing. They all should be rounded up and gutted. Especially those who preyed on children.

"How do you break an *apaswere* contract that was trans-ferred to elfin skin?"

"With great care," she said. "That is if it can be undone." She jerked her chin toward the morbid piece. "Burning won't work. It could even backfire and cause the signers to die. Without knowing the spell, I don't think I can undo it."

"A spell you can't undo? I didn't think that was possible."

"Improbable doesn't mean impossible."

"What should we do?"

She fingered the lettering. A chill from it shot up her arm and into her mind, she saw the moment the *apaswere* allowed the ink to flow from his skin to the new document. There was life in that ink.

Life in the parchment.

Strange how that essence had a very particular smell. Like citrus soaked in brandy. Unmistakable. Pungent even. It was how she could track others without her potions. How she trained her potions to seek living creatures.

That unique essence.

"To break this, you'll have to divide it."

Masakage arched a brow. "How so?"

"I'm not sure. My guides are trying to tell me, but something is muzzling them." Her ears buzzed as she tried to push past the interference.

Her brother took her elbow to steady her. "Are you all right?"

"Not sure," she whispered. And she wasn't. Something was very off about all this. She felt her eyes flood with heat, which meant they were now glowing orange. "He's taken money from two monarchs. He was supposed to end the contract. But his goal is to make money."

She turned toward Masakage. "They intend to kill you and Xaydin. Gisela will be a hostage, and if her mother refuses to pay for her, Gisela will be killed as well."

"Do you see where his partner is?"

Cocking her head, she let her two shadowy guides lead her through shifting scenes that blurred together. This was the part she always hated. It was so hard to filter all the information bombarding her. Images flashed and blurred so quickly that often she had no idea what she was looking at or what her guides were trying to tell her.

"I see him..." But she couldn't quite hone in on where he was. "He's strong."

"No one's stronger than you are."

She appreciated her brother's confidence in her abilities, but it didn't change the fact that she couldn't push through the haze. Diflyn wasn't the fool he pretended to be. His powers were formidable.

"He wants vengeance on Dash."

Masakage widened his eyes. "Pardon?"

"Diflyn was among your group...but kept outside it. He has

a personal grudge against the lot of you. Dash in particular. He feels as if you abandoned him by not allowing him to be an Outlaw. He not only wants to prove himself worthy... He wants to destroy all of you."

And with that, she had to pull out before she caused herself permanent brain damage. As it was, her head pounded a second heartbeat that pumped pain all throughout her body.

She could barely keep her eyes open against the piercing light that sent shards of agony into her brain.

Masakage swept her up in his arms and carried her to the bed where he gently laid her down. "Sorry. I didn't mean to make you ill."

Grateful that he understood the toll her powers took, she patted him warmly on his arm. "Anything for you."

He used his powers to summon a bag of ice. "Here." He gently placed it against her brow. "Is there anything I can do?"

"Watch your back, brother. Diflyn will be coming for you and he could be anyone. He wants you and X dead."

"I'll be watching. In all aspects." Masakage watched as she finally closed her eyes to rest.

Her powers had always amazed him. While their mother was a sorceress of unparalleled power, Candara made a mockery of her abilities. Even as a child. Headaches had often rendered her unable to function. Her father had beat her unmercifully over them, thinking she used them as a reason to get out of chores.

But he understood. His own powers crushed him, too. But nowhere near as badly as they did her.

He went to the table near the window where he'd placed his ale. Reaching into his travel pouch, he pulled a tisane out and poured it into the cup. Stirring it slowly, he waited for it to dissolve. Then he took it to the bed.

"I have something for the pain." He lifted her head carefully from the pillow.

She scowled at him then glanced down to the cup. "Your potion or mine?"

He laughed at her belligerent tone. "Yours, of course. Mine aren't as effective."

"No, they're not." She took the cup and drank it down, then returned it to his hand. "Thank you."

"Always." He waited for her to return to her spot, then he placed a light kiss on her forehead.

Making sure she was fine, he put the cup back on the table and left the room.

Diflyn.

Out of habit, he reached into his bag and pulled out a coin. Five clubs. Conflict. Fighting.

Candara was right. He was out for their blood.

But there was something more. He felt it in his bones. Something neither he nor Dara saw.

It was coming for them.

This wasn't the time for his powers to be vague. As much as he hated seeing what would come, he hated not knowing even more.

They needed to lay hands on the mer prince as quickly as possible and get this contract broken so that Dash would be able to ratchet up the war with Meara and be done with her.

They all needed to be done with the centaur queen.

Sooner rather than later.

DIFLYN TRANSFORMED INTO HIS "NORMAL" form of a royal

courtier. Garyn thought himself so proper and prim. Bastard had no idea who or what Diflyn really was.

Not some second in command or flunkey.

He would never be subservient to anyone. The blood of dynasties flowed through him.

The only reason he traveled with Garyn was because he needed a flunkey so that he could stay in the shadows. Not out of fear. Caution.

Now, he had a report to make.

Approaching the castle gates as a centaur, he tugged at the lapels of his military coat to straighten it. The one thing about Meara, she couldn't abide anyone who wasn't immaculately dressed.

He inclined his head to the guards as he walked past them and across the drawbridge. He would give the queen credit, even in the light of day, there was order in her capital. No one rushed about. Children didn't play in the streets. Everyone went about their business in somber silence.

Some would find it appalling. He found it refreshing. The queen kept order. Not chaos. That was sorely missing in the other kingdoms he'd visited.

There was nothing like being home.

As he approached the steps to the castle, he was greeted with a full garrison of centaurs.

"What's your business?" a captain asked.

"Here to meet with the queen. I have news for her."

"And you are?"

"Her cousin, Diflyn of Naran."

His name didn't register with the captain, but the dark brown centaur was wise enough to accept it as fact. Shooing the others back, he allowed Diflyn to proceed with the captain at his side.

After all, Meara was nothing if not paranoid.

Which was why he was forced to wait in a gilded hallway outside her throne room while the captain went inside and left him to be watched by the eight guards.

All of them dressed in royal livery.

The bay to his right seemed a bit uneasy while the gray on his left appeared amused.

Diflyn would ask why, but he didn't really want to be friendly with those who ranked below his station.

That being said, he was impatient as minutes ticked by.

At the half hour mark, he was ready to leave. Only the knowledge that by doing so he'd invoke her wrath kept him standing quietly.

Inconsiderate bitch.

She was most likely doing this on purpose. It was what gave her great entertainment. To exercise her power and make others feel their lesser stature.

If only he had the courage to attempt her murder. But he knew he'd never be so bold.

Like everyone else, he feared failure. Because she would exact a brutal retaliation.

When going up against Meara, succeed or die took on a whole new meaning. And to be honest, he admired King Dash for his willingness to confront her.

But he wasn't stupid enough to think for one moment that Dash would be successful. Dash had a code of honor. Meara did not.

And in war, it was the soulless monsters who won. Morality was for nursemaids and farmers. Mercy for the weak.

Meara understood that. Respect was nice, but fear reigned supreme and kept everyone in line.

"Diflyn?"

He looked at the major domo who called his name. "Here." He stepped forward.

A dapple gray, the major domo was well dressed in a dark blue jacket that matched his wary eyes.

Diflyn could only imagine the terrors that equine must have seen in his service to Meara.

Without another word, the major domo led him into the queen's throne room where she rested in sternal recumbency at her desk. Even in that position, she was regal to the core.

Her long black hair was intricately braided around her auspicious gold crown that was laden with rubies and diamonds. She was a beautiful bay with white stocking. To be honest, he'd never seen any female more beautiful.

What a shame beauty of that magnitude was wasted on such a callous bitch.

"Majesty," he said, bowing low before her.

She glanced up from the papers in her hand to sweep a withering stare over him. "Speak and leave."

"I'm your cousin, Majesty. Through your father's sister."

That caught her attention. She set the paper aside and narrowed an angry glare at him. "Am I to be impressed that you learned some genealogy?"

Had she been paying attention, it would have told her he was a shape shifter. But by the expression on her face, he could tell that she thought he meant the king.

Not her true father.

His gaze went to the two guards standing behind her. This wasn't the time to let that out. The one thing he knew about the queen, she didn't like surprises or for anyone to know her secrets.

"Do you have business with the crown or not?" Impatience filled her voice.

"I have your contract, Majesty. The one between you and the High King."

That got her full attention. Rising to her feet, she stood even in height to him. "Where is it?"

"It's with my partner. He's the one who took it from the *apaswere* who was dying."

"I've never heard of such a thing. How is that possible?"

"Magic, Majesty. And magic guards it still."

"How so?"

"My partner has betrayed us. Instead of killing the *apaswere* as you demanded, he's transferred the contract and is keeping it safe."

"And you've done nothing about it?" Each word was spat out in staccato.

"I wasn't sure what to do, Majesty. Do you want me to bring the contract to you?"

She cast a furious glower to her men, then met his gaze. "Walk with me."

Knowing better than to walk at her side as an equal, he let her lead him from her throne room.

Her guards fell in far behind them so that they wouldn't be able to overhear, but close enough they could kill him if he posed a threat. How well trained they were.

Meara went into her stone-walled garden that held statues of those who'd opposed her reign. It was said that she had a sorceress who made sure she had an eternal record of all her defeated enemies.

Truly creepy. And it said it all about how she relished her cruelty.

Diflyn averted his gaze from them, not wanting a reminder of what could easily become of him.

Once they reached the center, Meara stopped to rake a less-than-impressed grimace over his body. "Fetch me that contract. I need it in my possession."

"And what of your assassin?"

"Kill them both. Garyn and Gisela. Bring me their heads along with the contract and you'll be most rewarded."

GISELA WAITED until Xaydin was fully asleep before she carefully pulled herself away from him. She hated leaving his side and would have preferred to stay with him for the rest of her life.

Naked in bed. Just the two of them.

If only they could.

How awful that the world wouldn't leave people in peace. No wonder love was rare. First you had to find the one you wanted to be with, and then you had to win their heart.

That was difficult enough. Then enter a world that was forever trying to destroy the bond between you.

Enemies. Friends. Those who envied the fact you'd found what they could only dream of.

Or those who just liked causing trouble.

The world shouldn't be like this, and yet it was.

Sighing, she dressed in silence as she watched the steady rise and fall of his chest. The fact he would sleep so soundly with her told her just how much he did care.

He didn't have to tell her. No one slept like that with someone they barely knew. Someone they didn't trust. She'd have never done such.

Yet she trusted him.

He trusted her.

I will never betray you.

It was a promise she prayed she could keep. And with that in mind, she headed downstairs to see if any of the others were about.

To her surprise, the inn was empty except for the garrison of soldiers.

Rob sat in the middle of the room with a platter of food. A smile curved his lips as soon as he saw her. He motioned her to take a seat with him.

Normally, she'd have refused, but since she didn't have anything else to occupy herself with, she accepted and did her best to ignore the curious stares from his men.

"Where is everyone?" she asked.

"Being trolls, I excused their normal clientele. They didn't need to be here while my cousin recuperates."

She hadn't thought about that.

"Are you hungry?"

"Famished."

He handed her a small plate. "Please... I have plenty to share."

Grateful for his hospitality, she made a plate while looking about the mostly empty room. "Where's Masakage, Ronan and Candara?"

"Haven't seen them. They went their ways hours ago."

Interesting.

Not knowing what to say to Rob, she ate quickly, then excused herself to return to Xaydin's side. Honestly, she was afraid to leave him alone for long. Since they didn't know where the imposter had gone, he could return and finish Xaydin off.

She still couldn't believe he'd been able to do what he did.

Trust no one.

Even the vigilant could fall.

She'd just sat down on the bed when someone knocked.

"Come in."

Ronan shouldered the door open. But instead of entering, he stood in the doorway. "How's he doing?"

"Resting."

"Good." Ronan hesitated. "May I come in?"

"Sure."

Still, he didn't do anything more than come in a couple of steps and close the door.

A tense silence filled the room as she waited for him to speak.

"Is something on your mind?" she prompted.

"Yes... I've been trying to figure out how you're a shifter if Cratus is your father. We don't just spontaneously come into this world."

He was right. They normally required two shifter parents to have a child with those abilities. It was rare for even a hybrid with only one shifter parent to be able to transform.

For her...

"My mother's father was a shifter."

The surprised expression was quite comical. "Beg pardon?"

"My mother's not the only one who steps outside the bond of marriage. Apparently, her mother had a voracious appetite herself."

"I'm trying to make sense of this."

She couldn't blame him for the struggle. It was a hard one.

"Who was her father?"

"She's never spoken of him. All I know is that she lied to me years ago. I didn't put it together until you mentioned the mark under the tongue."

"How do you mean?"

"My mother has such a mark. She told me that she had it put there so that we could always tell it was her and not an imposter."

Ronan went pale. "She said what?"

"I had no reason not to believe her. But..."

"You think Meara's a shifter?"

She shook her head. "She can't shift. I know that for a fact.

It infuriates her that she's stuck in a centaur's body." And now it made a lot more sense why that angered her. No doubt, she felt robbed by her genetic code.

"But you can."

"Exactly. I always thought it came from my father. But no one ever mentioned Cratus having those powers. If the shifting isn't from him..." She arched a brow.

"It has to come from your mother."

"Exactly," she said with a nod. "But have you ever heard of it skipping a generation?"

Ronan grew silent as he considered that. "No one knows much about us because they're always too busy trying to kill us. And there aren't that many of us left. I know in most mixed marriages, the children can't shift. Not always true...but it's uncommon for it to happen. It was why those marriages were forbidden while Lygaria stood. They were trying to preserve our race because even then our numbers were dwindling."

That made sense to her. But it didn't answer her primary question. "I know my grandmother wasn't a shifter."

"Do you? She could have been one of us who only lived as a centaur."

"You can do that?"

He nodded. "I have a friend who spends her life as a bird. She almost never shifts into any other form. It's not uncommon for shifters to withdraw from the world and live as something else. Again, it's why no one knows how many of us are left. We could be the insect in the room or anything."

"So, there's no way of knowing where this came from?"

"None at all."

Which made her wonder if her mother knew? "Do you think any of my other siblings are able to shift?"

"It's possible."

How would she know?

But if Ferox had been able to shift, he wouldn't have hesitated. His arrogance was such that he would have bragged about it to everyone and used it to intimidate and bully others. Her eldest brother was a royal ass.

As for the others...

They weren't that different and her mother had never treated them the way she did Gisela.

Which meant this was her birth defect alone and why she'd always believed the ability had come from her father. But neither Dash nor his sister, to her knowledge, could shift.

What was her family history? She'd never been that curious before. Now...

She wanted to understand who she was. Where she'd come from. What her powers were.

"When did you first shift?" she asked him.

"I don't remember. But normally our children begin when they're four or five. What about you?"

How could she forget? She'd been five and had sneezed. One moment she'd been a unicorn and in the next, human.

Her governess had screamed and run off to tell her mother—who had told others she was Gisela's guardian.

That had turned out to be a mistake as her mother's first act had been to kill the woman for witnessing her transition. Meara's next move had been to imprison Gisela until she'd learned to control her shifting.

To this day, she was traumatized by her mother's hostility and hatred. She'd always assumed her mother had reacted that way out of fear of others learning Meara had slept with a shifter and birthed his child.

But if this came from her mother's side of the family, it made even more sense. The centaur nobles could use it as a reason to overthrow their queen. While they were currently quelled by Meara's wrath, they might find courage to rise up against her if they realized she wasn't fully one of them.

Centaurs were terribly paranoid and they hated anyone who wasn't a pure blood. It was why Thassalia kept to themselves and rarely allowed others to live there. Or even visit. Why it'd been such a shock when Meara had allowed the hostages of other kingdoms to live in her lands.

And why the centaur nobles had been fine when Meara had used those hostages as public entertainment.

While centaurs didn't like others, they did like watching them suffer.

She'd never understood why. She couldn't stand seeing others in pain. But apparently, she was an anomaly. Other creatures thought pain was highly entertaining. Meara had made a fortune off the bleeding backs of those like Ronan and Xaydin.

And her.

Truthfully, she'd never understood why her mother had allowed her to live. It wasn't like Meara to leave anything undone or any witnesses.

Was it because she was her only daughter? Or because Meara couldn't torture Cratus, so she tortured his child in his place? Nothing in regards to her life made sense. It never had.

"Xaydin told me that you had questions about being a shifter."

She nodded. "Many. I know very little about that part of my abilities." Because her mother had forbidden her from using them unless it was while she was killing someone Meara wanted dead. Then...her mother was more than happy to give her all the leniency she needed.

Just don't fail me. Her mother's mantra.

"How do we spot others of our kind?"

Ronan shrugged. "You really can't. Not until they do something to betray themselves."

"If we take the form of someone else, do we get information about the person we...subsume?"

"No. Those who impersonate usually spend a few days following their target around. Either in the body of something small such as a fly or other insect. Once they believe they can pretend to be their target, they take them over."

That sent a chill over her. So the imposter had been with them, and no one had noticed.

Not even Masakage.

A shiver went down her spine. Did that mean that Diflyn could be with them even now?

"That being said," Ronan continued. "There is a scent that we carry unique to us. In certain forms such as a bloodhound or honeybee, it can be detected. So there are shifters who can and will pursue others of our kind."

"Are those the only two to beware of? Bees and bloodhounds?"

"There are other animals who can smell us out, but they're either cumbersome or disgusting to be, such as a rat. But any canid can detect us. Bloodhounds just have a better sense of smell than their cousins."

Good to know. She'd never thought to track as a dog or wolf. Mostly because she hadn't needed that level of skill to find her targets.

"What are you two scheming about?"

Her heart lightened at the sound of Xaydin's deep, resonant voice. It was good to hear him, however... "Shouldn't you be in bed?"

He scoffed at her chiding tone as he took the chair between them. "Bah. It was cold and lonely."

"I thought you liked being alone," Ronan teased before he took a deep drink of his ale.

"For many things." He motioned the innkeeper who came into the room to fetch him his own tankard.

While they waited, she held hers out for him. "How are you feeling?"

"Much better. Did Candara heal me?"

Ronan nodded. "Although I'm not sure what she did. But she had an awful headache from it."

He grimaced at that, then took a drink from Gisela's tankard. "I hate that I caused that for her. So, where's the bastard who knifed me? Still in the stable?"

Ronan refilled his cup as the innkeeper brought the tankard for Xaydin and then left them. "Aye. Still under guard."

"Good. I want a few words with him."

"I'm thinking there won't be a lot of talking, but rather a lot more satisfaction."

Xaydin clanged his tankard against Ronan's. "You know me too well."

Gisela scoffed. "You don't have to know you that well to know you're prone to violence, even on your best day."

"True." Xaydin sucked his breath in sharply, then rubbed at his side where she knew he'd been stabbed.

That made her heart stop. "Are you all right?"

"I'll live. My attacker won't be so lucky." Those words were cold and emotionless.

Not that she blamed him. She wanted blood from Garyn, too. And it was strange to her to be on this side of the matter. Strange how she'd never considered the family and loved ones of her targets before.

She hadn't cared.

And she now realized how wrong she'd been. Before this assignment, it'd been a job. She was her mother's sword. A mindless animal carrying out her queen's commands.

Now, she regretted every single life she'd taken in the name of a centaur who held no feelings for anyone.

Xaydin wasn't a monster.

She was.

Unlike her, Xaydin had never been an unfeeling weapon.

I don't deserve happiness. She was the same kind of beast Garyn was. Selfish and mindless.

Well, maybe not quite. Maybe that was a little harsh. She had never pretended to be someone's loved one. Never lived among the families of her targets. That was a terrifying level of callousness. To strike while knowing how it would impact those who loved her target.

Could she have done her job then?

No. She wasn't that unfeeling. Not yet at least.

"How many people do you think Garyn has killed?" she asked.

Her question surprised the men who turned to look at her.

"Does it matter?" Ronan asked.

Not really. "I was curious. Did he say how long he'd been serving my mother?"

"No. But to be fair, I didn't ask."

Xaydin poured himself more drink. "What are you thinking, love?"

"Trying to understand my mother. Something I've spent far too many hours attempting in my life."

Ronan sighed. "She's selfish. That breed doesn't think like the rest of us."

That was certainly true. A part of her felt sorry for the fact that her mother couldn't appreciate those around her. Gisela would have loved her mother as a faithful daughter had she ever been allowed to.

It physically hurt her that she'd never been given that chance.

All because her mother was incapable of loving anyone. Of reaching out and caring.

How sad.

Looking at Xaydin, she was grateful that if she'd learned nothing else by being with him, it was that she was capable of caring for someone else. Capable of loving them.

He reached across and lightly squeezed her hand as if he knew her train of thought.

You're not your mother and you never will be. His voice in her head startled her.

He had known her thoughts. Had they been written in her expression or was he that intuitive?

Suddenly, they heard a commotion outside.

With a stern frown, Xaydin slid back and rose before heading out to see what it was. She and Ronan followed hard on his heels.

Once they were outside the inn, she saw Rob's guards rushing about.

"What happened?" Xaydin demanded.

"Prisoner's escaped!"

Rage descended over her as she heard those words. Garyn was gone? "How?"

No one responded. Probably because it was a stupid question that didn't matter. All that was important was the fact that he was gone.

"I should have killed him while I had the chance," she growled out between her clenched teeth. How could she have been so stupid as to take mercy on him?

I should have cut his tongue out!

Ronan rushed ahead, into the stable.

She stayed by Xaydin's side. It was obvious he wanted to run forward, too, but his injuries were still too raw for that degree of mobility.

As they entered the stable, she saw the empty shackles that were still fastened.

"How did he get free?" she asked.

Candara pointed to the cuffs. "Someone removed the ward."

"His accomplice, no doubt." Ronan growled low in his throat. "Want me to hunt them down?"

Xaydin shook his head. "They haven't gone far. I can sense it." He glanced about making her wonder if they hadn't turned into a fly or something smaller.

By the expression on Ronan's face, she could tell the same thought was in his mind as well.

Ronan paused and met Xaydin's eyes. They were talking to each other.

Why don't I have that ability? She hated that she had no idea what they were discussing. Part of her was suspicious and felt left out. Had it been her mother, she would have definitely been on high alert.

With Xaydin...

She trusted him. As miraculous as it was, she knew he wasn't keeping her out because he was plotting against her or doing anything more than trying to protect himself and Ronan. He wasn't vicious or duplicitous.

While Rob and his men continued to search for Garyn and uncover clues, Ronan turned into a bird and flew off.

Xaydin offered her his arm so that he could lead her toward Masakage who'd just entered the stable.

He paused next to his brother, then kept walking. Masakage fell in line behind them.

"What's going on?" she whispered.

Not here. I'll explain in a moment.

Without anything more, he led them back to the inn and didn't speak until after they'd climbed the stairs to his room.

"Secure the room."

Masakage brought out a small wand that elongated into his staff that held the glowing blue ball on top of it. He tapped the bottom against the floor, causing the ball to turn so bright, it was blinding. A soft wave went through the room. One that rippled her hair and clothes before it settled down.

He inclined his head to Xaydin. "We're good. The room's sealed."

"Good. I sent Ronan out to search for the Ningyoan prince while we deal with this."

"Finding Garyn?" she asked.

Xaydin shook his head. "He's dead."

That shocked her. "What?"

"He was on the floor as an upside-down cockroach." Masakage crossed his arms over his chest. "I'm thinking his partner got to him so that we couldn't question him anymore."

Before she could ask why, they heard a scream from down the hall.

Masakage went pale. "Dara's being attacked!"

18

Masakage immediately vanished while Gisela and Xaydin rushed to Candara's room.

When they entered, they found her in the middle of the room with what appeared to be a shield made of light. Gisela had never seen anything like it. Larger than most, it was circular with writing on it she couldn't identify.

An extra-large troll stood in front of her and was doing his best to kill her.

Without thinking, Gisela turned into a troll and rushed the attacker.

Masakage appeared out of thin air and wrapped his arm around Candara's waist and pulled her away while Xaydin created a sword that he threw to Gisela. She caught the weapon, then twirled about with it to confront the troll.

He smiled as soon as he saw her there.

For a second, she thought it might be Garyn even though Xaydin had pronounced him dead. But something in his eyes didn't look quite right. Not that she had time to think about it. All she could do was react as she parried his sword strokes.

She lunged toward him.

As she did, Candara and Masakage hit him with glowing fireballs.

And just as she went for him again, he vanished.

"Are you kidding me!" Furious, she glanced around the ground, hoping to find him there as a roach or some other nasty bug she could stomp into oblivion.

But there was no sign of him.

She toed the straw, wanting to make sure.

Still nothing. Grinding her teeth, she met Xaydin's equally peeved glare. "I understand why you hate shifters." Because she seldom shifted, she expected the same courtesy from others.

Apparently, they were slippery buggers.

Without commenting, Xaydin turned to Candara. "Are you all right?"

Candara nodded. "He made me angry. No harm. But when we catch up to him...he'll wish he'd killed me."

As they left her room to return below, Rob met them in the main part of the inn.

"Forgive me, Cuz. I just received a message from your brother, the king." He handed it over to Xaydin.

His brow turned dark as he scanned it. Whatever news it held, Gisela could tell it wasn't welcomed.

"He's ordering you to find me and bring me in?" Xaydin asked incredulously.

Rob nodded. "Normally, I'd obey. But if anything happens to you, there's no telling what the populace will do. Most of the trolls and ogres I know would rather have you as king. I don't think he realizes what a threat you actually are. And he definitely doesn't realize the revolt that will happen if you're taken into custody."

"I should lead the coup just on principle." Xaydin folded the letter and returned it to Rob. "We'll get going."

"You're still wounded," Rob reminded him.

"I'm healing. The last thing I want is to see you executed for failure to follow orders." Xaydin scratched at his ear. "How much of that do you think is Zagrun and how much is Gregun?"

"Given that my father keeps Zagrun under his fist, I think you know."

Xaydin nodded in agreement. Rob was right. Zagrun would never dare something like this. Rob's father thought his position as advisor kept him from being targeted. But a shadow-king was still a monarch.

And it was obvious that he wanted Xaydin killed before he died.

Poor Rob to be caught in the middle of this fight.

"I never saw you."

Xaydin grinned at Rob's stern tone. "Understood. We'll be on our way in a few minutes."

There was a shadow in Rob's eyes. A suspicious troll might think it had to do with treachery and in Rob's case, it could be true. But for the moment, he decided to trust him.

He held his arm out toward his cousin.

Rob didn't hesitate to take it and shake. "Ride with the gods. I'll try and keep the others off your tail."

Because if a coup happened, Rob and his family could easily lose their lives too.

A reckoning would remove Xaydin's brother from the throne, and given Gregun's part in the death of Xaydin's father, he'd be the second troll they'd hang for treason. Then they'd go after all of Gregun's kin.

Gregun knew that and so did Rob. He would respect his cousin's desire to keep his father from losing his life, and protect his own family.

Would have been nice had Rob helped Xaydin's father keep his, but he wouldn't hold that against his cousin. Rob had been young back then. No doubt terrified of Gregun. After all, if he'd kill his brother, he was just as likely to kill his younger son.

Xaydin didn't envy Rob his position. At least he'd never doubted his father's loyalty or love.

He couldn't imagine being terrified that his father might kill him.

As bad as his mother was, she would never stoop that low.

Without another word, Xaydin led Gisela and the others back upstairs.

They had barely reached the steps when Candara stopped walking. Cocking her head, she appeared to be listening. Xaydin knew her expression. She was having a vision about something.

"What's going on?" he asked Masakage.

Masakage didn't answer. Instead, he swapped a scowl with their sister. "What are they saying?"

"Your enemies have changed." Candara turned a slow circle as if she were searching for something. She looked at Xaydin. "We need to go. Now!"

No one questioned her order. They quickly gathered their things and headed for the stable.

Gisela had tried to carry Xaydin's saddlebags, but he wouldn't allow it as he draped them over his shoulder. "Your pride is going to get the better of you."

"So be it. My father would come back from the grave if I betrayed the ethics he taught me." And with that, he took hers as well.

"I can do for myself."

He tsked at her. "This isn't because I think you're weaker or that you lack the ability to defend yourself. It's courtesy, princess. Plain and simple. Done because I care about you and respect you, not because I'm trying to belittle you."

Those words made her feel awful that she'd misjudged him. "I'm sorry, X. I'm not used to having anyone look after me."

"I know." He put his arm around her and gave a light squeeze. "You're not alone now, Gisela. Let someone fight beside you."

"I'm trying."

Xaydin leaned down to kiss the top of her head before he released her. He more than understood and wasn't offended by the fact that she had a hard time accepting his help. It was just as difficult for him to do the same. Too many years of being alone had a way of doing that.

Mistrust. Anger. Those were mother's milk to him. Which allowed him to understand why she could be equally as prickly. With anyone else, he'd be angry.

With her...

He was charmed.

There's something profoundly wrong with me.

He'd never argue that. It was something all the Outlaws had notated long ago.

Once they were in the stables, he handed Gisela her saddle-bags from his shoulder while he saddled his horse.

Or at least tried to.

Masakage used his powers to put the saddles and their saddlebags on for them.

"Show off," Xaydin chided.

He just smiled. "You'd do it if you weren't so used to hiding your powers."

Xaydin would have argued had it not been true. But he accepted the fact that when it came to those powers, he just didn't think to use them.

Candara shook her head at the two of them as she mounted and took her reins. Then she glanced over to Gisela. "You poor thing to be forced to travel alone with them."

Gisela swung herself up into the saddle, then situated herself. "They weren't so bad."

"Still, my apologies that they weren't fully home trained. We did try. Sadly, it didn't take."

"Should we be offended?" Masakage asked Xaydin.

"Probably." He swung himself onto the back of his horse. "You more so than me."

"How do you figure?"

"I enjoy being a ruffian. You like prancing around a lot more."

Masakage rolled his eyes. "Be glad you're wounded."

"Trust me, I am. I'll happily be wounded so long as someone kisses my boo boos." And with that, he kicked his horse forward.

Shocked, Gisela felt her jaw go slack. And by Masakage's expression, she could tell he was equally as surprised.

Heat flooded her cheeks before she averted her gaze and followed after Xaydin. She rode up to his side and passed him an irritated glare.

"I can't believe you just said that."

His smile was unrepentant. "If it makes you feel better, neither can they."

She intensified her glare. Not that it did any good. They both knew she was more mortified than angry. On the one hand, she should be thrilled that he was willing to make their relationship known. It meant that she was more to him than a simple one-time thing.

But on the other hand, she wasn't used to being part of a couple. Part of a team. The attention made her extremely uncomfortable.

She told herself that she didn't care what they thought of her. She'd never cared about that in her life. But they were Xaydin's family. It made them very different.

What if they hate me?

She'd been ordered to kill Xaydin. Why would they like her?

Candara rode up beside her and reached out to touch her arm. "Don't fret, Gisela. We're glad to see Xaydin happy. How something begins is nowhere near as important as how it ends."

She knew his sister meant to comfort her with those words, but they had the opposite effect.

Nothing ever ended well. That was the stuff of nightmares.

And how this would end, she had no idea. She wasn't stupid enough to think for one moment that they could be together. He was a tracker who hunted and killed *apaswere*. She was an assassin for a queen who wanted him and all his friends dead.

No, there was no future here.

But the thought of returning home and resuming her old life was abhorrent to her.

Do I have the courage to walk away?

Xaydin had been right. She didn't have to go home. There was nothing tying her there except a misplaced sense of obligation. She definitely owed her mother nothing.

Not even love.

But leaving behind everything wasn't easy, either. There was a lot to be said for familiarity. Even when it was bad. Better the devil she knew than one who could be worse.

What if there were no devils at all?

That seemed impossible. No life or situation was ever perfect. She'd be trading one set of problems for another.

The only question was if they'd be better.

Or worse.

While better was the fluff of her dreams, the worse was what terrified her. As bad as her mother was, she knew there were even greater monsters out there.

I can't let go. And that was her fault. She'd never have the courage to leave. Her mother would always anchor her to the hell that was her life.

Because at the end of the day, she knew that while Xaydin

may care about her now, it wouldn't last. She'd be on her own, and when that time came, she'd rather be on her own in her own kingdom than make an enemy of her mother who would banish her forever.

As wonderful as Xaydin appeared at present, he wasn't worth everything she knew and what little she had.

RONAN PAUSED as he neared the Vaskalian border with Tenmaru. Even though he was disguised as a peregrine falcon, he knew better than to cross into their kingdom. While Tenmaruns were exceptionally polite and had rigid rules regarding hospitality, they hated shifters as much as other kingdoms.

Perhaps more.

And just because he was friends with the Tenmarun princes, it wouldn't guarantee his safety if he were caught by certain oni or yokai who didn't follow etiquette. Rather, they ripped the wings off creatures such as he.

So he glided away from the current that was carrying above the treetops, down toward the docks that were just south of Tenmaru.

Gaharah was a bustling Vaskalian port. From here, it was easy to catch a boat to Cosaria, Umara or Oath Island. Each was within two days' reach from here.

Or for those with more courage, they could sail to any of the other kingdoms.

It was what made this port city one of the most important territories in all the kingdoms. News, supplies and goods from all over were brought to this port.

So it was here he'd ask after a certain mer prince who had an unorthodox relationship with a land-based creature.

He circled over the ships, then felt his heart lighten as he saw a familiar vessel. A small sloop flying Marauder colors.

What luck!

Ronan made straight for it.

For the most part, the boat was devoid of crew. So much so that he almost flew away.

But a flash of gold caught his eye.

Sitting with her back propped against the mast was the one he'd hoped to see when he spotted this vessel.

Dressed in brown leather and a black pirate hat, she was carefully peeling an apple with a knife far too large for the task.

Leave it to Mischief. She never did anything the easy way, hence her name.

Ronan flew to the deck and landed just a few inches from her booted foot.

She stared at him curiously, then shook her head. "Better be good news, Ronan. I've no use for you otherwise."

Same old Mischief. And she was a woman of great beauty. Dark skin that she painted with a large gold star on her forehead. Gold lines ran down from her dark eyes. He'd never understood why she painted her face like that. She was exquisite without it. And maybe that was why. The paint added roughness to her delicate features so that others wouldn't be numbed by her beauty.

Whatever the reason, he'd always found her fascinating.

She held an apple slice out toward him. "Polly want an apple?"

Laughing, he transformed into his human body, then used his powers to clothe himself. "You never change."

"I do not." She gave him a pointed stare, letting him know

how she felt about his shifter skills. "Are you here to recruit me for another Dash mission?"

"Not this time. I'm more curious about what you've heard on your travels these last few weeks."

"That is a long and mighty list. Care to narrow it down?"

"About a certain Ningyoan prince who's gone missing."

She paused, then put an apple slice in her mouth.

He knew that look. She was hiding information. "You've heard something. What is it?"

She sliced another piece while she slowly chewed the one in her mouth.

Aye, she was doing this to be annoying. He knew her tricks well and they always irritated him.

He reached down and took the new slice from her grasp before she could shove it into her mouth to keep from speaking. "What do you know?" he repeated before he ate the slice.

"Why are you asking?"

"Why are you being evasive?" Even for her, this was a new level.

Mischief shrugged. "I may or may not know much depending on your reasons for asking."

"It's for Xaydin. Mardyth wants his son returned. Enough so that he was willing to hold Masakage prisoner."

That caused her eyes to flare. "The king took Masakage prisoner?"

"Never said he was bright. Only desperate to get his son back. What do you know?"

"That the king might not get his wish in this. Did he tell you who the prince was in love with?"

"A land dweller."

She shook her head and laughed.

"What do you know that I don't?"

"He's in love with an Umaran prince."

That was the last thing he expected out of her mouth. "Pardon?"

"You heard me." She ate another apple slice.

Ronan sank to his knees as he digested that latest bit. There was so much to that, that he didn't know where to start.

"How did they meet?" he asked her.

She shrugged. "But if it makes it any better, the Umaran queen is offering quite a bounty on their heads, herself. She's no happier about the union than Mardyth is."

Especially since her son had been engaged to a princess. He imagined all of them were furious.

"We're talking Prince Evar, right?"

She nodded. "Marstyn and Evar. They've made quite the scandal everywhere."

Aye, they had. Especially given the hatred between their kingdoms. The merfolk hated nereids almost as much as the centaurs hated unicorns.

"Wow." He shook his head. "Where did you hear this?"

She gestured toward the dock. "Everyone's talking about it. How have you not heard it?"

"I guess news doesn't make it to my rock."

"Apparently not." She wiped her knife off on her breeches before she returned it to the sheath at her waist. "Are you really going to be so heartless as to break up a love match?"

He leaned back on his arms. "I would never be so cruel. Xaydin..."

"Needs to leave them alone and find his own happiness."

If only she knew how close to the truth she was.

Ronan touched the tip of his boot against hers. "How have you been, Missy?"

A hooded darkness descended over her eyes, making him ache for her. "Been a little rough. My father died and no one bothered to tell me."

He winced at the news. She'd always had a...capricious relationship with her father. Much like his own. It was hard to explain to those who didn't understand. The love you could have for someone who betrayed you. It was complicated always, but when it was a parent...

Hard to cut those ties.

"Anything I can do to help?" He didn't really expect an answer from her. She never needed anything from anyone.

So when she slid across the deck to embrace him, he was stunned. Closing his eyes, he held her against his chest and savored this moment. Mostly because he doubted it would ever come again.

I love you. Those words hung on the edge of his lips because he knew better than to say them out loud.

Mischief believed she was unlovable. That no one would ever be able to care about her. But the truth was, he'd been in love with her since they were kids.

For him, there had never been anyone else.

There never would.

If only she felt the same. But he knew better. They were friends. Nothing more.

It was all they'd ever be.

Gisela had just finished rinsing her hair when the door behind her opened. Without looking, she knew it was Xaydin. She could feel his presence like a physical touch.

They were heading to some northern dock city that she'd never heard of before. But she, Candara and Masakage had all agreed that he didn't need to push himself. Mostly because his wounds were taking longer to heal than they should given

Candara's magic. Apparently, the blade Garyn had used to harm him had also been charmed.

Magic healing magic always took longer than normal. It was also why they didn't dare portal. Candara wasn't sure if the magic still in his body would harm him or how it would react to going through a portal.

So against his protests, they'd stopped at an inn that was about a day's ride from the docks.

Irritated at them for "bullying" him, Xaydin had gone off to run errands while she'd stayed behind to bathe. His pouting demeanor had been strangely adorable to her.

Even now, he appeared peeved.

"Did you have a nice time?" she asked.

He answered her question with one of his own. "Are you trying to anger me?"

"Never."

Xaydin wanted to be mad at her. At all of them. They'd made him feel like a child as they'd gathered forces to make him stop when he wanted to get to the docks as soon as possible. He was even willing to risk a portal.

But they had insisted.

And it was hard to stay angry while she was dressed in a chemise that showed off every curve of her body.

Worse? Her hardened nipples stood out from the thin linen, begging him to taste them. She was irresistible.

And if he had to rest...then he had no intention of resting alone.

GISELA WATCHED as Xaydin took a commanding step forward and then faltered.

What the devil?

His gaze dipped to her lips and in that moment, she knew what he was after.

It was the only thing that ever made him hesitant. Her giant troll was fierce and steadfast, until it came to her. He was still bashful about them. How she loved that about him.

Closing the distance between them, she tilted her chin up and smiled. "Something you need, my lord?"

His eyes darkened as he pulled her against him and claimed her lips.

Gisela moaned at the strength of Xaydin's kiss. And to think she'd actually feared for him earlier this very day. But there was far too much power in that kiss for him to be seriously injured.

Her brave troll was going to be fine.

Without breaking their kiss, he backed her toward the bed then sat down, pulling her into his lap.

She jerked away from their kiss instantly. "Careful, X. You'll hurt yourself."

"I don't care," he breathed, pulling her lips back to his so that he could ravage her senses.

Gisela's heart leapt at his words and at the feel of his tongue sweeping against hers. The warm manly scent of him filled her head as she brushed her hands over his steely biceps that flexed and beckoned her with his power.

What was it about this troll that made her feel like this? Shivery hot and needful. Ever longing to be close to him when she knew deep in her heart that he posed the biggest danger to her life. To what she was supposed to do for her mother.

But she was lost now. Lost to the heat of his touch as she pulled his leather jerkin off before he removed his tunic.

She ran her hand over the muscles of his chest, feeling the way his flesh rippled and flexed under her palm. And she wanted more.

Leaning him back, she quickly removed his boots and pants, then returned to his lips.

Xaydin took her hand into his and led it down the length of his body until she touched his rigid shaft.

"Every time I'm near you, Gisela, all I can think about is being inside you again," he breathed raggedly in her ear. "Of you touching me until I'm drunk from it."

Gisela savored the sound of his voice in her ear and the feel of him in her hand. She ran her fingers to the tip of him where he was already wet. A shiver went through him that she felt with the whole of her body.

She found it hard to believe that this giant troll who could kill with a single blow could be so tender with her. That he could hold her like this and make her entire body burn for him.

Yet he did. He made her breathless and weak. And at the same time, he made her feel as if she could fly. No one had ever made her feel the things he did.

"I'm so glad you weren't killed, X."

"Are you?"

She nodded as she stared into those feral dark eyes. "Had you not survived, I would have used one of Candara's potions to bring Garyn back to life so that I could club him for eternity."

That brought an adorable smile to his lips before he nibbled her chin with his teeth as he slid his hands down her back to her hips.

Gisela sucked her breath in sharply as he lifted the hem of her chemise and bared her bottom to his questing hands. She growled deep in her throat as his hand found the part of her that throbbed for him.

Xaydin clenched his teeth at her sweet moisture coating his fingers. How he wished he could push her away...

But he couldn't resist her. He was addicted in a way he'd never imagined, and he needed to be inside her right now.

More than that, he had to have her, and he would kill anyone who tried to interrupt them.

She was the air he breathed.

Ignoring the pain of his wounds, he pulled her gently onto his lap and slid himself deep inside her waiting warmth. He closed his eyes and just savored the feeling of her surrounding him.

He could stay inside this woman forever. There was some foreign, inner calm he felt whenever she was near him. It was as if he could find no fault with the world.

No fault with himself.

It was a tranquility he'd never imagined could exist. And all from an assassin. It made no sense whatsoever, but then feelings seldom did.

Gisela gasped at the fullness of Xaydin inside her body. What she felt for him terrified her. What they were doing was madness given who and what they were.

She was an assassin. He was a bounty hunter.

And yet she was helpless against her body's desire for him. Her heart's desire to be near him. To soothe this man whose eyes were always tormented, like a stormy sea forever bereft of sunshine.

He guided her with his hands, showing her how to make love to him from above. She watched his face closely and wondered if her own features mirrored the pleasure he gave her.

His breathing was rapid as he bit his lip and growled while his hands urged her to move faster.

"That's it, love," he whispered as she found a rhythm that pleased them both.

Xaydin cupped her face in his hands while he let her thrust for both of them. Let her sate the longing he had to just stare at her beautiful body until he was drunk from it.

However, the last thing he wanted was for her to be embarrassed should someone interrupt them.

Closing his eyes, he shielded the room, hoping Candara wouldn't be rude enough to break his wards and enter. Masakage would know better.

His sister...

Gisela turned her face in his hands and kissed the inside of his wrist. His heart quickened at the gesture.

She was marvelous. Truly, an unexpected treasure.

He felt her body tightening against his shaft as she quickened her strokes. A smile played at the edges of his mouth as she came for him.

It was the most beautiful sight he'd ever seen. Her cries of pleasure filled his ears and warmed him through and through.

Pulling her down to his lips, he swallowed those cries before anyone else heard them and lifted his hips, driving himself even deeper into her body.

He could feel her heart pounding against his chest as he held her and thrust faster until he found his own release while she kissed him deeply and fully.

Hissing in pleasure, he savored the sensation of her wet heat until his body was completely drained and sated. There was nothing in all the kingdoms like his precious assassin.

No one could ever compare to her. Nor could they give him a more wonderful moment.

Gisela rested herself on her elbows so that she could stare down at Xaydin. She kissed her way along the edge of his whiskered jaw and just inhaled the warm, masculine scent of him.

She quickly checked the bandages over his stab wounds to make sure he hadn't started bleeding again. The last thing she wanted was to cause him any more pain. "Did I hurt you?"

"No, love. It'd take a lot more than your mere weight to harm me."

Good. Gisela lay herself over his chest and pressed her cheek to his heart that pounded and soothed her while he toyed with her hair that was fanned out over him. While he did that, he moved his other hand so that he could stroke her cheek.

"You are so soft."

She placed a kiss over his heart, then moved so that she could look up at him. "You're not, my monster troll."

He smiled down at her, his eyes hot and searing. "Tell me why I can't resist you, Gisela. Why I desire you when all my reason tells me I shouldn't?"

"If I knew the answer to that, X, then I'd understand why I'm here with you when I shouldn't be." Biting her lip, she pulled back from him. "What are we doing, Xaydin? Seriously?"

"I think we're falling in love."

Silence hung between the two of them as those words echoed in the quiet stillness.

He was right. Gisela knew the truth of it. She felt it with every part of her, and it made her want to run away in terror.

A tic started in his cheek as he continued to brush his fingers against her cheek. He let out a long, tired sigh. "The worst part is I can't afford to love you."

"I know. And I don't want to keep you away from your oath to hunt down the *apaswere*. I would never take you from your vengeance."

He winced at her words. "You're right. I can never lay aside my sword. Not so long as children are out there being hurt because they've lost the parents who love and protect them. And it's not just the *apaswere* who harm them. It's why my sword is pledged to Dash and to his war against your mother. I've no choice other than to do everything I can to help those who are targeted by his enemies."

"You can't save the world, X."

"If I save one person, then I've saved *their* world and the worlds of those who love and depend on them. Homes aren't made up of one single slab. They're the product of thousands of stones. If one storm damages a single one, then the entire house is compromised, if not destroyed. I might not save them all, but I have to save as many as I can."

And that was what she loved most about him. He thought of others and took nothing for himself. Just like what he'd told the *apaswere* when they were making their contract. He wanted nothing.

"I would never take you from your fight, X."

Xaydin kissed her lips, then withdrew from inside her. He moved to the side so that she lay beside him. He cuddled her tenderly as he covered them with the blanket.

"I wish I could give you what you want, Gisela. But I can't let Meara have an advantage over Dash. Not when so many lives would be destroyed."

Gisela glanced down to the nastiest wound in his side. She ached for him. Just as she ached for herself. "So what are we to do?"

"I don't know. Just savor the time we have and let it get us through the rest of our lives as sweet memories of what could have been had we been born someone else."

Tears welled in her eyes as she noted the deadness of his own. The last thing she wanted was to not see him.

Heartbroken, she swallowed hard against the sudden lump in her throat. If she had a choice, he would be it.

But that was a whimsical dream and she knew it. Prince Xaydin of Vaskalia was beyond the reach of anyone. So long as his need to kill his enemies remained, he'd never settle down.

"Very well." Gisela forced herself to get up and retrieve her clothes. If they couldn't be together, then there was no need in her torturing either one of them further.

It was best to leave now while she could almost bear the thought.

Although to be honest, the pain in her chest wasn't really bearable. It hurt and it cut. She didn't want to leave him, but just as he had said, she understood why it was necessary.

She only hoped the agony inside her ebbed eventually. Perhaps she might even one day find a way to smile again.

But some things weren't meant to be, and their relationship was one of them.

Leaning over the bed, she kissed his cheek and dressed.

Xaydin braced himself for the sudden coldness of his body as she withdrew from him. It was for the best, and yet his soul itself cried out for him to hold her close.

To keep her from walking out that door.

But it was over and he knew it.

With that thought slashing through him, he did the hardest thing he'd ever done in his life. He watched as she made her way out of the room.

Xaydin pressed his hand to his eyes and cursed beneath his breath. How had this happened? How had he allowed an enemy's assassin to slide her way into his well-guarded heart?

And yet she wasn't his enemy. Not like her mother. If she were, she'd have never conquered him so skillfully. She was merely a woman of great convictions. Bold, intelligent and determined. All traits he admired.

Now she was gone.

Pain the likes of which he'd never known consumed his heart.

"You have to be the greatest fool in all Thirteen Kingdoms." Candara's voice filled his ears as he realized when he dropped the ward to let Gisela leave, she must have entered his room. "Then again, I take it back. You're the greatest fool ever born."

Without uncovering his eyes, he growled at her. "Leave me alone, Dara. I've no patience for you at present."

"Good, because I don't have any for you, either. I've never suffered fools and I have no intention of starting now."

To his complete astonishment, she came over and slapped him across his uninjured ribs.

Xaydin grimaced at the unexpected pain and moved his arm so that he could glare up at her. "What are you doing?"

"Beating you for your idiocy. Be grateful you're injured. It's the only thing that's keeping me from doing more damage."

He snorted dismissively at her threat. "It'd take a lot more than your hits to harm me. Or even your potions."

"I don't know if I'd take that bet. Not with the anger burning in my soul at the moment. How could you let Gisela leave you?"

His gut tightened at the thought, even though his head understood the why. "It's for the best."

She slapped his side again.

"Have you gone mad?"

"I was born mad, but in the past, you always seemed to have more sense. You love that woman. So why are you pushing her away?"

"What do you know of it?"

She stood with her hands on her hips and her face showing every bit of her ire at him. "We're not stupid or blind. All of us know how you feel about her. It's no great secret, given the light that comes into your eyes at the mere mention of Gisela's name. Never mind the way you watch her like a hungry wolf whenever she draws near you."

"Centaur shit."

She rolled her eyes at him, then said something under her breath that he couldn't quite make out.

"Did you just call me an ogre?"

"I called you an ogre-headed troll."

"Why?"

She moved to slap him again, but this time he grabbed her hand before she made contact.

Instead, she kicked her foot against the bed and used her powers to assault him.

"Ow!" he snapped as something sharp struck his ass.

"You're my brother, Xaydin, and I love you, but I swear there are times when I could strangle the very life out of you." Candara turned away and headed for the door.

She paused and looked back at him. "Tell me something, Xaydin. When you're too old to carry your sword and battle for the weak, who will sit in the hall beside you to keep you company?"

He looked away at that. Honestly, he preferred not to think about his future. If he were lucky, he wouldn't have to deal with it. Some *apaswere* would make sure he died long before he grew old.

At least that was his plan.

However, his sister was in no mood to give him any sort of quarter from those thoughts. "You can't stop time from moving forward, nor can you defeat every demon who walks these kingdoms. All your life, you've been running from the ghost of your childhood, terrified of becoming as callous as our mother. But tell me honestly, X, what would have happened had our mother loved your father the way he loved her? Imagine for one moment, a marriage where two people live and die for each other. Both of them hopelessly in love for the whole of their lives."

How easy she made it sound. "Do you think it possible?"

"Masakage has told me that King Dash lives in utter happiness with his dragon queen. You've seen that yourself."

She was right about that. The two of them were deliriously happy.

But they were still newly married. What they had might last forever and it could end tomorrow.

"You make it sound so simple, Dara. But her mother would never allow her a life with me. She'd sic her dogs on us for eternity."

"When has being pursued ever scared the great Prince Xaydin?"

She had a point. That was his happy place.

"Besides," she continued. "Nothing is ever simple. Nor is anything worth having, unless you have to strive for it. But don't strive too long, Xaydin, or you may very well find yourself the loser in this. Have you given any thought as to how you'll feel when you see the woman you love off with some other man?"

That was just plain mean. And those words created an image in his mind so disturbing that he could barely draw breath.

No, he'd never once thought of that.

"Gisela would never be with another!" he called out after Candara. His injuries protested his raised voice by throbbing instantly.

Smirking, his sister stuck her head through the door so that she looked like some sick trophy. "Keep telling yourself that, brother, and on the day of her wedding, I'll make sure to find you and comfort you."

In that moment, he hated his sister for what she was doing. The last thing he needed to hear was the truth.

How dare she!

Throwing his pillow at her head, he then turned to his side and did his best to push her words out of his mind.

Gisela would never betray him like that and choose another man. Her freedom was too precious to her.

What if she loves another? Some centaur who might catch her eye...

That thought hovered in his mind like a demon plague. It could happen. Some other man could woo her. One who would stay by her side and give her his children.

The thought tore through him.

Set her free.

Xaydin cursed. It was what he should do. Look now how distracted he was and they barely knew one another. Imagine twenty years from now...

I would still love her.

He knew that. No matter what happened, she would always hold his heart.

Damn me.

She was his life and his soul.

And there could never be a future for them.

19

I hate my life. While that had been a true statement as far back as she could remember, it'd never been more true than now.

Gisela sat on a small bench, sharpening her sword in the stable.

Alone.

Was this really her future? Cuddling Brant's cold steel?

Her mother had offered her freedom for the contract demon. Now that she'd actually experienced freedom, Gisela better understood what she'd bartered for.

It was nothing like she'd imagined. Being surrounded by strangers in a strange land where she didn't know customs, laws or idioms. Because in her heart, she knew she didn't fit in with the other centaurs, and her mother would never allow her to stay in Thassalia. Gisela posed too great a threat for that. If she wasn't under her mother's thumb, her mother would have her killed.

She'd been in the inn earlier, watching the easy way Candara and Masakage had bantered.

That was what she wanted.

Friendship.

Ironically, she felt that whenever she was with Xaydin. "You just don't talk enough, Brant," she whispered to her sword. "I appreciate what a good listener you are, but our conversations are always one sided."

And rather boring.

Funny how that had been enough before this journey started.

Not anymore.

Sighing, she sheathed her sword and propped it up against the stall. She tucked her stone and cloth into her saddlebags and got up to store them on the door of the stall where her horse was eating hay.

She leaned against the stall to watch the equine. Because she was part centaur and unicorn, she'd never really paid much attention to horses before. Being equine herself, she'd never ridden a horse before this. For that matter, horses were rare in her mother's kingdom. They weren't needed.

But they were beautiful animals. Graceful.

Old legends claimed that centaurs had been created when an ancient sorceress had fallen in love with her stallion. She'd craved him so much that she'd transformed herself into a half-human, half-horse so that she could be with him.

Queen Taranilla. The first centaur.

It was said that all their people came from her and her stallion.

Gisela had never really paid attention to the old tale. It'd been something troubadours sang about and poets wrote odes to.

Now though...

She understood the queen. That hunger to be with what she loved. Had the queen ever been ridiculed for those desires? What had it cost her to become a centaur?

What would it cost me to leave it?

She'd lived as a human most of her life.

Sighing, she reached out to touch the horse's forehead. The coarse hair felt so strange and yet she liked feeling it. "You're a good boy, aren't you?"

The horse nickered in response.

Just as the horse raised its head to look at her, something sharp struck her across the back of her head. Nauseated, she tried to focus, but everything went dark.

"Gisela?" Xaydin entered the stable where he'd been told she was resting.

He saw their horses, along with the others who were being kept here. But there was no sign of her.

Not until he saw her sword propped against a beam.

"Gisela!" Panic gripped him. She'd have never left her sword behind. Not even to go to the outhouse.

Something wasn't right.

"Candara!" he called.

She appeared instantly. "You don't have to shout."

He picked up Gisela's sword and held it out to her. "What's happened? Gisela isn't here, and I know she didn't just wander off without her weapon."

Candara held her hands out around her. Her eyes turned stark white as she cocked her head to listen to the sounds of the universe and her guides.

Xaydin didn't move as he waited for her to do whatever it was she did whenever she searched for answers.

Her hands made graceful circles around her. In front and to the side. It was a beautiful dance in a very macabre way. He'd never understood why she made those gestures and whenever he asked her about them, she couldn't remember doing it.

Something takes me over and shows me what I'm seeking.

That was why he remained silent, waiting for her to do whatever it was she did.

"She wasn't alone." Her voice was barely more than a whisper. "Here, horsey. Let me scratch your nose." She turned around and scowled. "I don't want to lose him. Why can't we be together? I can't live without him."

Candara's white eyes met his. He knew she wasn't seeing him. Yet she was focused on his face with a stern expression. "He will leave. Everyone leaves. I don't want to be there when he learns to hate me. Ow!" She staggered forward, holding the back of her head in both hands until she sank to her knees on the ground and held her hand up. "Stop!" Then she fell forward, across the hay-lined floor.

Uncertain, Xaydin stood back, even though he wanted to help his sister.

Finally, she fell out of her trance and pushed herself up from the floor.

"Diflyn. He means to use her to draw you out."

Rage suffused his body so swiftly and bitterly that he threw his head back and roared.

"Where is he?" he demanded.

She shook her head. "We'll need a potion for that. I didn't see where they went."

"If he lays one hand on her..."

"He intends to kill you both."

Of course he did. "How did he capture her?" He couldn't imagine Gisela leaving herself open to attack.

"She was petting her horse when he rose up behind her with no warning. The coward bashed her in the head and took her."

And before he could say anything else, Masakage came rushing into the stable. "What's happened?"

"Diflyn took Gisela," Xaydin growled between clenched teeth.

His eyes flared at those words. "Then we will get her back."

Xaydin clapped his brother on the back. "Yes, we will. And I will bathe in his blood."

GISELA CAME AWAKE to an awful pain in her skull. It throbbed, sending so much agony that she could barely open her eyes. Worse, it made her sick to her stomach.

And as she came fully alert, she realized her hands and feet were tied.

Diflyn. She remembered him now. The quick glimpse of him right before she'd blacked out.

Bastard! She wanted his head for having humiliated her this way. How dare he sneak up when she wasn't looking!

He sat a few feet away from her, fire-watching. Scrying. Something her mother's soothsayer used to do.

Before her mother skewered the seer for having a vision that displeased the queen.

Personally, she'd never been able to see anything in the fire more than dancing flames, which made her wonder if they really saw anything.

Or if they simply made it up.

Obviously, Diflyn thought he could conjure the future. He stared as if he saw actors on a stage. And while he was distracted, she lifted her leg toward her hand. If she could just get to the dagger she had hidden there, she'd be able to free herself.

Don't breathe. If she made a single sound, he'd know. She had to move slowly, cautiously.

And get that damn knife...

It was so close. The tips of her fingers brushed it, but she couldn't quite get a grasp on the hilt.

Biting her lip, she had to force herself not to grunt or growl in frustration.

You can do it. Patience.

Fuck patience. She'd rather have reach.

Diflyn straightened as if he heard something.

Catching her breath, she lowered her leg and put her head back on the ground as silently as she could manage.

He snapped around to look at her.

Gisela feigned sleep.

Rising slowly, he approached her while she watched him from her barely opened eyes.

He squatted by her side, then put his hand by her nose and mouth.

She leveled her breathing in a slow and steady rhythm as if she were asleep. Her heart pounded as he remained by her side.

After what seemed to be forever, he rose and returned to his fire.

Only then did she dare let out a long breath to steady her nerves. She waited several minutes for him to become absorbed by the flames again before she returned to attempting to get her knife.

Just as she was certain it was a lost cause, she slid it from its sheath.

Victory!

It took everything she had not to shout in happiness as she quickly cut through the rope binding her hands. Watching Diflyn closely, she rolled silently and cut the bindings at her ankles.

She crouched low to the ground, keeping her knife in her fist.

Do I shift?

To do so would cost her the knife as she'd have no way to wield it. But to stay human...

It'd be harder to escape. Damn it.

Fine, I don't need a weapon.

Aggravated by the choice, she turned herself into a small robin. She hopped away from the camp, toward the brush on her left. Once she was clear, she turned herself into a falcon and took flight.

She'd barely made the tree line before Diflyn realized she was gone. Concealing herself in the leaves, she gave him time to scream and curse.

He looked up and right past her.

Thank the gods.

She settled on a branch and let out a relieved breath, then took a few minutes to try to get her bearings. Where was she?

Nothing looked familiar.

Surely, they couldn't have gone far. He had a horse, but it wasn't that much later than when she'd entered the stable. Maybe two, three hours most, given the position of the sun. It'd be dark soon.

Then she'd never be able to find her way back.

Suddenly, a blast landed on the limb above her. She looked down to see Diflyn staring up where she was concealed.

Was that a lucky shot or did he have a potion of some kind that helped him locate her?

Turning into a moth, she flittered away, hoping there was no way for him to find her in this form.

I have to go somewhere.

The sea wasn't that far away, especially not for a falcon.

Changing into a peregrine, she dipped and flew as fast as she could for the water.

To her shock, another peregrine headed toward her.

Diflyn. She knew it.

Furious, she went as fast as she could while trying to find a place to hide and escape him.

He was a crafty bastard to be so close to her now. Worse? He was gaining.

Did he know how to fight in this form?

She did not. For that matter, she wasn't used to traveling as a bird. She'd only used this form when she had to in order to spy or escape.

I hate heights!

And she did. Her heart pounded furiously. This was a last resort, and she wanted to be anywhere but here in the sky.

This or death.

Because she had a bad feeling that if he caught her, she wouldn't survive it.

I will not be broken by the likes of him.

Or captured, either. He was a coward who attacked from the rear when others were distracted. She had no respect for such a beast. There was no honor or decency in him.

She dove into an air current and used it to increase her speed. As she did so, Gisela saw a number of ships below. They were docked in a harbor.

If she could just make it to those, she'd have a chance of getting rid of her nuisance.

A screech sounded right behind her. He was almost on top of her now.

That left her one choice.

She turned into a squirrel and fell quickly toward the sea. Her descent was terrifying.

But what choice did she have?

Diflyn flew on as she went down. After a few seconds, she transformed again into a small fairy. At least like this, she could fight.

While fairies couldn't fly as high as a bird, nor anywhere near as fast as a falcon, they were warriors, too.

Fiercely so.

But the one thing she didn't think about as she landed on board a ship...

How many enemies the fairies had. Enemies who quickly surrounded her with drawn swords.

Shit. What have I done?

The captain stepped forward. In this form, she barely reached his knee. "Why are you here, fairy?"

By his dark skin and the symbols painted on his face, she knew he was a Marauder—one of several races that called Cosaria home.

Holding her hands up to let them know she was unarmed, she addressed the captain. "I was being pursued. Forgive me for landing without permission."

"Don't trust her. Fairies know nothing of the truth. I say we throw her to the sharks."

"I'm good with that," Gisela assured them. "Toss me overboard. I deserve it."

Since they had no idea that she could become a shark herself, that confused them. While she might not know how to swim as a human, she definitely could manage as a fish. It'd been what had allowed her to follow Xaydin to the merfolk.

She smiled at the Marauders. "I'll just dive right over the side here. No need to trouble yourselves." She inched her way toward the railing.

"Stop!"

She froze at the fierce shout.

"Do you think us stupid?"

How did she respond to that? "I don't know you well enough to make any judgment as to your character or intellect."

Drawing his sword, he narrowed the distance between them. "What game are you playing?"

"No games. I'm just trying not to die."

And before they could respond, something hit the boat hard and sent the bow dipping below the waves.

The crew cursed as they were thrown about. Several went overboard.

"Sea monster!" they screamed and shouted.

Gisela winced. Not a sea monster.

Diflyn in the form of a giant squid.

Shit and shit again. What was the predator for a kraken? Her mind went suddenly blank. Every creature had something that hunted it.

Dragon was the first thing to come to mind. Of course, she'd never tried becoming one of those before.

Could dragons swim? She had no idea.

Think, think, think...

How she wished she'd paid closer attention to her biology books.

Diflyn lunged at the ship again. Grabbing the masthead, it was obvious that he intended to take the ship down.

Gisela was just about to turn into a fish to escape him when a giant sperm whale broke the surface. Gaping, she watched as it snapped its jaw around Diflyn and dragged him toward the sea.

The two giant beasts fought each other while the Marauders did their best to save their ship. They dropped sails and tried to catch the winds that would take them to safety.

Gisela returned to her bird form to escape while the others were occupied.

But as she returned to the skies, she glanced back at the whale and squid.

Diflyn turned into an orca and when he did so, the whale vanished.

She gasped as she realized the whale had to be another shifter. One who'd been willing to help her. Why?

Wait a second. Could that possibly be...?

"Ronan?"

The odds seemed to be against it, but who else would have helped her?

At the moment, it didn't matter. She needed to get herself out of this mess as quickly as she could.

Flapping her wings, she headed for shore. As soon as she was past the docks, she returned to her human form, then conjured clothes to wear.

Sadly, she couldn't manifest weapons or do any other useful magic like others of her ilk could. But she'd take this, as it allowed her to blend in with the crowd. With any luck, Diflyn wouldn't be able to find her now. There were too many other humans about for him to locate her.

At least, she hoped that was true.

"Gisela!"

She paused at the call from an unfamiliar voice. It'd been a woman.

Turning about, she tried to find the source.

No one seemed to be paying any attention to her at all.

Maybe she'd imagined it.

That was her thought until she tried to turn down an alley. Out of the shadows a shorter woman emerged to block her way.

The gold star in the center of her forehead was similar to the one the Marauder captain had borne.

When she tried to step around her, the woman refused to let her pass. "Ronan sent me after you. I'm Mischief."

Of course, she was. It made perfect sense. "How did Ronan know I was here?"

"Xaydin sent word earlier that you were missing. We were about to begin our search when the giant squid attacked my brother's ship."

"Your brother hates fairies."

Mischief laughed. "You have no idea. But it's a hatred they deserve." With her hand on the hilt of her sword, she stepped back and gestured for Gisela to go first.

"Where are you taking me?"

"To wait for Ronan to join us."

Even though it made sense, she was reluctant to follow. She didn't know this woman. Why would she give a stranger her back?

Mischief quirked a grin. "You don't trust me."

"Why would I?"

"Fair point. But I mean you no harm. I am an Outlaw. I'm here to help you."

Another person her mother had ordered her to kill. That list was getting longer.

Which meant her life was getting shorter if her mother ever found out that she'd failed to do her duty. A smart assassin would kill them all and be done with it. Go home and return to the life she knew.

But that was easier said than done. She liked the Outlaws, more than she should.

You're betraying your mother.

In her mother's eyes, that was true.

But her mother had never trusted her any more than she'd trusted her mother. Not the way Gisela trusted Xaydin. She knew he'd be there if she needed him.

That the Outlaws would help her.

She wasn't so sure with her mother.

Gisela didn't want to be a betrayer. For that matter, she didn't want to be an assassin.

What do you want?

To be a protector like the Outlaws. To help others, not destroy them.

"What the..." Mischief's eyes grew wide as her voice trailed off.

Gisela turned to look over her shoulder to see what had the Outlaw so transfixed.

Then, she wished she hadn't.

Holy gods...

The street behind them was flooding with centaurs.

An army of them.

Dozens were coming in through portals, running down the street and striking anyone who got in their way.

Mischief pulled her into a nearby alley. "This is an act of war."

Maybe. "Meara doesn't have a contract with Vaskalia." The contract she'd signed with them had died with Xaydin's father. His brother had never renewed it because no one had ever dreamed centaurs would war on ogres, giants and trolls.

Shaking her head, Gisela peeped down the street to the growing army. "Why is Meara doing this?"

"No idea." Mischief took her hand and pulled her deeper into the alley. "We need to rendezvous with the others."

"Others?"

"Xaydin, Masakage and Candara."

"What about Ronan?" Gisela asked.

"He can take care of himself, and he'll meet us as soon as he can."

That sounded like a plan to her.

"Halt!"

Gisela turned to see a centaur behind them. Mischief turned to engage him.

"No!" Gisela stopped her from escalating the situation. "Get to the others. I'll take care of this."

Mischief hesitated before she nodded.

Gisela held her hands out as she kept the officer from pursuing Mischief. "What are you doing here, Captain?"

He angled an arrow at her heart. "On your knees."

"I'm Gisela of the Queen's Guard and I'm here on her business. Lower your weapon."

He hesitated. "Her majesty said nothing of this in her orders to us."

"What are your orders?"

"None of your business."

Aggravating beast. "Let me get my papers." Gisela slowly reached into the pouch at her waist. She pulled out her royal dispensation that bore Meara's seal, thankful that while she couldn't conjure weapons, she could at least conjure this.

She held the parchment out toward the captain.

A white equine, he had dark human skin and black, suspicious eyes. He approached her slowly until he was able to take the paper from her hand.

His lips moved as he read the decree that gave her authority to act on the queen's behalf. There were only a handful of them who held that document. Mostly because her mother didn't trust them not to get her into trouble with the High King who was already looking for any reason to go after her.

He examined the seal. "Gisela...are you her assassin?"

She nodded.

"Then you're under arrest."

Those words were so unexpected that it took her a few seconds to react as the centaur came forward.

"I serve the queen!"

"You're a traitor, and we're under orders to arrest or kill you."

Gisela lunged at him.

Shoving her away, he called out for others to assist him in arresting her.

She immediately returned to her bird form and launched herself toward the sky.

Arrows followed after her.

She dodged one, but the moment she did, it threw her into the path of another. Pain exploded in her shoulder as the arrow ripped through her wing. Unable to stay airborne, she tumbled toward the ground.

Gisela tried to catch herself, but the pain was too much. She hit the ground hard and then exploded back into her human body.

She tried to summon clothes but couldn't. The pain was too great and made it impossible for her to concentrate on anything other than maintaining her form. She heard the centaurs rushing her.

Get up! She shouted at herself, doing everything she could to crawl forward.

It was useless. Blood was smeared on the ground, all around her and her side was pouring even more.

So, this is how I die.

She'd always wondered when and how it'd happen. Strange how it left her cold and ambivalent.

The only thing she'd always known...

She was alone for the event.

"The queen wants her head!"

Of course, she did. No doubt her mother would add it to her collection.

These were the last minutes of her life and the only thing

that flashed through her mind was images of Xaydin. The memory of being loved and of loving.

Her only regret was that she'd never get to tell him that she loved him.

Closing her eyes, she waited for the centaurs to end her.

Just as they reached her, a blast sounded. One so loud that it was deafening. Sparks flew around her, lighting up the entire alley.

And then she felt it.

That massive presence that was so powerful it shook the air around him.

Xaydin.

Strong, muscled arms surrounded her before he lifted her from the ground and cradled her against his chest. Tears welled in her eyes as she met his tender gaze.

"No one shames my lady," he growled, pulling his black cloak around her.

With one kiss to her brow, he handed her over to Masakage. "Protect her."

Then he went after the centaurs who'd made her bleed.

Joy spread through her as he caught the captain with one vicious punch to the face.

Masakage laughed as Candara swept past him to help Xaydin.

Gisela bit her lip. "I should be with him."

"Not until we patch your wound. You can't help anyone if you're dead."

Probably true, but still...

Xaydin was here. He'd come for her.

"How did you find me?" she asked Masakage as he carried her down the street while she cradled her wounded arm.

"I don't know. Xaydin figured it out somehow. I've never seen anything like it. He was absolutely determined."

She hugged him, then kissed his cheek. "Thank you."

Masakage actually blushed. "Don't thank me for taking care of family. It's what we do."

Family...

While she had those she shared blood with, she'd never known the bond before. But he was right. Masakage, Candara, Xaydin and even Ronan were her family now.

She'd do anything for them, especially Xaydin.

Masakage took her to a small, empty sloop.

"Where's everyone?" she asked.

"This is Mischief's. She and her crew are helping fight the centaurs."

Of course they were.

Family.

A tear slid down her cheek. "I need to be with Xaydin."

"Xaydin needs to know you're safe. The worst thing you could do is endanger his heart."

"I don't understand."

Shaking his head, Masakage took her to the captain's chambers and placed her on the small bed.

He pulled the cloak back to see the wound that was high on her ribs, almost to her shoulder. The moment he saw it, he hissed. "That has to hurt."

"I've had worse, but it's a contender."

With a laugh, he used his powers to stop the bleeding.

When he went to do more, she stopped him. "Go to Xaydin and keep him safe."

"He wants me with you."

She put her hand on his. "I promise I'll stay right here. But I need you to take care of *my* heart. Please, Masakage. He's wounded, too. Bring him back to me in one piece and breathing."

Hesitation darkened his eyes before he nodded. "Remember, it's my life in your hands. Don't get up! Last thing I need is an ass-whipping from a pissed off troll."

She laughed, then grimaced as he conjured clothes for her and then left.

Xaydin had come for her. She still couldn't believe it. No one had ever done that for her before.

This was the most wonderful moment of her entire life.

Sighing, she pulled his cloak tighter about her and inhaled his masculine scent. Warmth spread through her.

She'd rather be wrapped in his arms, but this was a close second. Happier than she'd ever been, she pulled her clothes to her and dressed.

Just as she secured the last buckle on her jerkin, she heard someone walking across the deck above her.

Some of the Marauders must have returned. She hoped that meant they'd won the fight.

As she pulled the cloak back around her, the door to the cabin opened.

And Meara stepped in.

20

Shock riveted Gisela to the floor as she stared at the last person she'd ever expected to see. Indeed, the dead Garyn would have been less stunning had he appeared in her bed.

Gisela moved to confront the queen. Even if her legs were unsteady.

Dressed in black leather armor, her mother was as regal as always. Right down to that imperious sneer on her beautiful face.

"I knew this day would come. From the moment I birthed you and failed to cut your throat. I knew I'd regret it."

"Why didn't you kill me, Mother? Really. What was the point of allowing me to live?"

Something wistful filled her eyes. If Gisela didn't know better, she'd swear it was regret.

But Meara didn't answer her question. She closed the gap between them so that she could glare down at Gisela. "You had one task. One. Protect the *apaswere* with my contract on him. How hard could that be?"

Gisela wanted to laugh at her naive question. How hard, indeed...

"If it was easy, Mother, why did you send out another to kill the same *apaswere* you'd told me to protect?"

That question caught her mother off guard.

"I don't know what you're talking about."

Gisela scoffed. "Yes, you do. I can see it in your eyes that you're trying to find a lie to get you out of this. Is that why you want me dead now? So that no one else will ever know how duplicitous you are?"

Meara went to slap her, but she ducked and moved away.

"I'm not a child anymore. And you no longer command me."

"Ungrateful wretch! You're just like your useless father! Feckless and cruel!"

"Cruel?" Gisela was incredulous that her mother would ever apply that label to anyone other than herself. "Cratus—"

Her mother cut her words off with a high-pitched scream. "Never say that name out loud!"

"Why? Because he was a unicorn or because his parentage betrays the fact that you are a shape shifter?"

Fury darkened her mother's eyes.

"So, it's true. The mark beneath your tongue wasn't something you put there. You were born with it."

Her mother lifted her chin. "And I should have killed you at birth as I did your shifter siblings!"

That outraged confession stunned her. While she'd known she had three siblings who hadn't survived childhood, she'd never dreamed their own mother had slaughtered them over an ability they'd inherited from her.

The nightmare of that truth took her mother to a whole new low.

In that moment, she had an answer as to why she'd been

allowed to live when the others had been killed. The one thing that made her different.

"You planned on using me against my father, didn't you?"

"He wasn't supposed to die!" That honest shriek caught them both off guard.

It was probably the most honest thing she'd ever heard her mother say.

But that left her with one more question. "Once he was gone, why did you keep me?"

Fury caused her nostrils to flare. "I don't answer to you!"

No, she didn't and Gisela should have known her mother would never answer that question.

Before she could move, her mother unsheathed her sword and angled it at her throat. "I'm done with you."

Gisela barely had time to duck. But her mother's intent was clear... She intended to behead her.

On the one hoof, she was impressed. Meara didn't like to get her hooves dirty. This kind of execution was normally relegated to Gisela or another of her mother's goons.

On the other hoof, she was horrified that her own mother wanted her dead badly enough to do it herself.

Their relationship had just sunk to a whole new level of shit.

And if she'd ever possessed any hope that her mother might have held a modicum of maternal instinct, this extinguished it. The creature in front of her was completely devoid of compassion or love.

That knowledge and reality crushed something deep inside her.

Her own mother wanted her dead. She winced at the truth she could not deny. While Masakage, Candara and Xaydin might have issues with their mother, at least she wasn't actively trying to kill them.

SHERRILY KENYON

"Don't do this." The words were out before she could stop them. Worse, they were said in the tone of a little girl, and that made her hate herself.

It was a pleading tone. Not because she wanted to live, but because she didn't want to die by the hand of her own mother.

How pathetic is my life?

But Meara wouldn't be deterred.

Gisela ducked the next sword stroke and twisted away. This was when having two legs was beneficial. She was much spryer than her four-legged mother, and those two legs allowed her to run up the ladder to the main deck.

As she reached the walkway, her mother appeared behind her and buried her hand in Gisela's hair. "I told you not to fail me."

Yes, she had, and Gisela had known the price of failure. But she'd never dreamt that the price would come at the hands of her mother.

Gisela tried to pry her mother's hand loose from her hair. "Let go!"

Her mother raised the sword to cut her throat.

Just as her mother would have sliced, Gisela turned into a bee and flew around to sting her mother's back.

Meara screamed as she swished her tail, trying to strike Gisela.

Gisela flew toward the docks, but because she was injured, she couldn't hold her form. She hit the docks hard in her human body, then cursed the fact she was naked again.

The one thing she truly hated about shape shifting. Why couldn't they keep their clothes when they shifted back to human?

She barely had time to consider that before Meara appeared at her side.

Her mother kicked her to her back with one hoof. A hoof

316

she then put down on the center of her chest. She pressed so tightly that Gisela could barely breathe as pain exploded through her. It felt as if her ribs were breaking. She gasped for breath. An anguished breath that made her wound ache more.

It was over. She couldn't shift. Couldn't fight her mother off given the weight of her equine body.

If I'm going to die...

She wanted it to be in the body she was born in.

Closing her eyes, she exhaled and released all the energy she'd cultivated through her life to make sure she always appeared human. That she never once screwed up and became the thing her mother hated most.

A unicorn.

The moment she shifted, Meara screamed and backed up.

Gisela snorted and felt a new strength run through her. This was unlike anything she'd ever experienced. Warm and soothing. She was still wounded, but the pain wasn't so bad now. It was as if her body was so happy to be what it was born to be that it didn't care about anything else.

And that body gave her another gift...

A weapon.

Lowering her head, she charged at Meara.

Just as she would have reached her mother and stabbed her through her cold, callous heart with her horn, Meara vanished.

Rearing up, Gisela cried out in rage. *Coward!*

The word had barely gone through her mind before she realized she wasn't alone.

Xaydin was at her right side.

In front of her, Masakage and Candara stared at her in disbelief.

Well, not so much at her as they stared at her horn.

Pawing at the ground, Gisela snorted. "Anyone calls me a dart donkey and I'll skewer them."

Masakage laughed so hard he choked.

Candara rolled her eyes.

Smiling, Xaydin approached her so that he could stroke her mane. "That's the last thing I'd ever call you, my love."

"Well, we now know her paternal lineage, don't we?"

Gisela turned her head to see Ronan joining them. "What's happening with the centaurs?" she asked him.

"They're retreating. Guess your mother knew she couldn't stand up to the four of you." Ronan scratched at his neck. "Love to know who opened the portals for them...in both directions."

Gisela knew. "Her wizard brigade. I didn't see any among them, but she uses them in battle and must have brought some with her."

Which explained how she was able to appear on the deck so quickly.

I should have known. Just as she knew what her mother now planned. "She's retreated to her lands. But she will be back. And in greater numbers."

Xaydin nodded. "Sadly, we're well versed in her battle tactics."

Candara stepped forward. "But she doesn't have what she wants most."

"My head?" Gisela asked.

"I was thinking more about the contract with Dash. But sure, your head probably ranks up there. Her disappointments today were many."

"Which will only make her more determined." Gisela let out a tired sigh. "So where does this leave us?"

"Screwed and ass backwards," Ronan said nonchalantly.

Ignoring his comment, Xaydin scratched his chin. "We have an errant prince to return home and a contract to deliver. Let's take care of what we need to."

"We still don't know where the prince is," Gisela reminded them.

Ronan shook his head. "Not exactly true. Mischief knows."

Xaydin didn't comment as his hand dipped to stroke Gisela's side. It was then he saw the blood in her fur. "Are you all right?"

"I want to say yes, but... I need to lie down."

He immediately took off his cloak and wrapped it around her. "Change, and I'll get you to the inn."

More grateful than she could ever say, she shifted to her human form. Had Xaydin not been there beside her, waiting, she would have fallen.

He scooped her up in his arms.

Candara opened a portal. "We'll be along shortly."

"Thank you." And with that, Xaydin took Gisela through the portal to their room at the inn.

Gisela let out a sigh as he placed her on the bed, then went to find one of his tunics for her to wear.

He pulled back his cloak and cursed. "When did this new wound happen?"

"When I was running from my mother."

"I swear, I'm going to kill her. How could she be so vicious?"

Gisela wished she had an answer. Rather, she knew her mother as a rabid beast with no decency in her.

Xaydin gently tended her wound until he could stem the bleeding. The tenderness of his touch soothed her in ways unimaginable.

"I love you, Xaydin." The words were out before she could stop them.

He froze for a few seconds before he met her gaze. "What?"

She reached up to finger the stubble on his cheek. "I love you. I thought I was going to die, and I realized that I'd never said it to you. If I don't survive this, I wanted you to know how I feel."

Xaydin was humbled by her words and the earnestness in her tone. She meant what she said.

Cupping her cheek, he leaned closer to her. "I love you, too." Then he kissed her.

She growled against his lips as she balled her fists in his hair.

Right then, Xaydin wanted to be inside her again. But he wasn't that selfish. Pulling back, he smiled at her. "You need to rest."

She whimpered. "Now I know how you felt when I teased you!"

"Exactly... Except I weigh a lot more than you do, and you're too injured." He gently brushed the hair back from her forehead and kissed it. "I have the room warded. Sleep in peace. We are just downstairs and within earshot." With those words spoken, he left her alone with her thoughts.

Thoughts that drifted heavily as she thought about everything that had happened. It was a lot to come to terms with, especially since she could never go home.

Even though it hadn't been much of a home, it was where she'd grown up.

Everything familiar was there. Everyone she'd ever known.

Now...

She felt empty and vacuous. Lost.

Where do I go from here?

She thought about Xaydin and her mood lifted. He loved her. She could build a better home with real friends who cared about her and each other.

Suddenly, the world wasn't quite as scary. Daunting, but not as terrifying as it used to be.

But the one thing she knew about Meara, the queen never gave up. Right now, she wanted them dead. That was a threat that would never go away.

"Well, that was fun." Ronan signaled their server that they needed five tankards. "What's next? Pulling my entrails out through my nose? The old flaming poker up my ass? Or should we just stick to the good old iron maiden?"

"Given that it's Meara, I'd say all that plus a good gelding or two." Xaydin sighed. "I really want that bitch's throat."

"Your mother-in-law, you mean? Shouldn't you be a bit kinder?"

He glared at Candara. "Don't even."

Ronan cleared his throat. "Aren't we all ignoring the obvious?"

"That is?" Masakage asked.

"That Gisela's the daughter of Cratus... Hello? Shouldn't we let Dash know he has a sister?"

Xaydin really wanted to ignore Ronan's question, but he couldn't. None of them could.

Masakage took his tankard from their server. "Knowing Dash, he'll be thrilled to welcome her in. Especially after Renata's death."

How he wished that were true. But as decent as Dash was, there was one important bit to this that they couldn't overlook, and he waited until the server left them before he spoke. "She's the daughter of Meara. Given how much he hates her... I don't know if we should tell him."

Ronan took a deep drink. "Doesn't that make her an heiress?"

Xaydin frowned as he considered that. "If not for...what... three, four brothers? Anyone know how many kids Meara has?"

"No idea." Ronan sighed. "But Ferox might already be dead."

"Either way, Gisela doesn't want to rule. She'd probably slap me if I even suggested it to her. From what she's told me, she profanes all politics."

"Can't say I blame her." Ronan looked up, then scowled as his gaze focused on something behind Xaydin's back.

Xaydin turned to see what had caught his attention, then he fell silent, too. It was Mischief coming toward them with a tall, muscular man who dwarfed her in size.

More than that, his dark features were eerily similar to hers. They even had on matching brown leather armor. Distinctive in its own right by the leaf-like scaly appearance.

Brother? Maybe a cousin.

Whatever he was, he looked enough like her that they could easily be related. Right down to the gold star and streaks drawn over his face. Until now, Xaydin had assumed those were random patterns the Marauders liked to use.

Now, it appeared they might have more meaning than that. This looked more like some form of heraldry or family design.

Mischief didn't speak until they stood by Ronan's side, facing Xaydin. "My brother, Evar."

Xaydin wasn't sure which of them was most stunned by her declaration. All the years they'd known her, she'd never once mentioned her family.

Not a single word.

They'd figured that she must have some, and that, like all the rest of them, she was the bastard child of a monarch. It was what Meara had required as hostages to keep the peace of the kingdoms. A royal child and the child of one high-ranking noble from every king or queen had been sent to her for her so-called protection.

It sickened him to even think about it.

The Marauders had sent Mischief and a red-headed boy who'd died the first month of captivity. He couldn't even recall that poor soul's name now. Only how scared the boy had been and how sick he'd become within days of entering Meara's court.

Since Mischief had never mentioned her parents, everyone had assumed the dead boy to be a prince and her the daughter of a noble. Which made sense as most of the royal children hadn't been hearty enough to endure Meara's torture.

Only the Outlaws, and they had banded together to make sure they could stand against the bitch queen.

But the bearing of her brother was as regal as any royal Xaydin had met.

He rose to his feet slowly. "Pleased to meet you, Highness."

Instead of correcting him, Evar inclined his head imperiously. "My sister tells me that you're hunting me."

They all exchanged puzzled glances.

"Pardon?" Masakage asked.

"I'm the one Marstyn left his kingdom for."

That was unexpected. Not that Xaydin cared who or what Marstyn loved, he was just a little surprised by it. "I take it that you're here to tell us to go away and leave you alone."

"In a manner of speaking. But I know Mardyth won't stop until he drags Marstyn home. Neither of us wants that. What I was hoping for is a meeting where we may discuss the matter with the king."

Clearing his throat, Ronan looked down at his tankard.

Xaydin didn't need to read his mind to know what thoughts lurked there. Mardyth wasn't the most reasonable of creatures.

"I'd rather not be a hostage again. But I have to say that of all the places I've been held, I rather did enjoy Mardyth's palace."

He rolled his eyes at Masakage. "You want me to set it up?"

Evar nodded. "He won't listen to us or even return any message I've sent."

That made sense to Xaydin. "I take it that you don't want to go to his kingdom."

Evar gave Xaydin a droll stare. "Rather not, as I'm sure I wouldn't come back. At least not alive."

He was right about that. "I'll see what I can do," Xaydin promised.

"Thank you."

When Mischief started to leave with her brother, Xaydin called her back.

She hesitated at first, then excused herself from her brother to return to their table. "What?"

"Take a seat." Xaydin indicated the one beside Ronan.

"Do I have a choice?" she asked.

"Not at the moment."

Sighing heavily, she pulled the chair out and sat down, then waved at the server to bring another tankard. "Yes, I'm a princess. No, I don't want to talk about it. What else is on your mind?"

"So, so many things." Xaydin held his tankard in his hand as he tried to sort through what little any of them knew about her.

Except for possibly Ronan. The two of them had always been close.

"Did you know?" he asked him.

Ronan shook his head. "I had suspicions, but she didn't speak about it and I never asked. Always assumed she'd tell me what she wanted me to know, and if she didn't mention it, it wasn't any of my business."

She reached over and covered his hand with hers. "Thank you."

"I'm always on your side. You know that."

Arching a brow, Xaydin exchanged an I-told-you-so smirk with Masakage.

Like I didn't know, Masakage said in his mind.

True. Everyone knew Ronan loved Mischief. The only question was if she loved him back. She'd never given any real clues about her feelings other than to claim she had no feelings whatsoever.

Which they'd known was bullshit. But she did do a better job of hiding them than anyone else he'd ever met.

Xaydin took a drink. "We respect your right to withhold. However, how are we supposed to help your brother?"

"I have no idea. I told him this wasn't something he should do. But he's older, so he never listens to me." She cocked her head. "Kind of like you, X."

"Don't take it personally. I don't listen to anyone."

Ronan choked. "So not true. Have you not noticed you give total deference to Lady Gisela?"

"Princess Gisela," he corrected. "And you won't speak of her unless it's to lavish praise upon her glorious being."

They all laughed at him.

Until they realized he wasn't kidding.

"Nice to know you still have no sense of humor." Candara set her empty tankard down. "I'll work up a spell so that Mardyth can come ashore. But it probably won't last long. Maybe half an hour."

"That should be adequate. Any longer and he might kill my brother. The gods know I'm tempted to do it after ten minutes in his oafish company. No idea what Marstyn sees in him."

"I'll go talk to the king." Ronan pushed himself back from the table.

"Why you?" Mischief asked.

"Only one who can become a fish. Well, except for Gisela."

"No," Xaydin said firmly. "She doesn't like the water. And..." he glanced at Mischief, according to Mardyth, your brother is a nereid. Is there something else you'd like to confide?"

325

She actually blushed. "A lot of Marauders are nereids. But I don't like being in the sea. Just on it."

"Noted." Ronan put his coin on the table for his drink. "I'll be back as soon as I can."

Without another word, Mischief got up and went after him.

Xaydin shook his head. "I really wish they'd find their peace."

"They will." Masakage put one of his coins on the table. "But it won't be easy."

"Hate your coins." Xaydin picked it up to study it. It was three swords piercing a heart. "Looks like they won't make it."

"Bleeding and broken hearts heal. No one knows that better than you."

Xaydin hated that his brother was right about that and he prayed Masakage was right when it came to Ronan and Mischief. If two beings ever born deserved happiness, it was the two of them.

"You got a coin to tell me how this mess with King Mardyth will end?"

"I do, but I don't want to pull one."

Really? That had to be a first. "Why not?"

"Because I'm terrified of the answer. There are some things that no one needs to see in advance."

That made his stomach cramp. "Thanks, alley rat."

"Demon."

Normally, they'd play this game a bit longer, but Xaydin wasn't in the mood.

He needed to make peace with a sea king who was determined to war, avoid his own brother who wanted him dead, find a lunatic queen out to kill them and get a contract to Dash before Meara reclaimed it.

At the moment, he was hating his life.

Except for one part of it. A part he hoped would heal and survive the mother who wanted her dead.

21

Diflyn cursed at the fact that he no longer had his contract. Meara would kill him if she learned it'd fallen into enemy hands.

She'll kill me for not taking care of her daughter, too.

True. His life was basically over.

Damn it! He'd barely escaped them with his life. And he still wasn't in the clear.

It'd seemed so simple in the beginning. Kill the *apaswere* and then Gisela. How had they screwed up so badly? He could feel the executioner's blade on his neck. It was a terrifying sensation.

He pulled out a skin of wine while he sat on the side of the road, trying to figure out what to do. He'd just taken a drink when he heard the brush around him move.

Thinking it was a bird or some other small creature, he paid it no attention.

Not until a man appeared by his side with no warning.

Before he could shift into another form, the man snapped a cuff on his wrist. "You're not going anywhere, shifter."

Shit!

"Who are you? What do you want?"

The older man had a grizzled face, filled with lines. Long, scraggly gray hair framed a face that might have been handsome at some point, but that would have been decades ago. With his sunken brown eyes and sharp features, he looked more like a walking corpse...

Diflyn ground his teeth as he realized that was exactly what he was dealing with.

A lich.

But they didn't normally leave their own land in the far north. It was virtually unheard of to see them in the southern kingdoms.

"I want the contract."

A contract he wasn't about to part with, so Diflyn played dumb. "What contract? I have no idea what you're talking about."

The lich punched him hard. "The contract you transferred onto the skin of an elf. Did you really think they wouldn't find out and seek vengeance?"

That was exactly what he thought. "I serve Queen Meara. You better let me go."

The lich laughed in his face. "And I serve King Baldur."

That made his stomach tighten to the point he feared he'd be sick.

"That's right, shifter, shit your pants. My king has strict rules for those who trophy hunt his people."

"I didn't do it. I bought the skin from a peddler."

"I know. I killed him right after he told me about you and your partner."

Of course he did.

Terrified, he tried to think of anyone else he could blame this on. But his mind was blank. He could barely think at all.

"You're going to die for this, shifter. The only question is how much will you suffer before you do?"

THREE DAYS LATER

Gisela stood beside Xaydin as they waited for King Mardyth to appear.

Evar and Marstyn were seated at a small table in the back, dreading the king's appearance.

Tall and blond with gold eyes, Marstyn reminded her a lot of his father. Except he didn't have a fish tail or translucent skin any longer.

Honestly, he looked completely human. No one would ever be able to tell that he was Ningyoan.

And at the moment, he was holding hands with Evar who was the heir to the Cosarian and Umaran thrones.

Mischief stood beside her, looking as nervous as her brother. "I don't know what's worse about this. Mardyth or our father. I love Evar too much to see him in this kind of pain."

Xaydin glanced over his shoulder to where they sat. "He looks quite happy to me."

"You say that. But this could cost him both thrones."

Xaydin gave Gisela a smirk. "Don't think he cares."

"I care. If he abdicates the Cosarian throne, it falls to me, and I don't want it."

"That I understand."

"What do I do, X?" Mischief asked.

"Support your brother. Hopefully, he'll be able to do his duties, and you won't ever have to worry about being queen."

That seemed to cheer her.

Gisela squeezed her hand. Unlike Xaydin and the others, she understood Mischief's fears. As the illegitimate daughter of the king and one of his wife's ladies-in-waiting, Mischief had spent her youngest years avoiding a queen out to kill her.

So much so that she'd been taken aboard a ship with her mother's brother who'd trained her in piracy, not court graces. It was the life Mischief preferred over anything else.

And why she denied her royal heritage. Why she'd been the one chosen to go to Meara's court.

Gisela couldn't blame her. She well understood hating the life she'd been born into, too.

The doors to the inn opened slowly. Xaydin had paid for the innkeeper to close his establishment to the public so that they could have their meeting without any disturbances or curious onlookers and gossips.

Mardyth walked in with Ronan and Masakage. He looked less than pleased, though she wasn't sure if it was from being human or being here.

Although, given the confidence the king showed in his stride and demeanor, she suspected this wasn't the first time he'd become human.

Either way, he made his way slowly to the table in back where his son sat with Evar.

And with every step that took him closer, he looked less and less pleased.

More like he had a bowel obstruction and was about to spew bile.

Marstyn rose to his feet and cut his father off before he could reach Evar. "Thank you for agreeing to this. I know how much you hate the land."

"Why are you doing this?"

Biting his lip, he turned to look at Evar. "Because I have no choice. I love him, Father."

"Love is fleeting. You will regret this decision."

"It doesn't have to be. Just as you don't have to be stubborn."

His father's nostrils flared. "I'm stubborn? You understand that you will no longer be my heir?"

"I don't care about that. I just want to be your son. The throne has never mattered to me. All I want is for you to be king into eternity."

Those words seemed to work magic on the older fish. Before she realized what he was doing, he jerked his son into his arms and held him close. "I don't want you harmed. You know how land-dwellers are. I can't protect you here."

"But I can." Evar finally approached them. "I'll make sure no harm ever comes to him."

The king's eyes turned dark and determined as he stared at Marstyn. "You can always come home...and feel free to bring Evar with you. That was what I wanted you to know. You didn't have to flee like a criminal. You did us both a horrible disservice by assuming you understood my objections to this. As I said, love is fleeting, but you will always be my son, and I will never forsake you." And with that, he handed over the underwater breathers to them.

Marstyn hugged his father close. "Thank you."

His father stepped back and cleared his throat. "Visit when you can."

And with that, he came over to them and inclined his head to Xaydin.

"Thank you for finding him." He handed Xaydin another underwater breather. "I'll uphold my bargain. You'll now be free to travel over my kingdom."

"Thank you." He offered the king his hand.

The king shook it before taking his leave.

Gisela rubbed Xaydin on the back. "You did something wonderful."

"I didn't do anything." He really hadn't. "I'm just glad it worked out and there was no bloodshed."

"A rarity for us," Masakage added.

"Indeed."

Gisela watched as Evar and Marstyn followed the king out of the inn.

"I feel good about this. Anyone else?"

They all stared at Ronan for his question.

He held his hands up. "Don't kill the messenger. I mean we got the big guy—" He gestured toward Xaydin. "—squared with the fish king. All we have left is to kill Meara and deliver a rather sick hide to Dash. Day done, right?"

Masakage clapped him on the back. "And avoid a troll and ogre army between here and there. Good luck with that."

"I can fly." Ronan winked at them.

Not to be outdone, Candara spoke up. "I can portal."

Xaydin gave her an irritated smirk. "We all can portal provided Masakage doesn't abandon us."

Gisela looked about the empty inn. "How long do you think before your brother finds you?"

Xaydin shrugged. "So far, we haven't been betrayed, but that doesn't say much. For all we know, he could be hiding on the edge of the town, ready to strike."

That was her fear, too.

"Let's get the contract to Dash and then we go for Meara."

She liked the sound of Xaydin's plan, except for one thing. "What about your brother?"

"I'll deal with him later. It's not the first time he's come after me. Every blue moon, he feels a need to eliminate me from succession."

She felt terrible for him. It must be awful to...

What are you talking about? Your own mother is after you.

334

True. Her brothers had never seen her as a threat, so they'd never wasted any energy trying to kill her.

Provided they even knew she was a sibling of theirs. Given her mother's secrecy and her own, they probably didn't. It wasn't like she'd ever told a soul that she was their princess, and her mother had murdered everyone who'd witnessed Gisela's birth.

As far as she knew, no one at home had any idea Meara was her mother.

And she was good with that.

Rubbing Xaydin's back, she glanced at the others. "When are we leaving?"

"Soon as we're ready." Xaydin inclined his head to them. "Fifteen minutes? Meet back here?"

Ronan snorted. "Since I have nothing to pack, I'll wait here for all of you."

Mischief stayed behind while the others went to get their things.

For once, Ronan wasn't quite sure what to say to her. A novelty, as they'd never had an awkward moment between them. But something about her brother and his situation had put a hesitancy in her.

He hated that passionately.

"When will you head back to sea?" he asked her.

"I don't know. It hasn't been the same lately."

He gestured for them to take a seat at a table on his left. "What's wrong?"

"Hard to explain."

"Most things are."

She snorted at that. "What about you? Are you heading home?"

"What home?" He spent his time spying for Dash or running messages. While his father wanted him to return to

335

Sagaria and resume "royal" duties, Ronan had no intention of ever doing so. Had his father wanted him to play prince, he should have never traded him to Meara. Nor allowed his mother's kingdom to fall and his mother to be executed.

Since the day of their release, Ronan had refused to step foot in his father's kingdom. They could all burn in hell for what he cared. His loyalty was to the ones who'd been with him through the nightmare of captivity, and who'd helped him survive it. Not with the bastard who'd handed him over to be tortured.

His father was lucky he talked to him.

Mischief reached out and placed her hand over his. "You know you always have a place on my boat."

"True. A crow's nest always needs a crow."

She shook her head. "You know what I mean."

No, he really didn't. They'd always had a complicated relationship. "I don't even know your real name. Rather sure it isn't Princess Mischief."

She chuckled. "Actually, that is what my parents called me. More often than Penelope."

Ronan sat there in stunned silence. "Penelope?" he repeated, trying to reconcile that name with the beautiful bit of chaos in front of him.

She nodded. "Princess Penelope Augusta Victoria Vandermere of Cosaria."

"So Mischief it is."

She laughed. "Exactly."

He shook his head as he remembered the last time they'd met. He'd fetched her for Dash, along with Cadoc, another of their Outlaws from the port city where she'd docked her ship. She'd been horribly drunk when he found her. They both had.

"Are you doing better?" he asked.

"I'm only all right when you're around. I wish you wouldn't leave."

Those words hit him like a sucker punch to the gullet. She'd never said that to him before. "I thought you didn't want me to hold you back." That was what she'd said the time before when they'd run into each other.

"Why do you think I was drunk, Ro? You weren't supposed to leave."

"You told me not to bother you. Not unless Dash or one of the others needed you."

Her eyes glistened from unshed tears. "Because it hurts to see you. You weren't supposed to leave," she repeated.

Ronan pulled her forehead to his. "You are the most complicated person I've ever known." And he should have known that when she'd been so hostile.

Mischief was so afraid of being hurt again that she always pushed away what she needed.

"You know that I'm always here for you, Missy."

"But you left me." This time the tears were in her tone. "You weren't supposed to leave me, Ro. You promised."

He cursed himself for being stupid. "You hurt me when you told me to leave. I have feelings, too, you know?"

She nodded. "I always screw things up."

"No, you don't. And you can never screw anything up with me." He kissed her lightly on the lips.

The moment he did, she launched herself into his arms and met that kiss with more passion than he'd ever known.

Closing his eyes, he savored the taste of her. It'd been a year since they'd been together.

A long, shitty year where he'd missed her touch. Her warmth. She'd been the only woman he'd ever loved or that he ever would. A little bit crazy mixed with vibrant intelligence and a willingness to slaughter anyone who got in her way. There was no one like her, and he appreciated every moment of the chaos she brought with her.

Slowly, she crawled into his lap and deepened their kiss. This was what he'd missed most. Her passion and taste.

"Oh!"

Ronan pulled back at the startled gasp, then laughed as he saw Candara's red face.

"I didn't mean to interrupt..."

Mischief laughed as she extracted herself from his lap. "It's all right. We shouldn't have chosen such a public spot for our kiss."

Ronan scoffed. "Not like it's the first time, and that was rather chaste for us."

Mischief elbowed him hard in the stomach. "Don't make me beat you."

"Long as you're naked, I'm up for most things, as you well know."

"Would you stop! You're going to make the poor girl burst into flames."

She was right. Candara was practically glowing from embarrassment.

"I'm not used to those who are so casual with their dalliances."

Ronan wrapped his arms around Mischief and rested his chin on top of her hair. "Wouldn't have to be casual if she'd ever marry me."

To his surprise, Mischief leaned back in his arms and raised her hand to cup his cheek. "Are you willing to stay with me if I say yes? It would mean you'd have to finally put down the roots you so despise."

For a full minute Ronan couldn't breathe as he digested those words. Had she really said them?

Did she mean them?

"Are you serious?"

Mischief turned around in his arms so that she faced him. "If you're willing to settle down, so am I."

He couldn't believe that. Not after all these years of begging her to marry. "You're the only home I've ever known."

She smiled up at him. "Then promise you won't leave and abide by it."

Picking her up, he laughed. "Not even you will ever drive me away." He savored the way she felt against him as she kissed him again.

"What are we interrupting now?" Xaydin asked.

Candara clicked her tongue. "I think they're getting married."

"'Bout time. They've waited long enough to stop buzzing around each other. It's really annoying for the rest of us to watch."

Ronan set Mischief back on her feet. "I don't want to hear it from you, X." He slid a meaningful look to Gisela.

Xaydin pulled her to his side and smirked. "Didn't take me twenty years."

"Fair point." Ronan stepped back from Mischief but didn't go far as she caught his hand and held him there.

"Shall we portal, then?" Masakage asked.

"We can always go by way of my ship."

Xaydin shook his head. "That'll take too long. Better to update Dash on what's happening now than wait."

Ronan agreed. While he knew Mischief would hate to be without her boat, it would take days, if not a full week, to reach Dash's palace over sea.

The portal would be even faster than if he flew. And it wouldn't leave him tired on arrival. "Who's going to open it?"

"I will," Candara and Masakage said in unison.

Candara smiled at her brother. "Together, then?"

"Sure."

They joined hands and began to chant under their breath.

Xaydin braced himself as a small circle began to spin the air in front of them. He'd always hated portals. They were extremely disorienting.

Slowly the spinning red circle grew larger and brighter. Taking Gisela's hand, Xaydin stepped through to find himself in the courtyard outside of Dash's Clovenshire Castle.

It was a large dark gray fortress that spread out into a perfect square. Each corner was equally anchored by a tall, square tower.

That was the outside. Inside those formidable stone walls was a spectacular manor house.

Dash's ancestors had built this place over three hundred years ago to hold back those who wanted to invade and tear the unicorns down.

It hadn't been that long ago that the unicorn race had been relegated to only this area of their lands and had stood on the edge of extinction. Until they fought back.

Unicorns were nothing if not resilient.

And violent.

"Welcome to your ancestral home," he said to Gisela.

Stunned and amazed, Gisela turned around in a small circle as the rest of their party joined them just outside the beautiful manor.

This was so different from Meara's castle. And it wasn't just because there were no centaurs. Children ran about, laughing and playing. Some were in unicorn bodies while others were in human form.

And they all seemed so...

Happy.

A few appeared disgruntled, but nothing like the ones who inhabited Meara's lands.

"It's beautiful," she whispered, wishing she'd grown up here instead. How different would her life have been had she known these people.

People who would no doubt hate her for being blood related to their biggest enemy.

Shit.

Just as she was tempted to run back through the portal to escape those she was sure would demand her head, the portal closed.

Why did I come here?

What had she been thinking?

The centaurs and unicorns had been at war as far back as anyone could remember. They'd never been united in anything other than hatred.

She shouldn't be here.

"You're fine." Xaydin rubbed gently against her back as if he sensed her unease. "No one here will harm you."

How she prayed he was right. Especially as the door opened and an exceptionally tall, handsome man walked through it. His long black hair was pulled back from his perfectly chiseled face with a leather cord.

But the oddest part was the large crow perched on his muscular shoulder. He leaned against a long, twisted staff that held a crystal at one end similar to the one preferred by Masakage.

Dressed in a black jerkin and breeches, he held an air of authority and danger. Of raw power that dared someone to challenge him.

That someone appeared to be Masakage who approached him slowly and said something in a language she didn't understand.

Smiling, the man embraced Masakage, then turned to the

rest of them. "I want to say welcome, but seeing all of you here... my sphincter clenches. What's happened?"

By his regal demeanor, she thought him to be Dash, until her group climbed the stairs to where he waited.

Xaydin tsked. "Ryper...not like Dash to let you off the leash. Or should I say harness?"

"Ha ha, troll." His gaze went past Xaydin to her. "And you've brought a friend. Should I ask?"

There was a hesitancy in Xaydin that made her curious. It wasn't like him. "Her name is Gisela."

Ryper smiled and gave her a courtly bow. "Pleasure to meet you, fair Gisela." He stroked the head of the crow on his shoulder. "Allow me to present Chrysis and she is a crisis most of the time."

The bird made a caw that sounded offended by his comment.

"Prince Ryper?" she repeated as she finally realized who he was.

"Ryper, please. I hate titles."

This was the brother of King Dash.

My brother, too.

That made her feel suddenly awkward and terrified. She wanted to embrace him and tell him who she was, but why would he accept her when even her own mother refused?

No, she couldn't let them know. The risk was just too great. And why would they ever trust her? She was her mother's assassin. Didn't bode well for family bonding.

"Dash is waiting inside." Ryper headed through the doorway first to lead them.

Gisela wasn't sure what to expect, but the inside of the house was even more grand than the outside. The interior stone walls were covered with elaborate tapestries, banners and weapons. The whole place was commanding and fierce—and meant to intimidate all visitors. And she was intimidated.

Especially when Ryper led them into a huge, luxurious throne room where King Dash sat beside what had to be one of the most beautiful women Gisela had ever seen. Thick red hair framed a jovial face that she could tell was used to smiling and laughing. More than that, the queen was exceptionally pregnant.

She couldn't imagine being that happy. It actually made her heart swell with delight to know someone could be. She'd never seen anything like it before.

Her gaze went to the woman's left hand that was held by Dash's until he saw them and rose to his feet.

"Outlaws! It's good to see you. Or maybe not," he teased as he descended his dais to approach them. "Tell me you have good news?"

Xaydin looked down at her before he answered. "Define the word *good*."

Dash narrowed his gaze on the troll. "What happened?"

"For that, I don't know where to begin. It's been a hell of a thing. The good news is we have your contract."

Dash scowled. "There's no *apaswere* here or a head-shaped bag. I'm confused."

"So are we." Masakage pulled the contract out of his satchel and handed it to Dash.

Dash reached for it, then stopped himself. "Is that flesh?"

They all nodded.

"Whose flesh?" Dash asked.

Xaydin shrugged. "We have no idea, but we're sure it's elfish."

"And enchanted," Candara added. "No idea how to destroy it."

"But that's the only copy." Xaydin took it from his brother

and held it out toward Dash. "There's no *apaswere* now to enforce it."

Dash nodded slowly as he finally understood the significance. "Destroy the only copy and there's no contract at all."

His wife stood up and moved closer so that she could see the document. "Surely dragon fire could destroy it. There's not much that stands up to that."

Candara sucked her breath in between her teeth. "True, but it could be enchanted. Your fire might cause it to explode or do something none of us are expecting."

Eyes wide, the queen backed up. "How dangerous is it?"

Gisela understood her concern. If she were pregnant, she'd be terrified too. "I don't think it's designed to do anything unless you try to destroy it, Majesty. It's been harmless since we took possession of it."

The queen appeared instantly grateful and relieved.

"Who are you?" Dash asked as he finally realized she was standing in Xaydin's shadow.

She stepped slightly more behind him, fearing reprisal from the king.

Xaydin tried to gently nudge her forward.

Fear rooted her to the floor. "He'll hurt me," she whispered.

Xaydin gave her a fierce stare. "He'll have to come through me first. And I promise, he can't do that." Then to her utter horror, he turned back to Dash. "She's your half-sister, Gisela."

Dash took the news without any change in his expression.

But Ryper turned toward her and swept a curious stare over her entire body. "Is this true?"

She tried to run, but Xaydin wouldn't let her. "It'll be all right, Gisela. I'd never endanger you."

Still, she was afraid of them. She was in their home, and all too well, she knew how her mother dealt with threats and unexpected words.

344

Xaydin turned around and cupped her face with his hands. "Show them who you really are. I'm right here and we won't let anything happen to you."

Biting her lip, Gisela nodded. Never in her life had she trusted anyone. No one except Xaydin.

I can do this. She believed Xaydin could keep her safe.

With a deep breath for courage, she turned into her unicorn body.

The moment she did, everyone gasped.

Well, not the ones who'd seen her form before. Just the ones who'd never guessed her real form.

Gaping, Ryper approached her. "It's true."

Dash nodded. "Where has she been all this time?"

Xaydin stroked her mane. *I'm with you, my love. If anyone moves to harm you, I will kill them.*

She took comfort and strength from his presence and words. "I'm Queen Meara's daughter."

Gisela expected them to attack her. To order her execution. She expected hatred and ridicule.

Instead, Dash buried his hand in her mane. "You must be terrified. I can feel you shaking."

"Her heart's pounding," Ryper added.

Dash pressed his forehead to hers, just below her horn. "Welcome home, sister."

To her shock, Ryper pushed Dash away so that he could do the same. "We're glad you're here."

Tears racked her so hard that she accidentally turned human.

Xaydin covered her with his cloak and helped her stand. "It's all right, love. Your brothers aren't Meara. They don't attack without threat."

She saw that now, and it angered her that she'd listened to her mother's lies for so long. That she'd allowed her moth-

345

er's poison to consume her life and scare her into submission.

They weren't the enemies Meara had claimed.

They were the family she'd always wanted.

"Thank you," she breathed.

Dash stepped back and held his hand out for his queen to join them. "Tanis, we have a sister."

Queen Tanis smiled brightly. "About time. I'm tired of being the only female here. Not that they aren't wonderful. They are, but I need someone to shop with who knows something about fashion."

Gisela laughed, then embraced her. "Thank you. But I'm afraid I know very little."

Her smile turned even brighter. "Then I'll teach you. I'm still learning about it myself."

Frowning, Ryper took her hand and looked at her palm.

Gisela had no idea what he was doing until he spoke. "You're a warrior."

"She was the Ryper in Meara's court. But her mother has turned on her and sent assassins after her."

Tanis winced at Xaydin's words. "I know your nightmare, Gisela. In my case, it was my sisters out to end my life after they killed my brother. I'm sorry for the pain I know you're in. Nothing hurts more than being pursued by the ones you love."

Gisela brushed her tears away. "Thank you, Majesty."

"Tanis," she corrected.

She smiled in spite of the pain. "Thank you for proving Xaydin right."

Dash signaled his steward. "Have Renata's chambers prepared for Gisela."

"Yes, Your Majesty." He left immediately.

Gisela arched a brow. Everyone knew that the High King

had worshiped his sister who'd been murdered by enemies. "Are you sure about that?"

"She would insist upon it if she were still here."

Tanis cleared her throat. "In the meantime, let's get you some clothes."

She let out a relieved breath. "A thousand thank yous."

Laughing, Tanis took her hand and led her through the opulent manor.

"Scary, isn't it?"

Gisela wasn't sure what she meant. "Pardon?"

"It wasn't that long ago that I was the stranger here. It's very different from my father's castle."

"May I ask which kingdom?"

"Indara."

Gisela stopped walking as she heard that. "The dragon kingdom?"

"You didn't know? I thought everyone did."

No. This was something that hadn't made its way to her mother's kingdom.

Tanis smiled warmly. "I was given the gift of choosing to be in a human body or my dragon form, and I can switch as I choose. Thankfully. It's hard to navigate the hallways and rooms here as a dragon."

"I can only imagine."

"If I wasn't wearing a crown, I could show you a lump or two on my head."

Gisela laughed. She really liked her sister-in-law. Tanis was a breath of fresh air in the dismal world Gisela had known. "Why are you all so friendly?"

"Because you're family, and it's something the boys don't have a lot of and it's something they highly value."

"I'm not used to that."

"Neither was I. Dragons aren't particularly...friendly as a

rule." She took Gisela's hand and squeezed it. "Don't be afraid. They only say what they mean, and they don't play games with others."

She hoped so much that was true.

Tanis took her to the queen's chambers.

Her breath caught in her throat as she saw the enormous room with floor-to-ceiling gilded windows. There was a huge bed in the corner with a navy brocade spread that looked as regal as any queen's.

"This is beautiful."

Tanis inclined her head. "I felt the same way the first time I saw it, but wait... You'll really love this."

Taking her by the hand, she led her through a door on the left and into a dressing room every bit as large as the bedroom. Dresses of all shades and fabrics hung against the four walls. There was a dressing table in the center, along with a huge chest filled with drawers.

"Pick anything you like."

Gisela had to close her gaping mouth as she stared at the luxury. "I have no idea what to pick. I've only worn the garb of an assassin."

"I understand. It took me a long time to learn to wear a court dress myself. Even now, I sometimes find it tedious and uncomfortable." Tanis led her to the far-right corner where there were garments made of leather. "You'll be more comfortable in one of these. Take your time, and I'll be waiting outside when you're through."

Gisela was overwhelmed by the generosity. Especially when she realized that Tanis was right. These were clothes more akin to what she normally wore.

And there was one made of burgundy leather that beckoned her most. The leather corset matched the pants and had an intricate burgundy and gold overcoat that fastened at the waist with brass buckles. The way it was cut was to be more like a dress, and yet it allowed her freedom of movement.

"I like this."

Biting her lip, she quickly pulled it on and went to the free-standing mirror next to the table.

It was wonderful. Far more feminine and elegant than anything she'd ever owned.

Now, if they could only find shoes...

Glancing about, she saw another door that led to a smaller room where the shoes were kept. Again, it was extravagant. There were dozens of shoes and boots to choose from.

Gisela found a black pair and was relieved when she pulled them on to find that they were the size she needed.

Standing up, she smoothed the open skirt that draped around her pants, and went to find her gracious hostess.

Tanis waited near the windows. When she turned, she sucked her breath in sharply. "You are absolutely beautiful."

"I can't thank you enough for the clothes."

Tanis waved her gratitude away. "I more than understand. Believe me, you and I have a lot in common."

She was beginning to realize that. And as she started to speak, there was a knock on the door.

"Enter," Tanis called.

Candara pushed the door open. "Sorry to interrupt. I have a gift for Gisela."

"Really?" Gifts weren't something she received.

Crossing the room, Candara handed her a long box.

She had no idea what could be inside until she opened it to find a long golden wand that reminded her of a unicorn horn. "What is this?"

"The wand of Queen Amandine. I gave it to my brother because something told me he needed it. But I think it was because I sensed your presence with them. As such, it should go to you. I think the queen would be honored for her descendant to have it."

"Shouldn't it go to Dash?"

Candara shook her head. "The wand wants you."

More honored than she could express, Gisela took the horn into her hand. The power of it made the hair on her arm stand upright. It sizzled in the air around them.

Never had she felt anything like it.

Terrified of what it could do, she returned it to the box. "Thank you."

Candara inclined her head to her. "I think you're both home, where you should be."

Funny, it didn't feel like home. It was wonderful and more beautiful than anything she'd ever seen, but it wasn't where she belonged.

Honestly, she didn't want to stay here. There was only one place she wanted to be.

"Can I see Xaydin?"

"Of course." Tanis led the way to the door. "Is he still in the throne room?" she asked Candara.

"They were when I left. But I don't know if they're still there."

"Then let's stalk them and see what they're up to."

XAYDIN SAT in a chair in Dash's council room across from where the High King sat at the round table.

He glanced around at Mischief, Chrys, Masakage, Dash, Ryper and Ronan.

His family. Some by blood and some by shared torment. These were the people he cared about. The only creatures he cared about other than Gisela and Candara.

And a few other Outlaws.

He would give his life for any of them, but especially Gisela.

They would do the same for him.

Without hesitation.

"I've sent word for Dove." Dash gestured at the contract that was laid out on the table before them. "Given that it's elfin, I know he'll want to return it home and let his people deal with those who are responsible for this travesty."

"It's grisly," Ryper agreed. "How could anyone do such a thing?"

Masakage sighed heavily. "Fairies write spell books on human skin...anthropodermics...a lot more than anyone should be comfortable with."

Dash nodded. "Don't get me started on those who collect unicorn horns." Especially since his sister had lost hers to such a bastard.

Xaydin felt for his friend. He could only imagine the horror. Personally, he'd rip the heart from the chest of anyone who did that to Gisela. "I don't understand trophy hunters."

"If only," Ronan scoffed. "These are mercenary bastards who do it for profit."

Mischief poured more wine into her cup. "So what are we to do with Meara now? The contract's broken, right?"

"I still have a contract with her. It's just unenforceable in this state."

"Meaning we can invade her lands?" There was way too much eagerness in Ryper's tone.

Dash nodded. "And thanks to Xaydin, we have someone we can put in power who won't be so quick to war."

Xaydin shook his head. "I doubt Gisela would accept such an offer. She wasn't raised to be queen, and from what I know of her, she won't relish the idea of it."

"Can you talk her into taking the throne?"

Xaydin stared at his friend. "Are you out of your mind, Dash? Can you talk Tanis into something she doesn't want to do?"

He had an amused smirk that said he might be able to accomplish that miracle. "The alternative is to put one of Meara's sons on the throne. They'll be right back, attacking us."

"And if you put Gisela on the throne, they'll be after her as an imposter. Not to mention the fact that she's part unicorn. All their people will hate her for her paternity. I won't subject her to that."

"Maybe you should ask her?" Mischief gave him a pointed glare. "You're making assumptions about what she wants. I say we pitch the idea to her and see what she says. Let her make up her own mind."

"I would prefer that."

They all turned to see Gisela in the doorway with Candara and Tanis.

Xaydin rose to his feet. "I didn't mean it like that."

She offered him a smile. "I know you didn't. I'd never accuse you of imposing your will on me. But it would be nice to be consulted about my future."

As Gisela neared him, he held his chair out for her and let her sit down. Then, he went after a spare chair that he pulled in beside hers.

While he did that, Tanis took a chair next to Dash and Candara moved to sit between Masakage and Mischief.

With a heavy sigh, she looked at Dash. "I don't want to be queen...but what you said about my brothers is correct. There's not a one of them who could be a decent king. They'll exact revenge on any and everyone around them. For any small slight or whim. Real or imagined. They're as cruel if not worse than my mother."

"Is there anyone else you'd put in power?"

Gisela tried her best to think of someone.

In the end, she had to face the harsh truth. "There's no one."

At least no one she'd trust with that kind of power. A few, such as Ferox, would be worse than her mother.

Gisela sighed. "The Thassalians are doomed."

Dash shifted his gaze to Xaydin.

"Don't even think it. I won't sit on my own throne, why would I sit on someone else's?"

"I wasn't planning to crown you. Rather I'm thinking you'd be an excellent bodyguard for a queen."

Still Gisela shook her head. "I'm an assassin, not a politician. Is there not one Outlaw capable of taking our throne?"

Ronan laughed bitterly. "No. The one thing we all learned while in your mother's custody was never to trust a centaur."

It was hard for her to argue that when she'd come away with the same lesson.

Dash let out a tired sigh. "We have a choice. Leave Meara in power and endure her constant scheming and attacks. Or we find someone willing to take the throne who is able to keep the centaurs from rebelling. Anyone know anyone? I'm open to all suggestions."

There weren't any.

Gisela took Xaydin's hand in hers. "If I do this, I don't want to be alone."

"If you do this, I'm in it with you. Because I'm stupid that way."

She laughed at his dire tone. "And apparently, so am I." Cutting her gaze back to Dash, she already regretted the decision she was making. "I'll do this, but if I'm overthrown and beheaded, I'll be haunting you for eternity."

Xaydin snorted. "And I'll be beating the shit out of him."

22

ONE WEEK LATER

In centaur form, Gisela stood with the whole of Dash's army at the border of her mother's lands.

This had been the last thing she wanted. But Dash had been right. Meara would never stop.

Not until she was forced from her throne.

I hate war.

Yet here she stood, side-by-side with men and women ready to lay down their lives to end her mother's bloody reign.

Her mother's army was ready. They were in the valley below, waiting for the cry to begin killing.

Dash's army was primarily unicorns, but he had a number of soldiers from other races, including two dragons who were friends of his wife.

Because she was pregnant, Tanis had stayed at home where it was safest for the baby she carried.

As the war drums pounded a rhythm that went all the way through her body, the fetid wind blew through their ranks, ruffling the banners of their army and her hair and tail.

She'd never fought in her centaur form before. But it seemed somehow right. Natural even.

How she hated to think of the number of their soldiers who'd die today. The number of centaurs who'd pay for her mother's greed and cruelty.

And for what? A hollow crown?

She'd never cared less for it. Never dreamt she could be queen, yet here she was, willing to die to make sure no more innocent centaurs suffered.

Xaydin stood at her side in his full black metal armor. He was a troll of great power and beauty.

He took her hand and kissed it. "Don't die today, my love."

"Nor you. I'd much rather have you than a crown, because I can definitely live without it. And the last thing I want is to find out if I can live again without you."

"Same. I would tell you to stay behind me, but I know you better. Just watch for arrows."

"And swords and spears."

"Indeed." As soon as he said that word, the drumming stopped and a shriek ran through the enemy ranks.

En masse, they attacked.

"Hold position!" Dash's criers warned.

The plan was to let Meara's forces exhaust themselves by running uphill.

At least it was the plan until Meara's squadron of wizards portaled into the midst and started hurling fireballs. Damn it! They'd forgotten about Meara's Wizard Brigade.

Dash's wizards returned that assault as the dragons launched and laid down their own fire over Meara's army.

Utter chaos exploded.

She followed Xaydin down the hill, toward the enemy, taking care to make sure nothing and no one harmed him. She was used to fighting from the shadows and striking unseen.

This was a whole new way to fight, and honestly, it scared her. There was so much noise, and the ground quickly became slick with blood and other things she didn't want to think about.

Her heart pounded so loudly that she could no longer hear the drums. And she was grateful she stood on four legs instead of two. She needed the extra stability. It was also awkward to have arms with hooves. Her entire center of gravity was different and she didn't like it.

Even so, Gisela ducked a blow before she came up and stabbed the attacking centaur through the throat. His dying scream rang out, losing itself among all the others who were screaming in pain while they died.

She felt completely nauseated. Was this really the only way to remove her mother from power?

A queen who stayed back from her army to watch them die in her name, from a safe distance.

It made her sick that her mother would ask so many to die horribly on her behalf while refusing to fight with the rest of them. At least Dash was in the thick of it.

And Xaydin didn't seem to mind at all. In fact, he cut through the centaurs with an ease that was frightening. It was obvious that he was a creature of battle. At home here, like many of them.

But that didn't mean that they should be so comfortable slaughtering others.

And for what? To keep a vain woman in power. One who so obviously cared nothing for those around her.

Meara was in this for her own glory. For her own needs and wants.

Gisela was ashamed that they were related. She didn't want to watch soldiers die for her.

No. She wanted the blood of only one creature.

Meara.

"Candara!" she shouted, trying to find the mystic among the fighters.

Scanning those throwing fireballs, she finally spotted her between Masakage and Ryper, who'd chosen to fight as a human and not a unicorn.

Gisela made straight for her. But it wasn't easy to reach her. It seemed like half the army used it to try to attack her.

She was almost there when four attackers surrounded her. She was fighting two at once when the third went to slice her legs. She felt a slight sting before the centaur was sent reeling.

Gisela smiled at the sight of Xaydin protecting her as he moved past her shoulder to take on the two she'd been fighting.

That left her able to deal with the fourth one. With two sword strokes, she was finally able to move forward again.

"What are you planning?" Xaydin asked.

"Get to my mother and end this. I need Candara to open a portal to where she's standing."

Xaydin wasn't sure he approved of her plan, but if they could reach the queen, it would stop the fight and end the war.

It was a bold move.

If anyone could carry it off, it would be Gisela.

Still, he wasn't keen on putting her in that kind of danger. Especially since they were winning. In time, they'd take this field and have the queen on the run.

But he understood Gisela's desire to save as many lives as they could. He wasn't thrilled with the losses they were taking on either side.

While he didn't mind a good brawl every now and again, battles had never been the thing he craved as he was well aware of the cost. What monarchs asked their citizens to bear when they marched to war.

It was brutal. It was bloody.

And in the end, no one ever really won.

If only there were another way to settle things. But unreasonable creatures forced them to do what they must to protect their people and to keep the real monsters at bay.

He protected Gisela from the centaurs who were bent on killing her until they reached his sister.

Candara had a cut along her brow but otherwise seemed unhurt. "What's wrong?"

"Nothing." Gisela gestured in the direction she'd last seen her mother. "Can you teleport me to where Meara is?"

"Us," Xaydin added. He had no intention of letting her go after her mother without backup.

"Are you sure about this?"

"I am."

Candara looked at him and nodded. "All right. Stand back for a second."

Masakage and Ryper covered her while she conjured her portal and made it large enough for them to pass through.

Gisela considered changing forms, then thought better of it. The Thassalians needed to see her in this form. It would make it easier for them to tolerate what she had to do to protect them.

She and Xaydin left the portal and appeared behind her mother whose attention was on the battle below.

Gisela angled her sword toward the guards who stood on each side of her mother while Xaydin did the same. "Enough, Mother. End this."

The queen turned around, wide-eyed. "You're attempting to overthrow me?"

"I'm taking you prisoner."

Her mother laughed, then ran for the battle. Her two guards rushed them.

Normally, Gisela would have engaged them, but she left them to Xaydin so that she could pursue her mother into battle.

Because she was still in centaur form, the rear troops didn't realize she was after Meara.

Not until her mother spun around.

"Kill her!" her mother roared, shoving the centaur closest to her toward Gisela.

Gisela froze as she realized this might not have been the brightest plan. Her heart pounded as she glanced toward her allies. She was a far cry from Dash's army, and she had no way to cast a portal and escape.

I'm an idiot.

Gisela stepped back and felt a strong hand on her spine.

I'm with you, love, to the bitter end. You're not alone. I'm right here, by your side. Xaydin's words meant more to her than she could even begin to express. This was more than she'd ever expected or could hope for.

"I don't want to hurt your soldiers, Mother. You need to answer for all you've done."

Instead of attacking Gisela, the soldiers glanced about nervously.

"Did you not hear my orders?" Meara roared. "Kill her or die in her stead."

That didn't have the effect Meara had hoped. Instead of prompting them to do her bidding, they turned their swords on their queen.

Obviously, they were as tired of taking her threats and orders as everyone else.

"What is this?" Meara roared. "I'm your queen!"

"Are you really her daughter?" the soldier closest to Gisela asked.

"She is," Xaydin said. "It's why Meara has kept her in secret. Unlike her brothers, Gisela is fair-minded and decent."

There was suspicion in their eyes, not that she blamed them, given all the decades of torment they'd suffered under her mother's brutal fist. She couldn't blame them for thinking she'd be the same.

"I may be of my mother's blood, but I'm not of her ilk. Detain her for King Dash, and I'll establish an elder council of noblemen and generals to vote in the next ruler of Thassalia...as they did in the old days."

That swayed their minds instantly.

Her mother started to run, but her own soldiers kept her in place. "I'll have all your heads!"

Gisela snorted. "Your days of threatening others are over." She looked to the highest-ranking soldier, a colonel. "Tell the centaurs to retreat before we lose any more lives."

He ran to obey.

Two soldiers took her mother by the arms.

She saw the defiance in Meara's gaze, but she knew better than to try anything. Her army had betrayed her.

So had her daughter.

Queen Meara was finished.

"You did it, my love." Xaydin gave her a hug that meant everything to her.

It was over, and as word spread to the army, the centaurs withdrew from battle.

As soon as their retreat was seen by Dash, he recalled his own warriors from the field. The two dragons circled over their heads, eyeing everyone below.

With Xaydin by her side, Gisela and the guards walked her mother through the army, toward Dash.

To her mother's credit, she held herself with every bit of regal dignity she possessed. Even with her hands tied before her, she walked through the bedraggled army as if it were a grand ballroom.

The saddest part was that she knew her mother would never allow someone she'd defeated to be allowed this much dignity.

Rather, she'd make a show of belittling them with every step. Of dragging them through the mud just to shame them.

I'm not my mother.

Defeat was enough humiliation for anyone. No more needed to be added.

She held on to Xaydin's hand until they reached Dash and his brother. Still in her equine form, Gisela bowed low before him. "My liege, we've captured the queen and tender her to your custody."

A rumble and curses went through the centaurs.

But Dash silenced them by holding his fist in the air. "Warriors of Thassalia, you fought bravely today. Honorably. You should take pride in defending your country. This is not a defeat. It's a new beginning for all Thassalians who will no longer be held beneath Meara's hooves."

A roar went up among their army. She could feel their enthusiasm and excitement.

Their seven generals rode forward under a white pennant.

Once they stood before Dash, they bowed to him in deference.

The Major General then saluted Dash. "What are your orders, Majesty?"

"Princess Gisela of Thassalia will be in charge. Until a new coronation, she will be Thassalia's monarch."

The general inclined his head. "All hail Queen Gisela!"

His call was taken up by the rest of their forces.

But inside, she didn't rejoice. She was terrified. All she'd wanted was her freedom.

Now she was queen?

"It'll be all right, Gisela. Just breathe."

She took Xaydin's hand and allowed his strength to flow into her.

Because he believed it, she believed it.

It would be fine.

"This is not fine!" Gisela shut the doors and transformed into her human body. "They're animals and not just because they're part horse! They're pigs!"

Xaydin laughed. "Council giving you grief?"

"Giving me a migraine! Now I understand why my mother took their heads all the time. Terror makes it easier to negotiate with them."

"I won't argue that. I find a swift kick in the ass and punch to the throat a remarkable way of adjusting certain attitudes and tones."

She gave him a droll stare. Though to be honest, she was coming around to his way of thinking. "I won't be my mother."

"No one thinks that. Want me to slap them around in your stead?"

At the moment, yes. It was a lot more tempting than it should be.

"No. But keep it in mind."

Someone knocked on the door to her bedchambers. Gisela returned to her centaur body. "Enter."

It was the eldest member of their council. "Forgive me, Highness. We didn't mean to distress you."

"All's fine," she lied, hiding her agitation from him. It wasn't...

Actually, it was his fault in part. He'd egged on the others.

Clearing her throat, she moved past that. "What brings you here?"

"We've taken another vote."

Oh goody! This she couldn't wait to hear. "Another tie?"

"No. We decided to stop voting on our own council members...or any of Meara's sons."

That should make her happy, and yet his tone made her stomach shrink.

"Our newest vote was unanimous."

Gisela had to keep herself from wincing as she dreaded his words. "Please tell me it wasn't for my mother to return to power."

The general laughed at her dead tone. "It wasn't for Meara or the princes who have all been found guilty of treason. Rather, we've chosen the best creature for the job. The one who has led us this past month without the drama, fear, threats, or any of the chaos of Meara's reign."

Even though she heard those words, she couldn't quite fathom them.

Confused, she glanced to Xaydin who watched her with an amused quirk to his lips. "Do they understand that I'm not a full centaur?"

"Neither was Meara nor her father before her."

"You didn't know that at the time," she reminded him.

"True, my queen. Very true. But you've shown yourself to be all we could dream of in a monarch. You've been honest and kind...most of all, you don't crave power. Again, it was unanimous. Once your name entered the vote, all were in agreement. You, alone, have the full support of the council."

Xaydin couldn't be prouder for Gisela, who locked gazes with him.

"I won't do this alone. Do they understand that I will come to them with a foreign prince at my side? I will not forsake him for another. Not even my country." Especially since she'd never wanted a crown.

"Your terms are acceptable to us. We await your decision on the matter." And with that, he took his leave.

Xaydin smiled at her as she resumed her human body. "Queen Gisela of Thassalia. I love the sound of that."

She arched a brow at his giddiness. "You'll be King Xaydin."

Laughing, he shook his head. "They didn't vote for me, love. I'll be Prince Xaydin, consort to the queen. That throne is yours, not mine. And if you accept, one day it'll belong to our son or daughter."

Gisela felt a lightness in her heart at his words. She had yet to tell him that she was expecting. Did he know or was he merely guessing?

And how could she say no? Really?

Xaydin was still being hunted by his brother, but if she took the throne being offered, they wouldn't have to run. Xaydin and their child would be safe from the troll king.

Forever.

While she'd never wanted to rule, this was the best outcome for them all.

Especially the baby growing inside her.

"I will assume the throne, but only on one condition."

"That is?" Xaydin asked.

"You will have to marry me before the coronation."

He laughed at her request. "I've already told you that. I will marry you whenever you wish and however you want."

True. He'd said it many times, but she'd kept delaying in case he changed his mind and wanted to leave. She couldn't blame him for it.

He hated being trapped. Nothing was a bigger noose than a crown.

But if she were to stay here, she couldn't do it on her own. She'd need someone she trusted. Someone she could confide in.

And there was no one else she trusted.

This place had birthed her. It'd shaped her.

Now, it would be her future.

I had no control over my horrible past.

But the future was entirely up to her.

I will make it one worth living.

Not just for her, but for the ones she cared about and loved. And for her people.

They were home and they would make it the best one possible.

EPILOGUE

Gisela sat on her throne with Xaydin seated in the one beside her. Not as king, but as her full partner in all things.

She had more than she'd ever dreamed. They were married and three weeks ago, she'd been crowned.

For the first time in her life, she was deliriously happy and was looking forward.

Around her now were bright yellow walls, hung with tapestries that told centaur history. It still seemed a bit strange that they'd welcomed her as queen, knowing her parentage and that she was part unicorn and shifter. But she wouldn't argue it.

So far, everyone seemed happy with their choice. She only prayed that it lasted.

As she started to rise, a portal opened on the floor just below her dais.

Xaydin immediately rose and placed himself between her and the hooded figure who stepped through.

He didn't relax until the hood was lowered to show them Masakage.

"What are you doing here, brother?"

Masakage took a deep breath. "I wish it was good tidings. Sadly, I'm here to warn you that Ferrell escaped."

Gisela cursed. Ferrell was Meara's youngest son. She'd made the mistake of sparing him because he'd sworn that he didn't want the throne and that he'd leave them in peace.

Obviously, he was as big a liar as his mother and brothers.

She gaped. "What? When?"

"Sometime in the night. One of Meara's loyalists freed him. We captured the culprit, but Ferrell vanished and is no doubt reconciled with the traitors."

Which meant he'd be coming for the throne.

Damn it.

"I knew we should have killed him." Xaydin growled deep in his throat. "Why didn't I kill him?"

Gisela agreed. She should have been the assassin and not a queen showing mercy. Of all the mistakes to make...

"He'll be heading this way." Gisela signaled her guard at the door. "Please advise the council we need a meeting and tighten the guards at the gate."

"Yes, my queen." He rushed to do her bidding.

Regret spread through her. "If he's anything like Meara, he won't give up." It was a reality Gisela knew all too well.

Xaydin nodded. "Don't worry. He won't reach us."

"Dash wants to know if you need reinforcements?" Masakage asked.

Gisela rubbed the slight bulge in her stomach where her child was growing larger every day. She wanted to accept but knew unicorn help wouldn't be welcomed by her people. They might even see it as an invasion.

While most accepted her, there were still some who feared being conquered by Dash and absorbed into his kingdom, especially given that they were siblings.

"Tell Dash, thank you. But not at this time. Ferrell's our problem and we will take care of him."

Masakage inclined his head, then opened another portal and left.

Xaydin took her hand in his and held them entwined over his heart. "He won't return. We will make sure of it."

"But he'll try."

"And we'll defeat him just as we did your mother. Trust me."

Gisela smiled for one reason only. She trusted him, and she knew so long as he lived, she would have peace.

And they would rule these lands as would their children after them. Let her brother come.

This kingdom was theirs and so it would remain.

Forever.

Fire & Ice

Born of Shadows

Born of Silence

Cloak & Silence

Born of Fury

Born of Defiance

Born of Betrayal

Born of Legend

Born of Vengeance

Born of Blood

Born of Trouble

Born of Darkness

THE LEAGUE: EVE OF DESTRUCTION

Eve of Destruction

Born of Blood

Born of Rage

Eve of Ruin

DARK-HUNTER

Night Pleasures

Night Embrace

Dance with the Devil

Kiss of the Night

Night Play

Sword of Darkness

Knight of Darkness

Death Doesn't Bargain

At Death's Door

LORDS OF AVALON

(written as Kinley MacGregor)

Sword of Darkness

Knight of Darkness

STANDALONES & COLLECTIONS

Dark Places

ABOUT THE AUTHOR

Defying all odds is what #1 New York Times and international bestselling author Sherrilyn Kenyon does best. Rising from extreme poverty as a child that culminated in being a homeless mother with an infant, she has become one of the most popular and influential authors in the world (in both adult and young adult fiction), with dedicated legions of fans known as Paladins— thousands of whom proudly sport tattoos from her numerous genre-defying series.

Since her first book debuted in 1993 while she was still in college, she has placed more than 80 novels on the New York Times list in all formats and genres, including manga and graphic novels, and has more than 70 million books in print worldwide. Her current series include: Dark-Hunters®, Chronicles of Nick®, Deadman's Cross™, Black Hat Society™, Nevermore™, Silent Swans™, Lords of Avalon® and, The League®.

Over the years, her Lords of Avalon® novels have been adapted by Marvel, and her Dark-Hunters® and Chronicles of Nick® are New York Times bestselling manga and comics and are #1 bestselling adult coloring books.

Join her and her Paladins online at QueenofAllShad-ows.com and www.facebook.com/mysherrilyn.

OLIVERHEBERBOOKS

A small press bound by the belief that every voice matters.

Sign up for our newsletter to learn about new releases and more.
https://oliver-heberbooks.com/subscribe/

Follow us on social media:

facebook.com/oliverheberbooks
instagram.com/oliverheberbooks
amazon.com/oliverheberbooks
youtube.com/@OliverHeberBooksPublisher